Battered Roses

Christina Rozeline

Christina Rozeline

Copyright © 2023 by Christina Rozeline

All rights reserved. No portion of this book may be reproduced in any form without written permission from the publisher or author, except as permitted by U.S. copyright law.

While Battered Roses is a work of fiction, your experience is not. If you find yourself in a situation similar to this, please seek help.

Domestic Violence Hotline
800-799-7233

Suicide and Crisis Lifeline
988

First Edition: November 2023
Printed by Chrstina Rozeline in the USA
www.christinarozeline.com

Copy Edited by: Lauren Loftis with Tally Ink
Proofread by: Lauryn Hatten
Header Art by: Comicrons on Instagram

Paperback ISBN: 979-8-9891154-1-9

Library of Congress Control Number (LCCN): 2023916961

Contents

Dedication	VII
	VIII
1. ONE	1
2. TWO	8
3. THREE	14
4. FOUR	16
5. FIVE	23
6. SIX	28
7. SEVEN	31
8. EIGHT	35
9. NINE	39
10. TEN	46
11. ELEVEN	50
12. TWELVE	53
13. THIRTEEN	61

14.	FOURTEEN	66
15.	FIFTEEN	69
16.	SIXTEEN	77
17.	SEVENTEEN	81
18.	EIGHTEEN	87
19.	NINETEEN	90
20.	TWENTY	95
21.	TWENTY-ONE	98
22.	TWENTY-TWO	104
23.	TWENTY-THREE	111
24.	TWENTY-FOUR	116
25.	TWENTY-FIVE	118
26.	TWENTY-SIX	121
27.	TWENTY-SEVEN	126
28.	TWENTY-EIGHT	131
29.	TWENTY-NINE	136
30.	THIRTY	139
31.	THIRTY-ONE	145
32.	THIRTY-TWO	151
33.	THIRTY-THREE	157

34.	THIRTY-FOUR	160
35.	THIRTY-FIVE	164
36.	THIRTY-SIX	171
37.	THIRTY-SEVEN	176
38.	THIRTY-EIGHT	183
39.	THIRTY-NINE	188
40.	FORTY	193
41.	FORTY-ONE	197
42.	FORTY-TWO	203
43.	FORTY-THREE	208
44.	FORTY-FOUR	211
45.	FORTY-FIVE	216
46.	FORTY-SIX	219
47.	FORTY-SEVEN	223
48.	FORTY-EIGHT	226
49.	FORTY-NINE	232
50.	FIFTY	236
51.	FIFTY-ONE	242
52.	FIFTY-TWO	245
53.	FIFTY-THREE	248

54.	FIFTY-FOUR	255
55.	FIFTY-FIVE	266
56.	FIFTY-SIX	273
57.	FIFTY-SEVEN	279
58.	FIFTY-EIGHT	282
59.	FIFTY-NINE	289
60.	SIXTY	294
61.	SIXTY-ONE	296
62.	SIXTY-TWO	300
63.	SIXTY-THREE	304
64.	SIXTY-FOUR	312
65.	SIXTY-FIVE	315
66.	SIXTY-SIX	326
	About the Author	338
	Follow Me!	339
	Acknowledgements	340

To my mother, who never stopped believing in me, gave me the gift of dreams, and the ability to realize them.

𝄞

Battered Roses

ONE

Rosaleen wakes with a start to Todd throwing another one of his morning fits.

No, not again.

He scavenges through his dresser drawers, slinging clothes all over the floor. "Where's my damn undershirt? I'm going to be late for work!" He slams the drawer shut, and Rosaleen pulls the blanket up to her chin. *Please find one. Please.*

"Get up and help me!" he says, jerking the covers off her.

She jumps out of bed. "I put them to dry last night," she says, quickly passing in front of him. "I'll go grab you one." *Don't hit me.* She squeezes her eyes together, cowering as he walks towards her.

He sneers and steps back. "Hurry up!"

Rosaleen hates how Todd gets into her head without even having to hit her. *It's not funny. I wish he wouldn't make this a game.*

Opening the dryer, she pulls out his shirt. *Why can't you just check the laundry before throwing your little tantrum?* She takes a deep breath before bringing it to him. *It's okay. I'm okay. He has his shirt now, so he should calm down.*

As she walks back into the bedroom, Todd jerks the shirt from her hand. "Took you long enough."

Hurry up and go to work! 7:30 can't get here fast enough.

"Can you not see these wrinkles? Are you trying to make me look bad?" Todd shoves the shirt in Rosaleen's face before throwing it on the floor. "You're worthless."

She picks the shirt up, noticing blood. *Did he bust my lip?* Checking the tender flesh, she looks at her finger. *I'm bleeding. Not that it's anything new. Now I'll have to cover this up, and he'll get mad that I'm wearing makeup again.* She walks over to the ironing board and turns it on, hoping he doesn't see the red spot. *I'm so sick of everything being my fault. It's just a stupid undershirt.*

She takes a rubber band off her wrist and pulls her long, brown, wavy hair into a messy bun so it doesn't get in the way as she works.

Rosaleen watches the steam rise from the iron as she grips it tightly. *What if I just stick this to his face?* She imagines his flesh melting under the hot metal while he screams in agony, though she knows she'd never do it.

Or would she?

She shrugs. *It's a nice thought, but I won't risk going to jail for the likes of him.*

"I'm running late for work again, because of you!" He jerks the shirt from her hand and inspects it. "You can't even wash clothes!"

I hate being your housewife.

He throws his undershirt onto the bed and grabs his work shirt.

He left his shirt on the bed! That whole fit was for nothing! There is no winning when it comes to Todd.

"You'll never be a good housewife!" Todd yells, buttoning his shirt as she follows him out of the room.

He kisses her harshly, her lip still stinging as he slams the front door on his way out.

Rosaleen rests her back against the door. *At least I get an eight-hour break from him,* she thinks, letting out a huge sigh. With the sleeve of her shirt, she scrubs the spot where his lips touched her skin until it starts to burn, disgusted that his kiss was not out of love, but only a habit.

Years ago, she couldn't resist his dark hair and green eyes, and she remembers how lucky she felt to have such a good-looking man want her. Even now, when they go places together, she notices other women looking at him. *If only they saw the ugliness buried under his good looks. Would they admire him then? If they could know what I hide every day?*

Attempting to push all thoughts of Todd aside, Rosaleen walks over to the shelf that holds her porcelain angel collection, sighing, "I miss you," she says, dusting off her favorite blue one as she remembers the morning her grandma gave it to her. Rosaleen had been crying when her grandma arrived at her house.

"What is it dear?"

"Todd and I had another argument today. After I told him I wanted a couple of weeks to think our marriage

through, he called me horrible and left. I don't even know where he went this time."

"Honey, we don't get married and then leave when things get tough. Look at me and your grandpa. Just hang in there and give Todd time." Her grandmother didn't know he had been hitting her, or she would have never told Rosaleen to hang in there. Rosaleen thought her grandmother was right about marriage being hard. She had hoped it would get better, but it never did. Rosaleen fell into her grandmother's warm embrace.

"There, there, dear. This will cheer you up," her grandma said, pulling something out of her purse.

"What is it, Grandma?" Rosaleen sniffled.

"You'll have to open it to find out. Now dry those tears so you can see."

Rosaleen unwrapped the figurine. "Your last angel. But Grandma, you aren't supposed to give me this until my birthday." Rosaleen held the angel up, watching the glitter dance over her wings in the light. She was wearing a sky-blue dress, Rosaleen's favorite color, and the angel's white hair matched the cloud she sat on.

"That one is my favorite one, so I saved it for last."

Rosaleen hugged her grandma goodbye later that evening, not realizing that it would be the last hug she'd ever give her. She still remembers the scent of her grandmother's strong perfume like it was yesterday.

Setting the angel back down, Rosaleen follows the hall to her room and gets dressed.

She slips her hand under the mattress, feeling around until her hand comes in contact with a small container.

Days like today make me thankful for these, she thinks, popping out one of her birth control pills and swallowing it down with the bottle of water sitting on her bed side table.

That chore done, Rosaleen proceeds to get dressed to go into town. Her mom, Bonnie, asked her to stop by on her way there the night before, and Rosaleen walks into her mom's house without knocking.

"Sure is hot out there." She says, wiping the sweat from her forehead as she watches her mother attempt to pull down old curtains.

Her mom struggles with the poles, turning to look at her. "I swear we live in hell and not Louisiana."

"Mom . . ." Rosaleen rolls her eyes. "At least we don't live in Northern Louisiana."

"I'd never eat their gumbo. That's for sure."

They both laugh, and Bonnie drops the curtain to the floor.

"Hey, you got a new dress?"

"Yes, I'm glad you noticed. It was on sale." Bonnie says, curtsying playfully.

Her mom always wears the softest t-shirt dresses with bright colored flowers. She is a bit larger than Rosaleen, but the added weight looks good on her.

Rosaleen doesn't think her mother's hair was as gray the last time Rosaleen saw her—or maybe it was, and Rosaleen wasn't paying attention. When she visited, she'd had just left home after another one of Todd's meltdowns. She'd left a mug on the tableside, and he chunked it against the wall. When she got to her mothers, she couldn't even think straight. She was just glad he'd hit the wall that time and not her.

She doesn't even remember what they talked about that day.

"I made tea cake. Let's go sit in the kitchen and drink some coffee with it. It's been a few weeks since I've seen you."

"I know. We've just been so busy."

I hate lying to her.

Rosaleen twiddles her fingers. "Hey mom, I can't stay long. I have a lot to get done before I get Todd's clothes," Rosaleen says, feeling guilty for not being honest with her own mother. She just really needs to be alone with her own thoughts, drinking a nice, hot latte.

"You two are the cutest couple. So young and in love. You are lucky to have landed such a loving husband. But is something going on? You're not as happy as you used to be."

"It's just Todd's job." Rosaleen forces a smile. Every time she starts to tell her mom how bad he really is, she feels like a failure. Rosaleen doesn't want to disappoint her, so she lies instead.

There's no use upsetting her.

"I'm your mother, I can tell when something is off."

She sees the concern on her mother's face. "Didn't you just hang those?" Rosaleen asks, abruptly changing the subject.

Bonnie sighs.

Rosaleen hopes her mom won't press the issue.

"I'm not feeling the beige like I thought I would. I'm already tired of the color." Bonnie says, holding up a yellow set of curtains. "I see what you're doing by the way."

"What?" Rosaleen says, laughing the conversation off. She grabs the new drapes. "But mom, they are almost the same color."

Standing, Bonnie starts to hang them "So," Bonnie says casually, "I would love to turn your old room into a kid's playroom one day."

Rosaleen rolls her eyes. *It never takes her long to bring up grandchildren.* "I've already told you. We've been trying for three years with no luck." *Another lie.* She sighs.

"Can't you visit a gynecologist and see what options are available?"

Rosaleen shrugs, "Todd stays busy. Besides we aren't in any hurry. If it happens, it happens."

Lie. Lies. I'm nothing but a liar! It's never going to happen with him.

Rosaleen won't tell her mother she's on birth control. She knows her mom has always wanted grandkids, but with her situation, she feels it's unfair to bring an innocent baby into a toxic home.

With all her secrets, Rosaleen can't get out of her mom's house fast enough. She needs to get to The Hideout. Rosaleen loves the name of the little coffee shop she visits each morning, and she can't wait to hide from all her problems back at home.

TWO

Rosaleen parks on the outskirts of town, walking down Main Street toward The Hideout. Main Street is technically the whole town, with only a few shops lining both sides of the road. But the stores served their purpose, and they were all the small town of Chesterfield felt like it needed.

Finding the coffee shop, she waits in line to order.

"Good morning, Rosaleen! What will it be? The usual cinnamon and caramel hot latte?" The bubbly barista remembers her order, but Rosaleen can never remember her name. It doesn't help that her name tag only has a golden bell on it.

"Yes, ma'am, please." Rosaleen pulls out some cash to pay. She always keeps a little secret cash hidden, so Todd can't track her every movement.

With all I put up with, I deserve this small cup of joy.

"That won't be necessary. The gentleman in front of you paid for your coffee," the barista says, smiling as she winks. "He's a looker too. You should go thank him."

Rosaleen holds her left hand up, showing the woman her wedding ring.

"Oh, that's nothing. You're just saying thank you." She hands Rosaleen her coffee.

Breathing in the freshly brewed coffee as she walks away, Rosaleen lifts her cup and gives a gentle nod of thanks to the man who bought it for her.

Instead of sitting in the lounge today, she makes her way outside to enjoy the fresh air, feeling cooped up from all the rain they've had over the past week. She sips her coffee, sighing with relief. No one here yells or jerks her around.

I don't know how I would unwind without this place.

A bird looks at her and chirps, flying out of sight from the patio's tree.

Rosaleen sits and watches stay-at-home moms walk by with their young ones—too young to be in school yet.

One mom passes by with her little boy. He tugs her hand toward the ice cream shop. "Okay sweetie, but after we play at the park." She picks him up and plants a kiss on his cheek.

Another little girl splashes in the puddles left over from last night's heavy thunderstorm. Her little rain boots light up every time she lands, and her mom pulls her arm. "Come on Camille, you're going to get dirty."

Rosaleen tries not to judge her, but if she had a little girl, she'd more than likely jump right along with her.

Rosaleen stares after them as they walk off, longing for kids of her own one day. She wants a little boy or girl she can sing lullabies to before bed and walk to the park with. *Why does Todd have to ruin everything?* Sometimes, she wonders if having kids might fix them—if Todd might become nicer—but she doesn't want to risk it.

She takes the last sip of her coffee before tossing it in the trash.

I guess it's time to do my duties, Rosaleen thinks, rolling her eyes.

She stops and picks up Todd's clothes from the dry cleaners, wondering why she doesn't make him get his own stupid clothes.

Dry cleaning in hand, Rosaleen walks back to her car, slowing as she nears the Town of Chesterfield's Tax Firm. Doing her best to appear calm, she passes the same window she's peaked through each morning for the past three months on the way back from The Hideout. She looks forward to the handsome, blonde-haired, blue-eyed man who sits at his desk. Attracted to his smart, subtle look, she especially loves the days he's wearing his glasses.

I can see us snuggled together, reading a good book by the fireplace.

The man picks up his mug from his desk, taking a sip from it.

Who am I kidding? It's too hot down here for fireplaces.

An elderly couple holding hands passes her, and she wonders if she'll ever experience that kind of love.

She looks back through the window and imagines what life with him might be like. She'd drop a coffee by his office every morning after she leaves The Hideout. At home, this man would walk up to her, wrap his arms around her, and dance with her in the kitchen as they bake up a warm dessert. He would playfully rub food on her face and kiss it off.

The warm, loving, wholesome though makes her tingle inside.

Oh, Bryan, she sighs.

Rosaleen knows that's not his real name, but she likes to imagine it's something similar. Maybe it's because she studies his familiar face every day or because of the stories she creates in her head about him. But whatever it is, she feels like she's known him for years.

This is nothing like the life she has now, where Todd couldn't care less about her. The only time he treats her well is when they're together in public. Those occasions used to give her a tiny bit of hope, but she's finally accepted the truth. He will never love her for who she really is.

She can only crave the life she imagines with Bryan. *What would it be like to wake up to a caring face instead of a war?* All she wants is love.

Rosaleen notices a 'We're Hiring' sign in the tax firm's window, and after her morning with Todd, something inside her snaps. *This might be my way out!* Wanting to take control of her life, she sets Todd's clothes down on the bench by the door and walks into the office.

The lady at the front desk looks at her funny. "Do you have an appointment with someone?"

"Um . . . are you still hiring?"

"Not currently. I'm sorry."

"Oh, I saw the sign in the window . . ." Rosaleen tries not to look as disappointed as she feels.

"Oh dear, I need to remove that. I'm sorry. We just filled the spot this morning, but I can jot down the website where you can go apply online the next time we're hiring.

Attach your resume with it." She leans forward and whispers, "Don't say anything, but a little birdy told me there will be a new position opening very soon. We have a new owner, and the firm will be getting a new name." Her eyes light up with excitement as she hands the written website to Rosaleen.

Instantly regretting her impulsive decision, Rosaleen awkwardly grabs the woman's note. "Thank you, ma'am," she says, folding the paper and putting it in her pocket.

That was so stupid of me!

Walking out of the office, a speeding car throws a wave of water onto her. "UGH!" she shouts. Just when she thinks things can't get any worst. *This is my favorite dress!*

The man from the window looks up from his work, glancing towards the commotion. As their eyes lock, he grins and looks back down at his computer.

He actually looked at me!

Her heart flutters, her face reddening with embarrassment. *Of all times for him to notice me!*

Rosaleen turns around, grabbing Todd's clothes and checking to see if any water splashed onto his suit. Relief fills her when she sees it's untouched by water. *What an afternoon that would have caused,* she thinks, hurrying back to her car before anything else can happen to her.

When Rosaleen gets home, she goes straight into the kitchen to make a sandwich, not caring that she's still in her wet, dirty clothes. The only thing sitting in her stomach right now is coffee, since her nerves were too bad to eat anything that morning.

She starts walking to the icebox, stopping when she notices the sink. *I better get these dishes cleaned up before Todd gets home.* Rosaleen makes a mental note to get it done, setting her keys on the counter.

She makes a sandwich and sits at the kitchen table to eat, forcing each bite. It's barely noon and she's already had quite a day. She thinks of Todd's earlier behavior. *What kind of mood will he be in when he gets home?*

Rosaleen forces herself to eat the rest of her food, thinking that she'd better clean up a bit before he gets home.

Rinsing her plate, she starts loading the dishwasher. After Rosaleen finishes, she throws her dish towel over her shoulder and reaches into her pocket to pull out the paper from earlier.

It would be ridiculous if I did this.

She hesitates as she unfolds it. Going to her computer, Rosaleen fills out an application before she has the chance to change her mind.

THREE

A few days later, Rosaleen's on her couch folding laundry when she receives a phone call.

She places the unmatched socks down before answering "Hello?"

"Ms. Hart?"

The use of her maiden name throws Rosaleen off for a moment. "This is she."

"Hi there. This is Easton Rivers with Easton's Tax Firm. I'm calling in regards to your application."

Oh yeah, I used my maiden name to apply. Why am I not talking? Say something.

He clears his throat. "Ms. Hart? Hello?"

"Yes, sir. I'm sorry. Did you say Easton's Tax Firm?"

"Yes, ma'am, we changed the name of the firm. I'm the new owner."

"That's right." Rosaleen stands, pacing the floor. *He's about to tell me I'm not qualified. I just know it.*

"I received and reviewed the materials you submitted a few days ago."

"Yes, sir." Her palms begin to sweat.

"I was wondering if you could come in on Monday for an interview? Say, around 9:30?"

What? Rosaleen fumbles with the phone, quickly putting it back to her ear. "Yes, sir. That would be great."

"Perfect, I'll see you on Monday."

Hanging up, she slowly releases the breath she was holding in.

"I did it!" Rosaleen squeezes her phone in her hand, jumping up and down.

Since being with Todd, she's always had to rely on him. For once in her three years with him, she did something on her own.

Rosaleen really didn't think she'd get a call.

Wait...

Rosaleen sits back down. The excitement disappears as fear floods over her. *I can't just make this kind of decision without Todd's approval. If I tell him, there will be so many consequences for going behind his back.*

What do I do?

Getting up, Rosaleen grabs Todd's stack of folded clothes. *First, I better put these away before I forget.*

Walking into her room, she tucks his clothes into his drawers, hanging the shirt he left on their bed on a hanger.

He's so sloppy.

As she puts it in the closet, she notices a red smudge on his collar.

It isn't the first time she's seen the color on his shirt, but today is different. She sees the shaped outline of lips.

Lipstick.

She's in denial as she backs away. *Todd would never cheat.*

FOUR

On Monday, Todd kisses Rosaleen goodbye as he heads out the door for work. It's a relatively good morning. Not all mornings with Todd are completely horrible, but still, she has the urge to bite him when he kisses her or knee him in the groin. "Have a nice day at work." She fights through the temptation to follow through on her urges as he leaves.

As soon as she sees Todd's truck disappear around the block, she quickly goes to her room and gets dressed for her interview.

Rosaleen pulls an old dress out from her closet and sits on her bed, staring at it with resentment. Todd picked it out for her without her input, forcing her to wear it to a work banquet.

When they arrived, Rosaleen tried to open the truck door and get out, but Todd pulled her arm back. "Do not humiliate me. Sit right there until I walk around and open that door for you."

Knowing all too well that he hasn't opened a door for her since they got married, she sat back and waited.

Todd opened her door and held his hand out.

She grabbed it, letting him escort her out as he wrapped his arm around her.

Todd pulled her closer to him, whispering under his breath, "All I want you to do is sit, smile, and be quiet. You're such a pretty woman when you're smiling and no words are coming out of that mouth of yours."

Thinking of the consequences of what will happen if Todd finds out about her interview, she puts the dress back on its hanger. *I'm not going.*

She wonders if it'll be easier to break the news about the job if she actually lands it.

What seems like something he should be proud of, will probably end as long night of regret for Rosaleen.

She remembers the last time she dressed up was just to go to the local grocery store. She only wanted to feel pretty, since she wasn't allowed to put effort into her appearance anymore. She knew she'd get home and be able to wash the makeup off before Todd got home. Little did she know, he had gotten off early. She barely had time to make it inside before he ripped her clothes off and burned them. After he got done with her, she didn't leave the house for two weeks due to the bruises he left on her face.

No! This isn't how my life is supposed to be. She takes the dress back off the hanger. Hoping she can get it over her hips, she wiggles it up side-to-side. *It fits!*

Rosaleen applies makeup to her face, lining her eyes with black eyeliner and mascara to accent their honey tone. There isn't a need to apply blush because her cheeks are rosy enough as they are.

Excited that she finally has a reason to wear the dark red lipstick that she bought a few months ago, she applies it. Red has always been her go-to color. Its bold colors accent her bronzy skin tone, even if she bought it out of spite, knowing Todd doesn't allow her to wear such bold colors.

While on their honeymoon, Todd threw a wet washcloth at her. "Wash that off. You look like a whore."

"But Todd, I've always worn this color. Even you said I looked beautiful."

"Don't argue with me about it. That's final. You're my wife now, and you will do as you're told."

Rosaleen realized that day that she'd been conned into a controlling marriage.

Trying to tame her wild hair, she pulls her hair up using a few bobby pins. She steps into her black flats, hoping she doesn't get blisters on her heels since she always wears flip-flops or goes barefoot. Turning to the mirror, she is very pleased with what she sees staring back at her.

Grabbing her keys, she heads out the door and drives into town.

She parks directly in front of the office this time, not wanting to walk the few extra blocks to the office and give the Louisiana heat a chance to melt her makeup. Plus, she doesn't want to end up with sweat spots under her arms. Even deodorant can't save you in Louisiana sometimes.

"I got this," Rosaleen tells herself firmly as she touches up her lipstick.

Stepping up to the sidewalk, she twists her ankle, falling forward.

"OUCH!"

Fortunately, she catches herself before she faceplants. *I'm so clumsy!*

Rosaleen looks around in the hopes that no one saw her fall, noticing some freckle-faced boy laughing at her. *Oh, that's just Johnson's kid.* She sticks her tongue out at him and proceeds to the door.

Rosaleen walks over to the lady sitting behind the front desk.

"How can I help you?"

"I'm here for a job interview with Mr. Easton Rivers."

"I remember you from the other day. Good luck!" The lady points to Rosaleen's left. "He's expecting you. You can go wait in his office."

"Thank you," she says, passing a few small cubicles and trying to ignore the throbbing pain emanating from her ankle. She is glad it isn't a long walk. The office is fairly small, with only four workers in the entrance lobby. She looks down the short hallway and sees a few more rooms. *I wonder what's in there?*

Rosaleen enters Mr. Rivers office, sitting in an available seat to rub her ankle. She stills when she hears the receptionist speak to someone in the hall. "Your 9:30 appointment is here—Ms. Hart."

"Oh, she showed up? She's not really qualified, but this will give me an opportunity to learn interviewing skills for the more professional workers," Rosaleen hears a man reply.

First interview? Rosaleen releases her ankle. *Why did they invite me to interview if I'm not qualified?*

The receptionist lowers her voice. "Um, sir, she's in your office right now."

Ugh! I feel so stupid for even being here. She wants to run out of the room, but it's way too late for that.

Rosaleen's eyes widen as Mr. Rivers walks into his office. *It's the man from the window! He sounds different than I imagined.* Her heart skips a beat as he looks at her.

Rosaleen clears her throat and stands, her knees shaking. *It's just an interview.*

An interview I'm not wanted at.

"I'm Easton Rivers," the man says, looking nervous as he reaches out his hand.

"Rosaleen Ash—" She quickly corrects herself. "Hart." *I almost forgot I used my maiden name, she thinks, shaking his outstretched hand.*

"Have a seat, Ms. Hart." He extends his arm, gesturing to the chair in front of his desk. "You look familiar. Have we met?"

Her heart sinks into her stomach as he looks directly into her eyes.

Could he have noticed me one morning when I walked by?

Her thoughts race. "I don't think so," she says, almost losing her balance as she sits down, placing her hand on the arm of the chair.

"Hmm." He follows suit, shifting back in his seat. "So, I've looked over your resume. I see you didn't list any work experience."

"I may not have any work experience in this field, but I have some computer skills that will make me a good fit."

"Okay then, tell me, how well do you know Corptax?"

Rosaleen sits straighter in her chair. "I know my way around a computer, and what I don't know, I figure out quickly."

"A lot of the position you're applying for includes working with a few different computer programs like Vertex, Sovos, Corptax, Oracle Tax Reporting Cloud. They tend to be a bit difficult at times."

"Could I perhaps demonstrate what I do know?"

"That would be a little outside the scope of this interview, but why not?" Easton grabs a piece of paper from his desk. "Perhaps type this form up?" Easton stands up, pulling the chair out for her to sit. "You can use my computer."

Rosaleen gets up and takes his seat.

Easton hands her the paper, and she sets it by the computer. *Don't be nervous. I probably won't even get this job.* She moves the mouse, and the lock screen pops up. "Could you put your password in for me?" She tries to sound as professional as she can.

Easton leans over Rosaleen to type. She can't help but notice how warm his body feels, the smell of his cologne clean and woodsy.

He abruptly steps back, startling Rosaleen.

"What happened?" she asks.

"I'm sorry for getting into your space like that. I didn't mean anything by it. Working with me won't be like that." Easton says, sounding nervous.

He's so warm.

Rosaleen locates Microsoft Word, opening what she hopes is the correct document.

Oh, please be it.

She's relieved when the words on the paper match the document on the screen. Following the relevant prompts, she fills in the information written on the paper.

That was fairly easy. "So that's all I really know how to do, but I wouldn't let you down."

"Understandable. You haven't worked for years. I bet that's nice."

"Yeah." *Unless you're forced not to.* She moves back to her seat. *Why do people always think it's a luxury to stay home? He probably couldn't walk a day in my shoes if he tried. There's nothing nice about not working for me. Some people, yeah, it's a luxury. But for me it's a prison.*

"Ms. Hart, why do you feel you would be the right fit to work with us here at the firm?"

"I'm a hard worker, I really am. I'm worth more than just being stuck at home. I put so much effort into my work. I truly am a fast, eager learner." Rosaleen stops talking as soon as she realizes she sounds like she's begging instead of trying to land the job.

"Thank you, Ms. Hart, I'll keep that in mind." Easton reaches out to shake her hand. "I will call you within the next few days to let you know our decision."

Rosaleen shakes Easton's hand.

I'll never get the job now. Why'd I have to ramble on like that? Rosaleen wants the job more than she allows herself to think.

He'll never call me after I sounded so desperate.

FIVE

Later that evening, Rosaleen sinks into her couch, unable to get the interview off her mind. *Did I phrase everything correctly?* She grabs a throw pillow and hugs it close to her chest. *I did it all wrong. I'm so stupid.* She glances over to the pile of clothes next to her. *I should get these folded before Todd gets home.*

Rosaleen grabs one of Todd's shirts. *I bet Easton wouldn't make me wait on him hand and foot.* It would be nice to get to know him, but I know I'm not fit for the position. She sets the shirt onto a neatly folded stack of clothes. *He was so warm when he leaned over me.* A smile spreads across her face. *Not to mention he smelled good.*

Rosaleen startles when Todd slams his keys down on the table.

When did he walk in?

"Is everything okay, Todd?" Her voice quivers. *Please don't be in a bad mood.*

"What have you done all day!?" He glares around the room with a look of disgust.

"I went to visit Mom, and I just got home. The time slipped away. I'm so sorry," she lies.

Todd walks into the kitchen, storming back out with a plate. "There are dishes in the sink!" He slams the plate down.

She tries to sink into the couch, watching as the plate wobbles on the floor until it stops. *I'm so glad he didn't pick a glass dish.*

"Filthy!" He proceeds to point to the couch. "What are all those clothes on the couch for? I work all day, and you can't even maintain a few things around the house?"

Unable to hold it in, Rosaleen starts to cry. "I'm sorry, Todd. I'll clean it up right now. Please don't be mad."

She jumps from the couch as he approaches her, snatching the clothes up. "Lazy!" He throws them onto the floor. "You think I'm going to fall for them fake tears? Shut up already." He kicks the recliner, and his hands curl into fists. "You're telling me not to be mad? I can't even come home to a happy wife or kids waiting for me at the door. If you weren't so lazy, maybe you would've gotten pregnant by now."

Rosaleen grabs the laundry basket from the floor, rushing to pick up the clothes.

"Why bother? This house is a mess and you're the most worthless good for nothing piece of trash in here." Todd's words pierce through her as he storms off.

Rosaleen drops the basket and falls to her knees. *Why doesn't he love me anymore?* Rosaleen tries thinking back to the exact moment she messed up. *I wish I knew. I would go back and fix it all.*

She finishes cleaning up Todd's mess, relieved he didn't hit her this time. Although, if she had a choice, she'd pick the physical over the mental abuse any day. The bruises fade, but his cruel words always continue to beat her up inside. *****

I forgot to take my birth control yesterday while Todd was at work.

Rosaleen sits up in bed. She can hear Todd on the phone in another room, using his professional voice. *He must be talking to a coworker. I wish he sounded like that when he talked to me.*

She listens harder, making sure he will be on the phone long enough for her to slip in her medicine. *The last thing I want is to end up pregnant.*

She quickly grabs the pills from under her mattress and the water bottle from her night stand. She can't get the pill out of the container fast enough, and Todd walks into the room. She drops the package onto the floor and kicks it under the bed.

"What is that in your hand? Are you sick?" Todd looks at her hand, then at her.

"It's an allergy pill. I'm a little under the weather this morning." She hopes he will believe her lie. "Is work calling you in?"

"They told me I didn't need to go in. Now I can be home with you all day." He walks over to her, and she flinches when he leans in toward her.

Rosaleen thinks he is going to hit her, but instead he plants a kiss on her forehead. Little moments like these remind her of the reason she fell in love with Todd.

"You feel warm. You stay in bed, and I'll go make you some soup." He pulls the blanket over her and covers her up. "What kind would you like?"

"Broccoli soup, please. I love your soup." *This is going to be a good weekend. Maybe he really does love me, and he's trying to better himself.*

Todd kisses the top of her head. "Anything for you," he says, walking out the room.

Rosaleen picks up the package and places it back under her mattress. Her heart is pounding ninety to nothing as she drinks a little more water.

She starts to doze off, pondering why she stayed with him after high school. They fought off and on, but Rosaleen always went back to him. The only reason she thinks she stays is that he is her first for a lot of things. Sex. Marriage. She can't imagine building a life with anyone else and experiencing those moments again. *Todd does have his flaws, but he doesn't mean to be the way he is. I just need to work harder at being a good wife. I'm stuck here. I'm always going to be considered used merchandise anyway.*

Maybe I should have listened to my sister. She always warned me about Todd.

Who am I kidding? He wouldn't stay home and make me soup if he didn't love me.

A couple of hours later, Todd walks in and gently taps her arm. "Wake up, honey. Your soup is ready."

Rosaleen stirs and opens her eyes.

Todd holds a tray with a hot bowl and orange juice. A single red rose sits on the side.

"My favorite flower. You remembered." She smiles and sits up.

"Well, why wouldn't I?" He carefully sets the tray on her lap. "Taste it and tell me what you think." He scoops some soup onto the spoon and blows on it. "Careful, it's hot." He holds it up to her mouth and she tastes it.

This is better than having a plate thrown at me. She savors the cheesy taste. Todd always makes the best soups. He very rarely makes anything like that for her. The bad days seem to outweigh the good ones now.

She swallows. "It's delicious." She grabs the spoon from Todd and eats a few more bites. *Like the good ole days.* "You outdid yourself once again."

"I'm glad you like it." He rubs her arm. "I'll be right back." He walks into the bathroom and comes out with a cold rag. "Here, put this on your head and rest some more. I'll be in the living room if you need me. I love you." Todd grabs the tray and turns off the light.

"I love you, too." She doesn't have to force the words out this time. Their brief moment gives Rosaleen a little shimmer of hope to hold onto.

He loves me.

SIX

Monday morning.

Rosaleen goes to put her arm around Todd, then realizes he isn't in bed anymore. *His suit isn't hanging on the bathroom door, so he must have left for work. That's weird. Why didn't he wake me up?* She rolls over and checks the time on her phone. 6:30 and two missed calls. One is from Todd and the other is from the tax firm.

Rosaleen instantly panics. She runs her hand under her mattress. Her birth control is still there. *Does he know?* Not calling Todd back first isn't even an option.

"Hello?" a woman answers.

Did I call the wrong number? She looks at her screen, and confirming she didn't. She hears Todd laughing in the background and quickly hangs up. The last time she heard Todd laughing like that was when he used to try to charm her.

Barely even having time to set her phone down and register what she heard, she gets a call back.

"Hello?"

"What do you want?" Todd's tone is snappy.

"I was just calling you back, but some woman answered your phone."

"The phone lines are down at work, so the secretary is using my cell to answer and make calls."

"Oh okay. I just thought . . . Well, I heard you laughing when she answered."

"What are you insinuating? I can't laugh with a coworker?"

"That's not what I—"

"I'll handle this when I get home." Todd hangs up on her.

Rosaleen knows she crossed the line by mentioning she heard the other woman. *What did he call for in the first place?*

She covers her ears, rocking back and forth. *Please stop!* She wills her heart to stop thudding so loudly. She needs to call the tax firm back, but just the thought of doing so adds to the tension.

He's probably calling back to let me know I'm not fit for the job. Might as well make myself some coffee before I call back.

After she finishes, Rosaleen takes a sip of her coffee as she sits at the kitchen table and dials the office back.

"Easton's Tax Firm, how can I assist you?"

She remembers that handsome voice. "This is Ms. Hart. I missed your call about an hour ago."

"Yes, ma'am, we met the other day for your interview."

"Yes."

"The job is yours if you're still interested."

After rambling on like I did? How does he not think I'm the most ridiculous person out there? I made a fool of myself. "I . . . um . . ." She doesn't know how to answer. *I thought I wasn't qualified, though. Maybe my determination persuaded him. If they aren't desperate.*

"If you'd like, I can give you a day or two to think about it?"

Who are you kidding? He's literally offering it to you! This is my only shot! "Yes, I'd love the job!"

Without even considering the consequences, she accepts. "When can I start?" Rosaleen asks excitedly before giving Easton a chance to explain the details.

Easton tells her she can start the following Monday, and they say their goodbyes. A week from today. It will give her plenty of time to prepare and get a few outfits for work.

Rosaleen is excited. She so badly wishes she could walk right up to Todd and tell him. She imagines him taking her out to dinner to celebrate. *"I'm so proud of you." He'd tell her repeatedly.* This will never be the case, unfortunately.

I should be looking forward to this. She sits on the couch, worrying as she rehearses how she's going to break the news to him.

SEVEN

Later that evening, Rosaleen notices Todd relaxing and watching TV. She assumes he's forgotten about their call earlier since he is so calm. *Now's my chance to break the news.* She walks into the living room and stares at the back of his head. *Or I could wrap something around his neck and put an end to him. He'd never see it coming.*

She shakes her head in disbelief. *What's gotten into me?* Her negative thoughts are starting to outweigh the positive, scaring Rosaleen. Never in her life has she ever wanted to hurt someone. Now here she is, thinking of ways to end Todd. *I have got to get out of here.* She sits next to him on the couch.

Todd rolls his eyes and shifts his body away from hers. "What do you want?" He asks in a low, snappy tone.

"I have some good news to tell you."

"What good could possibly come from you?" He snarls, not even looking away from the TV.

Rosaleen immediately regrets her decisions and wants to get up and walk out of the living room. If she does, he will blame her for being vindictive. It will all turn back around on her somehow.

Rosaleen sighs and forces it out. "I applied at the tax firm here in town, and I got the job. I'm so excited!" She hears the bit of hope in her voice.

"You're joking, right?" Todd turns his full attention to Rosaleen now.

"It can help us afford a nice, long vacation or something," Rosaleen says, trying to sound convincing. It's a lie she quickly makes up to prevent Todd from exploding. It doesn't help. Nothing really helps.

"What the hell? You know that I just got a big raise!" Todd stands, grabbing Rosaleen by her arms. "You couldn't pass the idea by me before you applied for a job!?"

"Todd, I'm sorry. I just wanted to surprise you." She tries to jerk her arm away from him.

"First, you accused me of messing around earlier, and now you go behind my back and get a job without telling me?" He slams her against the shelf, the force knocking her porcelain angels to the ground. "I'm the provider in this household!"

Rosaleen watches pieces of her grandmother fade away as they shatter.

"Take care of my precious angels. These were passed down from my great-grandmother, and now they belong to you," her grandma says.

Her grandma's favorite blue one is the last to fall and hit the floor. It's the only angel that doesn't shatter.

"I'll call and tell them I've changed my mind. I don't want to work anyway," Rosaleen cries out, trying to calm him down.

"Oh no! You will work. You're not going to make me look like a fool by not showing up."

Todd looks at her as she glances at the unbroken angel on the floor.

Todd stomps on the angel, and a wing breaks off.

"NO!" Rosaleen cries out.

"Maybe if you cared about me half as much as you care about these stupid angels, things would be better between us! You don't ever care how I feel, do you?"

Rosaleen falls to the floor and tries to pick the angel up as Todd grabs her and shoves her back onto the couch. "I ought to break you too!" He raises his fist.

Rosaleen closes her eyes and lets out a terrifying shrill that not even she recognizes.

He punches the cushion next to her.

She opens her eyes and takes a deep breath, unable to hide her fear.

"Thought I was going to hit you, didn't you?" He laughs as he turns and snatches the angel from the floor. He holds it above her. "Is this what you want?" His eyes grow dark and cold.

"Please, Todd. That's all I have left of my grandma." Rosaleen wants the moment to end so badly. It seems like his outbursts get longer and longer each time.

He slams the angel through the wall.

Rosaleen can see the blood dripping from his knuckles. *If that had been my head, he would have killed me.* The thought makes her stomach queasy. She sits still, afraid to even blink. *Why did I do this!?*

"It's always about you! Never me!" Todd storms out of the house, slamming the door behind him.

The wedding picture of Todd and Rosaleen hanging above the door falls, and it too shatters.

As she stares at the broken picture, she feels a sense of relief.

She's never liked their wedding picture anyway. It's a constant reminder of the worst decision she ever made. The day she walked down the aisle in her perfect wedding dress and with a large bruise on her thigh, all anyone could see was how picture-perfect they looked together.

She gets up and walks over to the new hole in the wall. Another one to add to the many others in the house. She puts her hand through and grabs the broken angel. Luckily, all that broke off was her legs and the other wing. The other angels are too far gone, but this one can be pieced back together.

Rosaleen knew Todd would over-react to the news of her getting a job, but she didn't think he would blow up at her like that.

EIGHT

A week later, Rosaleen walks to her car, insecurely tugging at the bottom of her dress. She bought a knee-length black dress with a small slit in the back. The seam travels up her back with a hidden zipper. *If Todd sees me in this, he'll have a fit. Even though he probably wouldn't notice because he never looks at me anyway.* Distracted, she rips her pantyhose on a rose bush near the driveway. Sitting in her car, she pulls them off and tosses them into the backseat. *I'd be more comfortable in my house dress. Pantyhose are overrated.*

On the drive to her first day of work, Rosaleen listens to her favorite song. She pulls up in front of the office and gets out of her car. *It's too late to back out now.* Rosaleen walks into the office, and the smell of freshly brewed coffee hits her. A few workers are huddled together, chatting while holding foam cups in their hands. *Is it too soon to help myself to a cup? Or three?*

They all look up as she walks toward Easton's office, making her feel like a huge spotlight is on her. She awkwardly smiles at them, and they return the greeting.

One woman comes over to her. "Hi there, you must be the new lady. It's Rosaleen, right?"

"Yes, ma'am. What's your name? I know I've seen you around town, but I'm terrible with names."

"Oh, stop with the ma'am stuff." She puts her hand on Rosaleen's arm. "I'm too young for all that. I'm Dixie, by the way. I live with my husband and four kids down the road." She points off to the left, as though Rosaleen will know which house is hers.

"Well, nice to meet you. I look forward to working with you."

Dixie strolls back to the group of workers, and they carry on with their morning chat.

She proceeds into Easton's office. He isn't in yet. She is already nervous, and his not being here makes it worse. She spots a chair in the corner and sits on it.

A few moments later, he flies through the doorway. "I'm so sorry I'm late. The traffic was horrible," he says, out of breath.

He points to an old desk near his and tells her, "That is your temporary desk. You'll have your own office eventually. We are about to start repairing and remodeling the office down the hall. It was hit the hardest during the last hurricane season."

"Thank you," she says in a soft voice, and sitting at the desk. Papers are scattered everywhere, and dust covers the surface.

Her first day is relaxing. All she has to do is sort through her desk, shred what isn't important anymore, and file the rest.

As she works, Rosaleen watches Easton out of the corner of her eye, admiring how attractive and calm he is. *Todd used to look this good, before he became a monster.*

Easton comes off as someone who wouldn't even think about raising his voice.

Every now and then, Easton moves a certain way in his seat, and Rosaleen catches a whiff of his clean, crisp, woodsy cologne. *Todd smelled amazing when we first got together. Now his smell makes me sick.*

Over the next few weeks, Rosaleen learns to deal with Todd's outbursts after work, but it's all worth it. Each morning, she looks forward to being surrounded by the kind workers and Easton.

Ever since she told Easton how much she likes trying new coffee, he always makes the time to grab her some on his way to work.

Easton sets the coffee on her desk as she's working. "I've got you a brand-new flavor. Can you guess what it is?"

Rosaleen looks away from the computer screen. "That's too sweet of you. You don't have to do this every morning."

"I want to. No one else around here gets as excited about coffee as you do."

That's because you bring a new flavor every morning. She picks up the coffee and takes a sip. "Hmm. I taste cinnamon."

He doesn't give her a chance to finish guessing. "It's cinnamon bun. They just released it today."

Not used to a man being so nice, Rosaleen can't understand why Easton is so kind to her. He never grabs the other workers a coffee in the morning. *Maybe he feels obligated because we work in the same office together.* It's almost as if he is excited to see her when he walks in.

NINE

One evening, Rosaleen is finishing up her work and getting ready to leave when Easton chimes in, "Hey Rosaleen, can you wait behind?"

"Sure thing." She doesn't really want to stay since she's already late getting home. This will make her even later now. *How am I going to be home before Todd and have the house clean and supper cooked? I'm going to pay for this. I've never been late before.* She has always been too afraid of what he might do.

Easton walks over and sits on top of her desk. Right in front of her. She is so close, she can feel the warmth of his body.

He's going to fire me. Then, Todd will rub it in my face and say that's what I deserve. "Did you need something, Easton?" Rosaleen asks, trying not to let him hear the nervousness in her voice.

He points toward her hair.

She flinches back.

Easton pulls his hand back. "You have some fuzz in your hair." He laughs. "I didn't mean to startle you."

Why does he think startling me is funny? Rosaleen doesn't think the reaction is amusing. *I need to chill out. He doesn't know.* If Todd's hand moves toward her like that, it usually means she's about to get hit.

"You know, I saw you the day the car drenched you with water. I was hoping you didn't see me laugh."

"Yeah, I saw," she replies, and they both laugh off the awkwardness. *Where is he going with this?* "I really should be heading home. It's getting late."

"How about we hang out after work some time? You know, just to get to know each other better?" Rosaleen can hear the hesitation in his voice.

"I don't think my husband would like that," she replies.

Easton's eyes widen. "You're married?"

Why does he sound so surprised? "Yes, I am."

Someone bangs on the front door, startling them.

"Oh, wait," Easton says, hopping off her desk. "It's okay. I forgot that I asked Dixie to lock the door behind her when she left. She must have forgotten her keys." He walks out of the office to open the door.

Rosaleen hears him exchange words with another man, but she can't make out what they're saying.

A minute later, Todd walks in behind Easton. "Hey, sweetie, I'm just stopping by to see if you're okay since you aren't home yet."

Rosaleen can feel the color draining from her face. *Sweetie? Todd has never shown up at her work. This isn't good.*

"Rosaleen is okay here. We had to work a little over," Easton chimes in, not giving her a chance to answer.

Oh, please shut up, Easton. She knows that he isn't saying anything out of the ordinary, but it will cost her when she gets home. Todd has always been jealous if she so much as looks in the direction of another man. Now she's alone with one, and he's speaking for her. *This isn't good.* She has no clue what will happen. She's never been in this situation before.

"Sorry, Todd, I was just getting ready to leave." She stands, shuffling the papers on her desk into an orderly stack. *Stop it.* She drops the documents. *He's going to think something is up.*

If there's one thing Todd has actually picked up about Rosaleen, it is that she starts organizing the things closest to her when she's nervous. He finds it humorous, and he purposely starts doing things to make her react.

Todd fakes a smile. "Okay, we can go home together," he says eagerly. The way Todd responds tells Rosaleen she's in trouble when they get home. He only speaks to her like this when he's angry with her in public. She hears the insincerity in his tone, and she knows she's in for it.

"If you wait out front, we'll be done in a few minutes." Easton gestures toward the door.

Is Easton trying to get me killed?

Todd's jaw tenses, and he looks at Easton while addressing Rosaleen. "Sweetie, don't you think it's getting late?"

Rosaleen shifts her attention to Easton. "Is it okay if we finish up tomorrow? I need to get home."

"You can go. I got it from here," Easton says warmly, not taking his eyes off Todd.

The tension grows, and Rosaleen feels like hiding, wishing she could stay at work instead of going home.

She walks towards the door.

Todd steps next to her, placing his hand around her arm as they leave. Give me your phone," he says quietly when they near the exit.

Chills run up Rosaleen's back as she hands him her phone.

On the drive home, Todd follows Rosaleen's car closely. He's so close she can see the light from her phone through her rearview mirror. *He's probably going through my texts and call log.*

She knows he will accuse her of messaging Easton, even though she doesn't have his personal number. *There's no use explaining. He won't believe me anyway.* If he doesn't find anything on her phone, he will say she deleted it.

Todd's truck swerves into oncoming traffic lane. A logging truck lays on the horn, and she watches him jerk back into their lane.

Todd flips the driver his middle finger as they pass, confirming just how mad he really is. *He never has outbursts in public. It would make him look bad.*

Please, help me, God! Rosaleen thinks back to the night she told Todd about the job. *He's even more mad than that. I don't want to go home. I wish that truck had hit him!*

She clutches the steering wheel tightly. *I'm so afraid.* Tears slowly run down her cheeks.

As they pull in the driveway, Todd gets out of his truck, slamming the door behind him. Walking over to Rosaleen's car, he jerks it open before she can reach for the handle.

"Todd, the neighbor is outside." *Why am I protecting this man?*

The neighbor checks her mail, minding her own business.

Todd waves at her, then looks at Rosaleen. "Smile and wave before she thinks something is up," he whispers through his teeth.

Rosaleen paints on a smile and does as she's told.

The neighbor doesn't wave back. She just glances at them with a judgmental look. She closes the mailbox and goes back into her house. Rosaleen is almost certain her neighbor knows, but keeps it to herself. *Who wants to get involved in something like this?*

Rosaleen swallows the lump in her throat. *I should have screamed for help.* She doesn't dare, though.

Climbing out of the car, she walks towards the front door, with Todd trailing behind her.

Todd shoves her into the house. "Go to our room. I'll deal with you in a minute."

No, not there! "Todd, I'd like to shower first. I've been working all day," she says, trying to shift his attention to something else. *Maybe he'll forget everything by the time I get out of the shower.*

"Do what you want." Todd's tone scares her.

What I want is to run away. She knows from Todd's reaction that she'll be better off if she follows his instructions. He doesn't really mean she's free to do what she wants. What he means is that she better just do what he says.

As she waits for him, she paces nervously around the room. When Todd walks in, he's naked. "Take your clothes off," he demands.

With no choice, she removes her clothes and sits on the bed.

Rosaleen turns away from his stone-cold eyes. She is disgusted as he breathes heavily over her. Everything about their not-so-passionate moment makes Rosaleen hate him even more. She tenses as he grunts and thrusts inside her. *Please stop... This isn't love. I hate you so much!* Every time he does this to her, a little more of her slips away.

Todd climbs off Rosaleen and spits on her. "If you want to act like a whore, then I'll treat you like one."

Rosaleen cautiously gets up to grab her clothes, hardly able to move.

"That little work boyfriend of yours better watch himself."

"We just work together, that's all."

"I didn't ask you for your input." Todd shoves her down to the floor, stepping over her as he leaves the room. "Now go wash up so you can cook supper."

Rosaleen sits in the shower, holding her knees close to her body and rocking back and forth. She feels numb as the water beats down on her. *Three years of this. Three whole years of hell.* She scrubs her body until her skin feels like it's on fire. *He's disgusting! I want him to die!*

After a long, silent supper together, Rosaleen makes an excuse to leave the living room while Todd is watching TV. "I need to go do a load of laundry." She sneaks a bottle of water into the almost empty laundry basket as she goes into their room.

Even though she'd taken a pill after Todd left that morning, she decides to take another. *I will never get pregnant by this monster!* She grabs her birth control and takes one, carefully tucking it back away and making sure to leave no evidence. *I really need to start hiding these better.* She picks up Todd's dirty clothes from the floor and sets the basket in the bathroom. *He'll never know I didn't do a load.* She walks over to the bed and straightens the sheets. Lying down, she turns off her lamp, knowing it will be hours before Todd crawls into bed with her.

TEN

"Hey Rosaleen, I'm leaving for lunch. You should come with me," Easton says the following afternoon.

"I brought a salad. Thank you, though," Rosaleen declines politely.

"How about a coffee from The Hideout, then?"

Will he just go away? He's already done enough. Rosaleen knows it's not Easton's fault, but she still feels like he crossed a line by stepping between her and her husband. "I love their coffee, but I have a lot of work to catch up on."

"You can't even lie." Easton laughs. "You work in the same office as me. Just put the salad to the side and ride with me already."

"My husband might not like that." *Please take the hint.*

"By the way, what's up with that guy? He seemed a little uptight yesterday."

"He just gets worried sometimes. That's all." *Who am I trying to convince?*

"He was so worried that he took your phone when you left?"

Rosaleen's eyes widen. *I didn't think he noticed that.* "You saw that?" Rosaleen decides to escape to the break room.

Easton stands in front of the door, blocking it. "Rosaleen," Easton says, staring into her eyes.

Woah! What is he doing? The demanding stare reminds her of Todd.

No, he's nothing like Todd.

"I need to get past you." She tries squeezing between him and the door.

He doesn't budge. "I'm not moving until you talk to me."

Rosaleen walks back to her desk, organizing it. "You have no right to throw your opinions about my marriage at me."

He looks sympathetic as he stands there, staring at her like she's a lost puppy. "You know you deserve better than that."

"You don't even know me." She grabs the stapler and puts it away in the top drawer, slamming it shut. She starts counting the pens on her desk, trying to rid herself of her feelings of disorientation.

One . . . two . . . three . . . four . . .

The counting doesn't help; instead, her mouth grows dry, and her palms begin to sweat.

"You're right. I don't know you. But I know you well enough to see how scared you were to leave work last night. The way that man had his hand on your arm—I could have punched him."

"Well, I'm fine. Obviously." *Liar.* She scoops the pens up and puts them into the mug her mom got her for her new job. It says *I start working when my coffee does* on the front. She uses it as a pen holder, not wanting to mess it up through everyday drinking and washing.

"I was worried sick about you the whole night."

Why would he be worried about me? Rosaleen starts fiddling with a strand of hair hanging over her shoulders.

"You know it's true. Look how nervous you're getting just from listening to me talk about it."

Get off my case. Rosaleen remains silent, trying to hold back tears.

"Why are you so nervous right now?"

Anger drowns out her anxiety. "Excuse me?" She tilts her head to the side and puts her hand on her hip. *Is he really this stupid? He's literally refusing to let me walk out. Acting like this is perfectly normal and he's asking me why I'm so nervous. Well, I wonder why!* "Maybe if you'd get off my case."

"Look, I'm sorry if I upset you. I just feel like you should give me the chance to show you how a real man treats a woman."

"I'm married. That would be beyond wrong."

"I've already told you. Just as friends." Easton walks away from the door.

Rosaleen feels like a cage is opening. "But why do you want me to go out with you so badly? You know I have a '*husband*.'" She emphasizes the word on husband to get the point across.

"Because I think I'm falling for you." He sits in his chair, facing Rosaleen.

What? Has this man lost his mind? We just started working together. She remains silent, willing to hear him out.

"When I leave work, you're all I think about."

Rosaleen's heart stops. *Todd says that I'm nothing but old, used merchandise. Could he really care about me?* She ignores the red flags. *He's just concerned about me. He never meant to scare me.*

"You have no idea how wonderful you are. Your smile makes me weak in the knees, and I look forward to hearing your soft voice in the mornings. Something about you drives me crazy."

"Easton, I never meant to make you feel that way toward me. I was just being nice to you." She walks toward the door. "Now I'm going to grab my lunch. I'll see you in an hour."

ELEVEN

Rosaleen walks into the bedroom and notices Todd's phone lying on the bed. *He never leaves his phone behind.* She remembers the woman who answered her call the other day. *Would he cheat?* She sits next to his phone, picking it up.

She's never been allowed near it. Come to think of it, this is her first time ever touching it. *What if he catches me?* The thought of lurking through his phone makes her uncomfortable.

His phone buzzes, and she drops it back down. *This isn't worth it.*

A name pops up on the screen. Savannah. *Who's that?*

She hears the shower turn on in the bathroom. *He always comes out while he's waiting for the water to warm up.* She darts to the closet as he opens the door.

Rosaleen watches from the crack of the door as Todd walks out, a towel wrapped around his waist. He sits on the edge of the bed and grabs his phone.

She covers her mouth with a shirt sleeve hanging next to her, her breathing growing louder. *I can't get caught. How could I play this off? There's no reason for me to be in the closet with the light out.*

His face lights up with a smile, and Rosaleen assumes he's reacting to whatever Savannah wrote.

What does she do to make him happier than I do?

He sits the phone down and goes back into the bathroom.

Rosaleen waits until she can hear the shower door close before she rushes to his phone. *Now I really want to know who she is.*

She takes the opportunity to look through his phone. There are months of heated texts between Todd and Savannah. As she searches more, she finds emails with hotel room confirmations and receipts from a couple's spa. *He never brings me anywhere that nice.* The details in the text messages are what get to her the most. Todd's text to Savannah explains what he plans to do to her during their next hotel stay this coming weekend.

She's about to put his phone down when another text pops up.

It's Savannah again.

I can't wait to get my hands all over your—

The shower is still running when the bathroom door swings open.

Rosaleen tosses his phone down, hoping he doesn't see her going through his stuff.

Todd glances at the phone, Rosaleen, then back at the phone. "What are you doing?"

"Uh . . . just waiting on you. I thought we could spend time together tonight."

Todd rolls his eyes. "I'm tired." He yanks his phone off the bed. "Get out of my way so I can go to bed."

She feels like Todd has taken a knife and twisted it into her heart. *Why have I stayed with him so long and put up with all this pain?* She gets out of his way.

"Want me to lie with you?" Rosaleen asks.

"I already told you I'm tired." Todd turns over. "Why are you still here?"

Remembering the texts she read, Rosaleen tests Todd. "I was wondering if we could go out on a date this weekend?"

"I can't. Don't you remember? I have a business meeting in New Orleans," he snaps.

"Oh, I never get to go with you. I get lonesome sometimes." Despite the fact that she's only trying to gauge his reaction, it's also the truth. She really does feel lonely. *Being excluded by force is no way to live.*

"It's not up for discussion. This is for work, not a vacation. Turn the light out and go away!" Todd slams his fist against the headboard.

Not a vacation, huh? Rosaleen walks out, grabbing her phone from the living room.

She sends a text to Easton: **Still want to take me out?**

Almost instantly, Easton replies: **Yes! You won't regret it. Is Saturday around 7:00 p.m. good?**

Rosaleen types back: **Sounds exciting!**

She walks back into the bedroom and sees Todd smiling at his phone.

Almost tempted to ask him who Savannah is, she lies down next to him. "Goodnight."

"Yeah." He jerks the blanket and puts his phone under his pillow.

TWELVE

Rosaleen dolls herself up for her evening out with Easton. She doesn't want to call it what it really is—a date. That would be cheating on her husband. She'd always sworn to be faithful to him, regardless of her situation, but she no longer feels like he deserves it. She's ready to move on now that she knows Todd is cheating on her. The texts only prove what a total monster Todd is. *He hurts me, then goes and loves someone else. What did I ever do to make him hate me so much? What do I have to do to fix myself?*

Still, she's not ready for the dangerous part.

Leaving.

That has to be planned out very carefully. It isn't an overnight decision.

Maybe one day.

She slips on a blue, flowy dress that falls just above her knees. She let her long hair cascade down her back, since Easton has never seen it loose. Spinning in front of the mirror, her dress flutters around her, making her feel free.

Patiently waiting for Easton to pick her up, she paces around the living room until she sees car lights roll into the driveway. *It's too late to back out now.* Rosaleen takes a deep breath.

Easton is the type of man Todd tells Rosaleen she's not good enough for. Now here she is, going on a date with him. *Maybe I am worth more than Todd makes me believe.*

Easton gets out of his truck, walking to her front door. She meets him outside. He's wearing a dress shirt and slacks, and she can't take her eyes off him.

"Hey there. Are you ready?"

This is cheating. "Sure." Rosaleen knows what she's doing is wrong, and guilt floods her.

He walks beside her to his truck and opens the passenger door for her.

Wow! I can get used to this. Her remorse starts to fade.

"You look beautiful tonight." Easton fiddles with the steering wheel. "Not that you don't look beautiful every other day. You're always beautiful."

How do I respond to that? "Thank you..." She plays with the skirt of her dress. She isn't used to being complimented instead of ridiculed.

"So, what made you change your mind about going out with me?"

Rosaleen thinks back to the messages she read on Todd's phone. She remembers how betrayed she feels, how done she is, and how much better she deserves. "I just figured it would be fun to get to know you outside of work."

"Well, I'm glad you said yes."

"Where's this place you're so excited to bring me?"

"It's a nice seafood restaurant about an hour away. I hope that's alright with you."

"Of course."

"The people there are extremely nice, and they practically know me by name now. I go there at least once a month."

"You must really like this place." She adjusts herself in the seat, pulling at the strap of her seat belt.

"I do, and that's why I reserved my favorite table just for you."

Rosaleen forces a smile. *What am I even doing here? If anyone sees us together, Todd is sure to find out. How do I explain being alone with another man to him?*

When they arrive at the restaurant, a friendly greeter opens the door for them. "Evening, Mr. Rivers."

"Greg." Easton slips some cash to him as they shake hands.

Did he just tip the doorman? Rosaleen looks at the man as he tucks the money into his shirt pocket. *I wonder how much he gave him.*

They walk up to the podium, and Easton is greeted by the hostess. "The usual table, Mr. Rivers?"

Easton nods.

Rosaleen stands there, not knowing how to react. *Why are they calling him by his last name?*

"Follow me." The hostess grabs two menus. "I see you have a lovely date this evening. Special occasion?"

"It's our first date." He looks at Rosaleen like he's won a prize at the fair.

Is this what it feels like for someone to notice me?

"Ya'll have a nice dinner." The hostess smiles, walking away as they sit.

A server arrives at the table with a chilled bottle of wine and a pair of glasses. He sets the flutes down and proceeds to pour. "I'm Oliver, and I'll be your waiter tonight."

Disappointment spreads across Easton's face. "That's unfortunate. Where's Lenny?"

What? What's wrong with Oliver? He seems friendly.

"Sorry, sir. He fell ill tonight with the flu. Lenny did tell me you'd be here tonight, though." He sets the wine in front of Rosaleen.

Rosaleen chimes in before Easton can speak. "I'm sure you're just as good. We are glad to have you, Oliver."

Oliver takes a step back and bows. "I'll be back in a moment to take your orders."

"What was that?" Easton sounds as irritated with Rosaleen as he had with Oliver.

"I just . . . He looks new and nervous. I didn't want him to feel like we were disappointed with him."

"Who's disappointed?" Easton asks testily.

What's with his tone? Rosaleen lowers her head, afraid to answer his question. She knows to never challenge a man when they sound like that.

She learned that the hard way.

"Hey, Oliver is fine. He's already coming back." Easton winks at her.

Huh? I need to learn to stop reading too much into people. This is not Todd. I need to calm down.

Well into their dinner, Rosaleen can feel her cheeks glowing from the effects of one too many glasses of wine. Easton waves Oliver over to pour more as Rosaleen begins giggling at Easton's not-so-funny jokes. She knows it's the wine that's making her feel this way, but the loose feeling is one she hasn't experienced in years. It feels good to sit back and enjoy herself.

Rosaleen reaches over for a piece of bread when her arm bumps into her glass of wine, knocking it over.

Her eyes widen as Easton jumps up. "This shirt is new!" His shoulders are tense, and his fingers clench into a fist.

Rosaleen grabs the cup. "I . . . I'm so sorry," she stutters as she pats at the wine with her napkin. "I'm so clumsy." Her voice trembles.

"You need to be more careful." He wrings some liquid out of his shirt.

A few people at the tables next to them look over to see what the commotion is about.

Easton nods curtly at them, tugs on his sleeve cuffs, and sits back down.

It's not the reaction Rosaleen is waiting for. Todd would have blamed her for having too much wine and embarrassed her in front of the whole restaurant.

"I just—" she starts to explain.

Oliver rushes to the table. "It's okay, ma'am." He lays a towel over the table. "Let me get a new cloth."

Easton puts his hand up, stopping him. "That won't be necessary, Oliver. We were about to leave."

"Are you sure, sir?" he asks.

"Yes, just grab the ticket, please."

Rosaleen looks at Easton before glancing at Oliver.

Oliver chimes in, "For all the inconvenience, your dinner is on the house, sir."

"It isn't the restaurant's fault." Easton looks over at Rosaleen, his brows pinched. "Ticket, please."

The way Easton stares at her sends chills up her spine.

"Very well." Oliver walks off and quickly returns with their check, not giving Easton and Rosaleen a chance to speak. "Have a great night." Oliver gives Rosaleen a look that says, "good luck."

"Would you like to go to the boardwalk for a little stroll before I bring you back home? It's always pretty after dark." Easton stands and tucks his chair in. His voice sounds less irritated—more sincere.

Wait, I thought he was mad. He's bound to get revenge for embarrassing him here. Maybe he's just acting nice in front of everyone?

He walks over to Rosaleen's side and takes her clammy hand into his, helping her stand.

"Um, sure." Rosaleen is afraid to say no. Afraid what will happen if she embarrasses him further.

Easton pushes her chair in. "Are you okay? Hey, it's just a little wine." He shrugs, smiling at her.

Is he bipolar? "But what about your shirt? I'm sorry I ruined it."

"I have an extra t-shirt in the truck since I occasionally have to go on last-minute business trips."

Business trips? Just like Todd. She shakes her head. *No! No. He's not like him.*

"Relax, it's just a shirt." He nudges her playfully.

So, he's not mad? Maybe I'm just paranoid and overthinking.

Rosaleen and Easton walk out of the restaurant to the truck. After letting her in on her side, he walks over to the driver's side and grabs another shirt from a hanger.

Rosaleen's eyes follow Easton's hands as he unbuttons his shirt. *Wow.* He is definitely built differently than Todd. She regrets comparing the two back in the restaurant. *I wouldn't be too thrilled if someone spilled wine all over my new clothes either.*

"See, no harm done." Easton winks at Rosaleen as he buttons the clean shirt up.

Immediately, calm rushes over her. *See, he's fine. I just overreacted.*

After leaving the restaurant, they go to the lake's boardwalk.

As they are walking, Easton grabs her hand.

She nervously pulls it back. *This is wrong. I'm married.*

He grabs it again.

She lets him intertwine their fingers. She can't recall the last time she felt so secure. Todd never holds her hand this way.

"I love the way the moon reflects off the water." Rosaleen stares in awe at the rippling gold.

"I knew you'd like it." He rubs his thumb over hers.

"Thank you for—" He turns her to face him, cutting her off.

"Can I kiss you?" Easton whispers.

Craving love, she says, "Yes."

He presses his lips to hers, and she closes her eyes, falling into his kiss.

"Do you want to come back to my place?" Easton asks, cutting through her thoughts.

She pulls back, wanting more than ever to give into the feeling of his breath on her. "Easton, I can't. I want to so badly, but I can't."

"It's okay." He takes her hand. "You don't have to explain."

After walking along the lake for a little while longer, they head back to his truck, and he takes her home.

Standing in the doorway of her house, he gently pulls her hips into his body. "Sweet dreams," he whispers, kissing her forehead. He walks to his truck, gets in, and drives away.

Rosaleen watches until his lights are out of sight, touching the spot where he kissed her. *That was amazing!*

THIRTEEN

On Monday morning, Rosaleen sits on her porch, sipping coffee before work. Replaying the date with Easton over in her mind, she wonders if she actually has feelings for Easton or if she's using him for comfort. She's deep in thought when her phone startles her.

A disturbing text from Todd pops up: **Rosaleen, you worthless slut. When I get back you will regret what you've done!**

She feels the color drain from her face. *He must know about Easton.* Her mug falls from her hand, coffee splattering all over her legs.

"OUCH!" Rosaleen jumps, her leg burning. *What am I going to do now?* She watches the mug roll off the porch.

Maybe I can go stay with mom? Todd warns her all the time of the consequences she'll face if she ever tries to leave.

The first and only time she tried leaving, he held a knife up to her throat. *"I'll kill you if you even think about it."* Ever since then, she won't even look toward a door when he's on a rampage.

The confusion is overbearing. Should she stay put or risk it all by leaving? It is never as simple as it sounds.

I'm not leaving. He will kill me.

Rosaleen walks into the office, trying to ignore her coworkers. Her puffy, red eyes give away the fact that she's been crying all morning. Not to mention, she's twenty minutes late already. *All I want to do is try and make this a normal day.*

Dixie approaches Rosaleen. "Hey girl, you okay?"

"Oh yes, my allergies are just bad right now. You know, pollen. Thanks for asking."

"Well, if you need anyone to talk to about your *allergies*, you know where my desk is," Dixie says, emphasizing the word.

Rosaleen nods, walking off without saying anything else.

She's just trying to be nice. I didn't have to be so rude.

She heads toward her office and looks around. *Good, he's not here yet.* She grabs the makeup bag from her top drawer and touches up her mascara.

Just as she puts the bag back into the drawer, Easton walks through the door and shuts it behind him.

Easton glances at Rosaleen, then sits at his desk without saying a word, not even acknowledging she is in the same room.

Rosaleen works quietly for two hours, wondering what she did to upset him. She finally has the nerve to ask, "Easton, did I do something? Because I don't know how much more of this I can take."

He looks up at her with understanding. "Nothing at all. I could see you were having a rough morning. I wanted to let you take whatever time you needed until you were ready to talk. You can tell me what's going on. I'm here, Rosaleen. I really am here for you."

She swallows what little pride she has left and confesses. "It's Todd. I think someone saw us in the city together. I'm not sure if he had someone follow me or not. I want to leave him, Easton, and I don't know where to start. I'm scared." She buries her face in her hands and cries.

"Scared? What will he do?" Easton walks over to her and wraps his arms around her. "It's okay. Don't cry."

"Todd is a terrible man," she sniffles. "He's going to kill me if I leave."

He puts a finger under her chin, slowly lifting her face until their eyes meet. "You shouldn't have to live in fear of your husband. You need to leave."

"It's always easier said than done." She tries to move back, but Easton pulls her in closer until she gives in and rests her head on his chest. His steady heartbeat eases her mind.

"Go home and have the rest of the day off. I'll call you later and see how you are doing." Easton wipes a tear from her eye.

The whole drive home is silent as she drowns in her thoughts. *If I stay, maybe it won't be so bad. He always warned me that he'd kill me if I talked to another man. What should I do?*

"What's that?" She sees a vase of dark red roses sitting by her front door. *Aw, Easton must've sent these.* However, as she gets closer, she realizes there isn't a single drop of water in the vase, and all the flowers are dead. *Easton would never do this to me. Would he? There were a couple of times where he did overreact a little.*

She hesitantly picks up the vase, observing the roses. *Who would do this to me?* A thorn pricks her finger, and the realization hits her.

Todd wants me dead.

She lets go of the vase, and it shatters it into a million tiny pieces. Wilted petals scatter across the porch. *That's me. This is what Todd's doing to me. Killing me.* She looks down and compares how battered her life is, just like the roses below her.

Rosaleen starts to panic, Todd's text from earlier in the day echoing in her head. *You're gonna regret this.* She stares at the blood trickling from her finger. *Do I want to live the rest of my life like this?*

Rosaleen feels a tear roll down her cheek and wipes her face. *Todd comes back today.* She lifts the bottom of her shirt, drying the rest of the wet tracks before calling her mom.

"Mom."

Her mother immediately notices something is off. "What happened?"

Don't cry. Don't cry. Don't cry. "It's Todd." Her voice breaks as the words spill out.

"Is he okay?"

"Yes, mom." Rosaleen starts to cry. "I need to stay at your house for a little while."

"You know you are welcome here anytime."

"It will be just me. I'm leaving him, Mom." She feels like a baseball hits her in the chest when she says the words out loud.

"What? Why?" Concerned colors her mother's naturally sweet tone.

"Please just listen before you say anything. It's going to be a lot to take in."

Bonnie stays silent, waiting.

"Todd isn't who you believe he is. He's a monster, Mom. He's been . . ." Rosaleen takes a deep breath between sobs. "He's been hurting me, and I'm so scared he's going to kill me. I need to get away from him before he comes home."

Bonnie lets out a deep breath. "I'm on my way."

FOURTEEN

Rosaleen sits and impatiently waits for her mom. *Todd usually doesn't come back until late in the evening. But what if he comes home early because of me?* She fights every urge to start running and meet Bonnie further down the road. Just as she stands and turns to grab some clothes from inside, she hears a car speeding into the driveway. *It's Todd!* She pauses with her back to the driveway, afraid to look him in the eye.

"Rosaleen! What happened to your legs?"

Rosaleen turns at the sound of her mom's voice. *Mom.*

Bonnie is staring at the scratches on her legs. Rosaleen looks down and observes them, not realizing the glass had cut her legs like it did.

"Did he do that to you?" Bonnie touches her leg.

Rosaleen's scratches burn under her mother's touch. "No. I dropped that vase, and it cut me up. I didn't even realize it."

Bonnie looks at what's left of the broken vase, her worried face becoming angry. "I could kill him." She steps over the glass cautiously. "Let's go get your stuff."

"I don't know how much time I have left before he gets back. I can come back later while he's at work."

Bonnie ignores her plea and continues inside.

Rosaleen rushes in behind her, grabbing a few outfits. Just enough to get by the next couple of days. "I'm serious, "We have to get out of here."

As they start to leave, Bonnie turns and looks at the now empty shelf in the living room. "Where are all the angels Grandma gave you?"

Todd happened. Rosaleen looks away, feeling too guilty to look her mom in the eyes.

"Just wait 'til I see him. I'll give him a piece of my mind." Bonnie stomps the rest of the way through the house and out the door.

Rosaleen knows it will take her mom some time to process what she just found out. It is probably for the best that she doesn't try to calm her down. She just found out that one of her daughters is being abused. That is hard for any mom to fathom.

Rosaleen gets into the car with her mom and tosses her bag into the back seat, realizing she forgot her birth control inside. The thought of grabbing it doesn't cross her mind. *He won't think to look under there. I'll grab it when I go back in a few days.*

"Why aren't you going to take your car?" Bonnie asks, interrupting Rosaleen's concerns.

"Because it's one less thing Todd can use to control me. I want to be completely rid of him." *Too bad he can't just die. I'd never have to worry about him again.*

"I like your way of thinking." She pats Rosaleen's leg. "Buckle up, sweetie."

Bonnie's motherly tone helps Rosaleen feel safer. Any other time, Rosaleen would feel annoyed with her mom for telling her what to do in the car.

"Look, I have some money put away in savings, I can help you get a used car. Something to help get you to work and back. Just until you can get something more reliable."

More thankful than ever, Rosaleen doesn't have it in her to show her mom how grateful she actually is.

Rosaleen sends a text to Easton, lying and saying she has a sick family member and needs to take the next two weeks off. There's no way she can show her face at work and risk Todd showing up.

Easton texts her back sad face emojis and asks her to call him when she gets a chance.

Okay. She replies, turning her phone off.

The rest of the ride to her mom's house is silent as Rosaleen reflects on the price of leaving Todd.

Nothing with him ever comes free.

FIFTEEN

Give it up, Rosaleen. You already know you can't make it without me.

Rosaleen shoves her phone in her pocket as she rushes out the door to her car. Her phone has steadily been buzzing with harassing texts from Todd since the day she left. *I don't have time for this! I'm running late!* Rosaleen has an appointment with a real estate agent in thirty minutes, and she is already running behind schedule.

Frustrated, Rosaleen jerks on the half-broken handle of her run-down car. She flies backwards with the handle in her hand. "Are you kidding me?" She feels her phone buzz again. And again. *Now I'll never make it in time! I'm going to be late, and the agent will be mad.* "Todd's right. I can't do this without him." Being promptly on time or early is another one of Rosaleen's flaws. If she were to be late for Todd, there would be consequences. *This lady is going to think I'm a no-show.*

She throws the handle across the yard and kicks the rusted door. "Stupid car!" What felt like the perfect car two days ago, when her mom got it for her, is now turning out to be just as broken as she is. Rosaleen isn't trying to be ungrateful, but things just keep breaking around her.

"I can't do this." She puts her back against the car, sliding to the ground. *Why won't he let me go already?*

Her phone buzzes again.

Giving in, she checks the message.

I'll be waiting when you're ready to crawl back to me. I give it a month before you fall flat on your face.

Just what Todd wants. His text strikes a nerve. *I'll show him!*

She goes to the passenger side, this time making sure she's gentle with the handle. She opens the door and proceeds to crawl over to the driver's side. The whole way she tries not to curse him. *Regardless of whether I'm late, I'm still going!*

She cranks the car, but only little sputters come out. "Come on, girl. We've got to get there. We can't let Todd win." She pats the dashboard and tries to start the car again. This time, it starts up without any hesitation. "Now let's go prove him wrong!"

Rosaleen pulls up a minute late to her viewing in a town so small that there is no name for it. It's just in between Frogmore and Chesterfield. There are no other cars in sight. She lays her head on the steering wheel, feeling defeated. *I must've just missed her. I was so close.*

This could have been mine. She stares at the cute little wooden fence that wraps around the yard. *I've always wanted a picket fence.*

There's no harm in looking around. She gets out of her car and observes the outside of the large, blue Acadian-style home. Some paint is chipping, and shingles are sprawled out all over the ground. Trees and vines are taking over the front of the old house. The brick chimney that used to be on top of the house has partially crumbled to the ground. But the beauty of the Acadian house still shows through, no matter how run down it is. *The real estate lady did tell me it was damaged from the recent hurricane.*

A wooden wrap-around porch catches her eye. She has always wanted a wrap-around porch. As she approaches the front steps, she notices a porch swing.

She pictures herself sitting on it and casually swinging, sipping on iced tea from a mason jar. No one there to yell at her or disturb the beautiful sounds of nature. *This could have been all mine.*

She follows the porch around to the back. Some boards creak and sink, but that doesn't stop her.

Off to the side of the house is an old, massive oak tree covered with moss. The branches wave down and sit on the ground. On one branch is a wooden swing attached to a tethered rope.

She walks over to the swing and sits. She's certain it will snap as it pulls and tightens under her weight, but it doesn't.

She slowly starts to swing until she is high in the air. She can't recall the last time she felt so free, the wind blowing through her hair.

Rosaleen closes her eyes as she glides back and forth, imagining a loving husband playfully pushing her higher and higher.

She jumps off while high in the air and falls to the ground, rolling onto her back. She stares up at the beautiful, clear blue sky, and bursts out laughing. She envisions turning over to see her smiling husband lying next to her. It feels all too real as she imagines him running his fingers through her hair, pulling grass out from between the strands. He rubs his fingers softly over her cheeks and leans in to kiss her.

Down the road, a car honks, interrupting Rosaleen's perfect daydream. She stands, dusting herself off as she walks back around to the front yard. *It was good while it lasted.*

Just as she's walking to her car, a red Mustang pulls up behind hers.

Out steps a small-framed, large-busted woman. *Could that be the agent?*

"Hi there! I'm Barbara!" she introduces herself with a nasally, high-pitched voice that echoes in Rosaleen's head. "Sorry I'm so late. I had to stop on the way and bring another client some paperwork before coming here."

She doesn't even know I was late. Rosaleen extends her hand to the agent, trembling from excitement. *This is really going to happen!*

"Oh, we don't shake around here. We hug. Everyone is family 'round here. You'll get used to it." Barbara wraps her arms around Rosaleen and greets her with a smothering hug.

Ew, no! Her breasts are suffocating me! Rosaleen pulls back, feeling slightly assaulted.

Before Rosaleen has a chance to speak, Barbara cuts in, "You're just gonna love this house. The last hurricane kind of jumbled a few things up, but, with a little TLC, this will be the perfect house to raise all of your darling kids."

"Oh, I don't have any kids."

"Bless your heart. Maybe one day! Come on in and see this place for yourself!" She tugs at Rosaleen's arm as she opens the screen door. "Oops." Barbara catches the top half of the screen before it falls onto them. "This just needs to be screwed back into the hinges and sprayed with a can of PAM to stop the screeching."

"PAM? What about WD-40 or something?"

"Oh no, honey, who needs to waste money on that fancy stuff when we have cooking spray?"

This lady is insane. Rosaleen laughs and follows her in.

Inside the house, the walls are covered with old, flowery wallpaper. The floors still have the original wood. *It won't take much to sand and shine them*. In the living room, there are old, vintage couches that Rosaleen already knows she is going to keep.

In the kitchen, cabinets are painted a stale yellow. She follows Barbara up the stairs. A shiny silver beam catches her attention on the seventh step up to the bedrooms. *What is that?* The step creaks as she walks over it, and Rosaleen makes a mental note to investigate if she decides to buy the house.

The master bedroom is off to the right, with a bathroom separating her room from the two other rooms. *My future kids' rooms.*

"Well, this is it. It doesn't look like much, but she was one of the first houses built here. All the other houses around town are fairly new. I know there are a lot of repairs needed, but the owner is willing to lower the price. I think he just wants to be done trying to keep with the place." She pauses and looks around the yard, letting out a sigh. "It's a shame. This house used to be absolutely gorgeous before the last hurricane. It's been vacant for three years now."

Exactly how long Todd and I were together. The thought convinces her she wants the house. Three years of damage repair for herself and her new home. What a perfect combination. One step closer to the life she's always wanted. "I want it!" Rosaleen doesn't even hesitate.

"Don't you want to look at other houses or take a few days to think about it? This is the first house you've looked at. The town has a few more on the market."

Rosaleen understands the real estate agent's logic, but if there is one thing she's certain about, it's that she wants this house. "Absolutely not." Rosaleen claps her hands together, unable to hold in her excitement. "I want this one." It is the first time in a long time that she makes a decision without Todd's input.

"Well, if you really are serious, then come by my office this afternoon and we'll discuss numbers. I'll be there 'til about 9:00 tonight. I have a lot of work to catch up on."

Later that evening, Rosaleen goes to Barbara's office, which is no bigger than a backyard shed and smells like cotton candy inside.

Rosaleen knocks on the old, rusted door.

"Come on in!" Barbara sings.

Rosaleen eagerly walks in.

"Well, hey there! You still wanna do this?" Barbara puts her canned Coke down on her desk.

"More than ever." Rosaleen says, sitting down.

"Now, I forgot to mention that the owner has already agreed to repair the windows for you.

"Oh, okay." *That will save me money.*

Barbara slides a paper in front of her with a good amount of numbers on it. "Look at the bottom, honey."

A price higher than Rosaleen can imagine paying is listed at the bottom. "Oh..." Rosaleen's heart sinks. *I'll never be able to afford this.* "I might need some more time to think about this, actually."

"Well, before you go." Barbara grabs a red pen and scratches it out. She proceeds to write a new number and circle it several times. "This is the new price."

"Wow!" Rosaleen perks back up. "Did he say why he went so low on the price?"

Barbara grabs a tissue and spits her gum into it, tossing it into the trashcan next to her. "He just said he was so ready to get rid of the house that he was willing to let it go for hardly anything. It was too time consuming. I spoke to him earlier, and he said he was going to call and order the windows today since it takes a good bit of time for them to come in."

Rosaleen is thankful for the price decrease and window repair. Her monthly notes will be more than manageable, giving her more wiggle room for repair costs. "That's perfect!"

"The inspector should be out within a day or two, but it's my husband, so I know everything will pass." She winks at Rosaleen. "I think everyone will be glad the place is getting restored instead of torn down. She was a beauty back in the day."

Barbara hands her the paperwork, and Rosaleen grabs a pen, signing it without hesitation. She can't wait to escape her mom's house and have her own place again. While she loves her mom and is immensely grateful, she craves privacy given everything that's going on. Bonnie has been incredibly supportive, constantly trying to comfort her with baking and arts and craft projects. She hasn't left Rosaleen's side since she's moved in. She hopes to be half the mom Bonnie is to her one day.

Barbara stands and sticks out her hand. "Congrats! You're now the homeowner of your very own fixer upper—after approval of inspection, of course. But I know ole Tommy and you don't have a thing to worry about."

Wait, no hug? Rosaleen humors herself and shakes Barbara's hand.

All the house needs is a little bit of extra love. She's wrong, it's not a fixer upper. It's already perfect.

SIXTEEN

The next morning, Rosaleen returns to her marital home when she knows Todd is at work. Walking into her old bedroom, she starts gathering her clothes, a rush of feelings pouring over her. Hatred. Hurt. Resentment.

She catches herself starting to cry and looks at herself in the mirror. "No, Rosaleen, you got this. He doesn't deserve me."

"What don't I deserve!? A kid?"

She whips her head around so fast that she feels dizzy. "Todd . . . I . . . didn't know you'd be home."

Todd throws a small, pink container onto the bed. "Forget to take something with you?"

It's my birth control! Her heart skips a beat, and the color rushes from her face. *How could I forget this, of all things?*

"You were stupid enough to leave it here. Did you want me to find it?"

That's why he was mad the day I left. She thought someone told Todd about her and Easton going out together, but instead it was about her birth control. "I . . . I can explain" she says, backing up slowly.

She'd rather he knew about Easton than the fact she's been withholding children from him. Todd will surely take this more personally than her being with another man. She knows he'll see it as taking away his manhood, but no child deserves an unloving home.

Todd takes a step toward her. "You owe me for this, don't you think?" He moves even closer. "Come here."

"Todd," Rosaleen says, backing into the wall behind her. Her heart races as she frantically searches the room for an escape.

"You're stuck." He's standing face-to-face with her now. "I'll make this easy on you if you don't fight me."

"I can explain." She knows he isn't going to give her a chance. She needs to get out of here immediately. He's not going to let her off the hook so easily. "Let's talk about this, please."

"For three years, you kept me from having a child!" Todd grabs her arm. As she tries to pull away, he squeezes her arm tighter. "Then you run away and leave me, like I'm some kind of monster." He shoves her onto the bed, and she fights to get up.

Rosaleen knows what's going to happen if she doesn't escape. She begins to scream, swinging her arms and kicking him. Using everything in her, she tries to buck him off of her, but he's too strong.

As Todd unzips his pants with one hand, he holds Rosaleen down with the other, not giving her the chance to move.

"Todd, please . . . Please don't." Rosaleen can see the stone-cold look in Todd's eyes. Nothing is going to change his mind at this point.

He punches her in the mouth. "Shut up! Why would you deny me children like this?" It almost looks like Todd is about to cry, but then the anger returns. "You will give me what you kept from me all these years!" He rips open her shirt. "You've been off your precious birth control for over a week now, haven't you?"

"Todd, not like this. Please. This isn't love."

He ignores her plea. "Nothing can protect you now."

A rush of adrenaline sweeps over Rosaleen. "I won't let you destroy an innocent child!" She bends her leg and jams her knee into his groin.

Todd sinks to the floor and curls into a ball. "Dammit!"

"Todd, I will never give you kids." Rosaleen stands over him and kicks him in the side. "Ask yourself why!"

Todd cries out. "You're going to pay for that!" He starts to stand up. "You'll be sorry now."

Rosaleen takes off, running as fast as she can through the house. She can hear Todd's heavy stomping behind her.

Without looking back, she runs out the front door to her car, jumps in, and locks the door just before Todd reaches her.

Hitting the window repeatedly, Todd spits on it, kicking her door. "Open this door right now! You won't be able to hide for long."

Todd runs over to the front passenger's side.

Rosaleen has just enough time to reach over and lock it before he can open the door.

"I'm going to kill you for this!"

Todd holds the door handle tightly, even as she starts the car and backs up as quickly as she can. He falls face down onto the ground when her handle breaks off. *Great! There goes my other one.*

As Rosaleen looks into the rearview mirror, she can see Todd standing up, dusting himself, blood running from his nose.

"That's what you get, you conceited bastard," she shouts, knowing he can't hear her.

A few miles down the road, Rosaleen pulls over and jumps out of her car. She barely makes it to the ditch before she throws up what little food she has in her stomach. She wipes her mouth and smears blood across her arm. The metallic taste makes her huddle over and throw up again.

Rosaleen climbs back into her car and looks around for a bottle of water. Unable to find one, she uses her ripped shirt to clean blood and vomit from her mouth.

Before putting the car into drive, Rosaleen throws her hands up and cries out, "Why me, God? Why!" She doesn't understand what she did to deserve this punishment.

SEVENTEEN

Rosaleen picks up her phone and glances at the screen.

Five missed calls from Easton. *I'm assuming he knows something is up.*

It's been almost two full weeks since she requested leave from work. There's no way she can get away with taking any more time off, if she goes back tomorrow, Easton will surely question the marks all over her body. The bruises on her arms and stomach can be covered with long sleeve shirts, but she isn't ready to explain why she has a black eye, gash above her brow, and a busted lip.

I'll worry about work later. She sits her phone face down. She's still waiting Barbara to call. She is supposed to drop off her new house keys, since the owner had agreed to let her move in before the deal closed.

Rosaleen curls up on her temporary bed.

"Here, put this on your eye." Bonnie walks in with an ice pack. "I'm so sorry I couldn't protect you," she says, rubbing Rosaleen's head. "You get some rest while I make you some chicken and dumplings."

Rosaleen can see the sadness in her mother's eyes. Without saying a word back, she grabs the pack. As soon as her mom walks out, she hugs the quilt her grandmother made her when she was a child. "I really miss you," she whispers.

Sometimes, she imagines her grandma sitting in her old rocker, quietly quilting. Occasionally, her grandma would stop and look up from her work, making eye contact with the wide-eyed girl staring at her from across the room. *"Rosaleen, I want you to know I'm hugging you every time you use this quilt."*

Rosaleen wakes up to a gentle tap on her shoulder.

"There's a lady named Barbara here to see you," Bonnie says startling Rosaleen.

"I must've dozed off. I'm coming."

When Rosaleen enters, she sees Barbara pacing around the living room, looking at the old family photos that hang on the wall.

Barbara looks over at her. "Oh my, you get into a brawl?"

"Huh?" Humiliated, she turns her face away. "I was moving a shelf and some books fell on me." *Liar.* She's still in the habit of hiding Todd's part in her injuries. It's always embarrassing to make up stories about what happened, but it is much easier to lie than tell the truth. Lying means she doesn't have to relive the trauma or see the pity in people's eyes. She doesn't want anyone feeling bad for her. She's sad enough as it is.

"Bless your heart." Barbara steps closer, examining her face.

"I hope I didn't leave you waiting long." Rosaleen says, retreating.

"That's okay. I was preoccupied with these family photos your mom has decorating the walls. Cute family." She points at the pictures. "Won't be long until your place looks just as good."

"Thanks." *Can she just cut to the chase and give me the keys?* There is something about Barbara's voice that rubs Rosaleen the wrong way. Or is she just mad at the world right now? Rosaleen can't recall ever feeling as frustrated as she has lately.

"Well, here are your keys to your very own house now!" Barbara sticks out her hands with three keys hanging on a key ring. "I'm not sure which key goes to what door, but you'll have it figured out in no time."

"Thank you so much, Barbara!" Rosaleen grabs the keys from her hand.

"Don't hesitate to call if you have any questions. I personally know the previous homeowners so I can help answer anything you want to know." She blows a bubble with her gum and pops it with her long, red fingernail.

Rosaleen cringes. "I'll keep that in mind."

Barbara smiles at Rosaleen and turns towards Bonnie. "Nice house, ma'am. I'll see y'all around." She smacks her gum as she walks out the door.

On Saturday, Rosaleen brings her meager belongings to her new house. As she pulls up and gets out of the car, she notices the field across the street is filled with beautiful, yellow wildflowers and huge, old oak trees. With so much on her mind, she hadn't seen them the other day.

It's going to be okay soon.

Rosaleen's phone buzzes, and she pulls it out of her pocket, seeing three texts from Easton. She puts her phone away. *Will he just stop already?*

Rosaleen hears footsteps behind her, and she jumps, her fists up and ready to defend her from Todd.

"Whoa there, girl!" a woman holding a basket says with a deep, southern twang. "I didn't mean to startle you. I'm your new neighbor, Patsy Berkeley." She's about five inches shorter than Rosaleen and a lot pastier in color.

"Nice to meet you, ma'am. I'm Rosaleen." She releases her fists, relaxing.

"I brought you over this here basket full of my home-grown vegetables." Her short red hair looks on fire in the sunlight as it bobs while talking.

Rosaleen looks at the basket and sees a few cucumbers, bell peppers, and carrots.

"You can make some stuffed bell peppers with these. Perfect size."

She grabs the basket from Patsy. "Thank you so much. That's very nice of you."

"I've already washed them for you. So, you can just slice and enjoy!"

"How kind of you."

Just then, two freckle-faced, red-headed boys pop out from behind their mom. They're looks are almost identical to Patsy.

"Well, there y'all are." Patsy grabs one boy, raising him up her hip. She looks back at Rosaleen. "These are my twin boys, Hunter and Beaux. Don't try to learn which is which. They look too much alike. Just yell, 'boys,' and they'll come to you."

The twin Patsy is holding sticks his tongue out at Rosaleen, and the other whispers, "Beware, your house is haunted." He holds his hands up and proceeds to mimic a ghost.

Rosaleen's skin crawls. *An annoying, chatty neighbor with creepy kids. Just lovely.*

"Get down, Beaux. You're heavy." Patsy peels him off her as he tries to cling back on. She focuses on Rosaleen. "You have kids of your own?"

Overridden with guilt, Rosaleen forces a smile. "No. No kids yet."

"Don't have 'em'. They'll drive you insane." Patsy laughs.

That's the first time someone hasn't insulted me for not having kids yet. Patsy rounds her two boys up, and they head back over to her own yard.

Rosaleen goes to the front door and sets the basket down. "Now, which key goes in which lock?"

The third key finally unlocks it and she quickly figures out that one of the other keys is for the back door. *But what is this last key for?* She searches all over the house and can't find a match. *Maybe it's a spare key to a family member's house?*

Slipping the third key off the ring, she places it in a drawer in the kitchen that stands off to the side. *My very first junk drawer!* Todd always demanded she organized the drawers. She wasn't allowed to store anything without permission.

Remembering to check the shimmering step she note on the walkthrough, Rosaleen walks up to it and tugs at the top. The board comes up with no hesitation. Inside is a small hollow space and silver paper. "Ribbons. Cool!" She pulls out some old, rusty scissors and glue sticks. It looks like a spot where someone once kept their art supplies. "My new craft holder." Rosaleen feels satisfied with her house as she places the board back. *I can hide my last angel here.*

She's about to cry and stops herself.

"I've got to be strong."

EIGHTEEN

Rosaleen kicks old, fallen roof shingles to the side of her property, clearing a path to the mailbox. *I'll clean these up eventually.* She looks up at the boarded windows. *But I'm not even thinking about those right now.*

Heading back towards her house, she glances up, noticing the neighbors that live to her right are outside. *An elderly couple doing yard work together? What an ideal marriage.* They remind her of the childhood days she used to spend with her grandparents.

The old man is patiently raking leaves into a small pile beside the fence line. He stops and nods toward Rosaleen. As the old lady is watering her flowers, she looks over and waves her tiny, wrinkled hand with a warm, let-me-bake-you-a-cake kind of expression.

Embarrassed about how messy her yard is compared to their pristine bit of land, Rosaleen pulls some old sales papers from the mailbox, smiles at them, and goes inside.

She hears a knock before she even has the chance to settle on her couch. *I just made it through my door and sat. Who could that be?* She rolls her eyes.

Patsy's voice rang through the door. "Hey girl! I was waving, and you didn't see me. I figured I'd just walk on over and say hi."

Rosaleen sees Patsy peak through the porch window. *Oh, please, does she ever just go away?* Rosaleen gets up, opens the door, and steps outside. "Oh, hey, Patsy. I was just about to start cleaning a few things."

"Do you need any help?"

"It's kind of personal, actually."

"Oh, okay. You're more than welcome to join us for dinner sometime. What about tomorrow?" Patsy asks her to come over and visit every time she sees her outside.

Rosaleen normally politely declines, making up some excuse as to why that day doesn't work. Now, Rosaleen can't think of an excuse fast enough. "Well, okay," she says, dreading the words as she utters them. "Tomorrow around 6:00 is good for me. I won't be able to stay too long, though. I have so much stuff to get done here."

Patsy's face lights up like a child's. "You won't regret it!"

Oh joy. I just can't wait. Rosaleen hopes her sarcasm doesn't show. "Alrighty then. I'm going to get back to my house-work."

"See you tomorrow." Patsy turns and walks off toward her house. She turns to say one final thing. "Oh, and don't come in your best wear. My cooking tends to get a little messy."

Rosaleen fakes a laugh and walks back inside, shutting the door behind her. She rolls her eyes as she plops back down onto her couch, mocking Patsy. "See you tomorrow."

Rosaleen sees her phone light up on the coffee table and glances at it as a text pops up. **Hey! Everything okay?** It's Easton. *I don't have time for distractions right now.* She ignores the text and turns her phone over.

Rosaleen hears a strange creak giving way to a thunk from upstairs. *What is that?* She gets up and walks to the end of the staircase. *Is someone up there?* It sounds like someone slowly walking across the attic floor. *Old wood creaks sometimes, but never repetitively.* The sound stops as quickly as it started.

Rosaleen stares at the ceiling, waiting for another sound, but nothing else happens.

What was that?

NINETEEN

The next day, she walks over to Patsy's house for the first time. Brick layers the base of the structure, giving way to a style that reminds Rosaleen of camping. Patsy has planted forget-me-nots along the skirt of the porch, all neat and perfect—without a single weed in sight. *Her house looks like something out of the Better Homes & Gardens Magazine,* Rosaleen thinks.

Before she reaches the top step, she hears a little voice. "Did you find the ghost yet?"

Rosaleen jumps back. *What in the world?* Something about the way the boy spoke creeps her out.

Patsy walks out to greet her. "Shoo! Run along and go wash up. Supper is just about through." She shifts her attention to Rosaleen. "Well, come on in, stranger!" Patsy warmly welcomes her.

Rosaleen steps into her living room and stares at several deer heads mounted on the wall. *I feel like I'm in an animal cemetery.*

"You like that buck? I shot that ten-pointer last year. Made the best fried back strap covered in white gravy."

This lady's crazy. Rosaleen, not quite used to country life, grins and nods her head as if she understands what Patsy is talking about.

She decides to change the subject. "I like the log cabin feel you have going on with your place."

"Why thank you, ma'am. My dad helped me treat and stain the logs before we remodeled the inside." Patsy pats the wall closest to her like it's her pride and joy. "Well, come on in the kitchen. I have some gumbo made up. I make the roux myself. You can help me peel potatoes for the potato salad."

"You had me at gumbo!" Rosaleen follows Patsy, trying to avoid making eye contact with the deer. *Yuck.*

Once the salad is prepared, they sit at the table, eating. Rosaleen's phone starts ringing, and she pushes the side button to silence it.

"Girl, you can answer that. I won't think it's rude." Patsy gulps down some sweet tea.

"I don't plan on answering it."

"Oh, is it an ex or something?"

"Not actually. It's this guy I work with. He's getting rather annoying." Rosaleen spoons potato salad into her gumbo and takes a bite.

"Oh, one of those clingy guys?"

"Yeah, kind of." Rosaleen knows Easton has been worried about her since her altercation with Todd, but she doesn't know how to tell him it isn't any of his business without coming off as rude. Avoiding him still feels like the easiest option.

Plus, it's not like we are a couple. I don't have to explain myself to him.

"So, if you don't mind me asking, why do you live alone?"

Rosaleen looks over at Patsy's twins. One is sticking rice in his nose and eating it, while the other is hanging upside down in his chair and swinging his legs. "Well . . . it's not appropriate to discuss why in front of your boys."

"Beaux, Hunter! Go on upstairs, wash up, and get ready for bed."

"That isn't necessary."

"Oh, they've been done." Patsy's boys race each other out of the kitchen, tugging on each other's shirts.

Patsy focuses on Rosaleen. "Okay then, why did you jump around so easily the day I introduced myself to you? That's all too familiar to me."

"I just get easily startled." *Jeez, she's nosey.*

"Honey, you can't lie to me. I had the same scared look on my face a couple of years ago. Let me tell you. If you bottle it up inside, that hurt is gonna turn into anger. It'll turn your heart to ice."

Can I trust her? I don't even know her. Patsy's insights are right, though. Maybe she will understand what I'm going through? Rosaleen slides her bowl to the center of the table. "I loved him, you know." She put her hands over her face, letting the tears flow.

"Oh, honey. We all did at some point. Let it out."

"I should've been a better wife. Then maybe he wouldn't have hit me as much." She raises her shirt, revealing the bruises Todd left on her stomach.

A concerned look spreads across Patsy's face. "What's his name?"

"Todd." Rosaleen replies, lowering her shirt after wiping her face with it.

"Now, now."

"This was my fault."

"Hey now, you look at me." Patsy's face is stern.

Rosaleen glances towards her and then looks away quickly. The shame she feels is overpowering.

"That's what they want us to believe." She waves her fork around as she speaks. "You quit thinking that, right now. You hear?"

Rosaleen nods.

"You're gonna get through this, just like I did. I'll be there for you every step of the way. No one deserves to heal on their own."

Like she did? She seems too tough to have been in my situation. Maybe it is all in Rosaleen's head, but when Patsy said that, Rosaleen instantly feels like she isn't as alone.

Rosaleen looks at the time on her phone. "I really must be going." She wipes her face with her sleeve.

"You don't have to run off so soon." Patsy picks up their bowls and sets them in the sink.

"I still have so much to unpack." She hands Patsy her cup. "Supper was great, by the way. You'll have to cook some more gumbo for me soon."

As soon as Rosaleen enters her house, she hears the faint creaking from upstairs again. *This is my house!* Rosaleen slowly walks up the stairs, checking each room. The sound still sounds like it's coming from the attic. *Did Todd find out where I moved?* "Who's here?" She grabs a shoe and throws it at the ceiling. "Show your face, you coward!"

The creaking doesn't stop.

What if Patsy's twins are right? Could my house really be haunted?

Over the next couple of weeks, Rosaleen and Patsy start to become the best of friends. A little at a time, Patsy reveals small bits and pieces of her past to Rosaleen. She mentions how she was in the same situation as Rosaleen and how she doesn't have any family other than her kids. She understands why Patsy is as tough as she is now. She had to fight an unexplainable war for herself and her boys. Knowing her story makes Rosaleen thankful that she snuck birth control behind Todd's back. She can't imagine having to protect little kids, especially when she can barely take care of herself right now. The only upside to Patsy, is that her husband disappeared and has yet to be found.

"Aren't you worried that he'll come back and take your kids when you least expect it?" Rosaleen asks Patsy one day as they sit on Rosaleen's porch swing, visiting.

"Oh, no, honey. I haven't seen him in years." Patsy never gives her his name, and Rosaleen doesn't care to give the man one, so she never asks.

TWENTY

On Saturday morning, Patsy bursts through Rosaleen's front door. "Come on, girl! I'm ready to paint!"

"It's barely even 6:00," Rosaleen grumbles.

"That's my point. Half the day's been wasted away. Get up." Patsy tugs at Rosaleen's blanket.

"Shh, I'm sleeping." Rosaleen pulls the blanket back, batting at Patsy's hand. "Go away."

"This house isn't going to fix itself." Patsy walks over to the window and draws back the curtains, letting the sun beam into the room. "It sure is pretty out there!"

"Let me sleep," Rosaleen groans, turning away from the light. "It's too bright."

"Now, I'm not gonna let you sulk in your bitterness. Get up before I treat you like my boys and throw a cup of iced water on you."

Rosaleen knows from past experiences that Patsy is a woman of her word.

Just last week Patsy called Rosaleen to come over and quit sulking.

"I don't wanna go out in the rain to get there."

"You've got five minutes to get here before I drag you out."

Five minutes later, Patsy stormed through Rosaleen's front door with curlers in her hair. "Get up!"

Rosaleen stood, startled. "Patsy! Your hair!" She laughed at Patsy.

Patsy jerked her by the arm. "I told you I was coming! Now my hair is gonna fall flat and my pajamas are wet!" She dragged Rosaleen up. "Out!"

They walked in between their two yards and stood in the pouring rain without moving.

"I don't have it in me, Patsy!" Rosaleen yelled over the rain.

"You think I never feel weak? We can't just stop!" Patsy yelled back.

"There's nothing left in me!"

Patsy raised her arms in the air. "Feel that?"

"Yeah, it's cold!"

"But you feel it. You are here right now, feeling this. You're going to get through this."

They both cried in the rain for the next ten minutes.

Patsy patted Rosaleen's shoulder. "Now, let's go inside and dry up."

Rosaleen doesn't want to push Patsy again. "Okay. Okay. Let me go get some old clothes." She kicks off her blanket and stands.

Patsy looks her up and down. "My word. You already look raggedy. Why not just stay in what you're wearing?" She laughs.

Rosaleen playfully throws a pillow at her. "Hey, now! Just so you know, these holey pajamas are comfy. They still have a couple of years left in them."

Patsy throws the pillow back at Rosaleen. "Say, why don't you sleep in your bed? It's gotta be more comfortable than this old couch."

"Eh, I'm still getting used to the place. Plus, I keep hearing this weird sound upstairs. I think it's coming from the walls."

"You've lost your mind. Now go get dressed so we can start painting outside!"

If it weren't for Patsy's kids making me believe my house is haunted, I wouldn't be losing my mind right now. "Ugh. You won't stop bugging me until it gets done, now, will you?"

"Well, yeah. I'm tired of looking at this old house. It looks haunted at night. Plus, as one of your neighbors, I can say that we've suffered long enough looking at all this." Patsy waves her hands at the house.

"Okay. Okay. If it'll shut you up." Rosaleen acts inconvenienced, but she secretly looks forward to Patsy's company every day, never admitting it because it always seems too good to be true. Patsy's friendship is rare and hard to come by. Plus, having fun and making messes makes the company more exciting.

TWENTY-ONE

Easton bumps into Rosaleen as she walks through the back door at work.

"Hey, Rosaleen!"

It's too early for this. "Oh, hey, Easton".

"I'm glad we ran into each other. I have something to show you."

"Whatcha got? I have work waiting on me," Says trying not to sound too inconvenienced.

Out of nowhere, Dixie runs up to Rosaleen, interrupting Easton. "Rosaleen, follow me! Your office is finally ready!"

"I was going to tell her that right before you walked up. Here, I'll take her." Easton cuts in.

"Okay, but I'll swing in later to see how you're liking it in there." Dixie says, her voice cheerful as she walks off.

Rosaleen knows Easton is using the opportunity to ask her something before he even speaks. "I wanted to see if I could take you out on Saturday."

"I have so many repairs to get done at home. Now really isn't a good time."

"We could celebrate your new house." Easton gives her a pleading look.

His begging her is a turn-off, and she doesn't appreciate that Easton won't take no for an answer. She recalls how much she thought she would like him, but now that she knows him better, she finds him clingy.

"Well?" Easton asks again.

Rosaleen avoids his question as she walks into the nearly empty office. Her desk and chair are the only things that sit in the middle of the room.

Easton steps in front of Rosaleen. "So, you never really gave me a direct answer about Saturday."

Can I just enjoy my new office without him bugging me? "I like the space. I might be able to get more work done now that I won't have anyone bugging me."

Easton laughs, but Rosaleen is serious.

I got it. "You know what would make this perfect?"

"You going on a date with me this weekend?"

Rosaleen rolls her eyes. "Not really. But I'd love a coffee from my favorite shop to enjoy in my new office." Rosaleen knows Easton will do just about anything to win her over right now, so she'll gladly take advantage. Anything to get him to leave her alone.

"I'm right on that. What flavor would you like?" he says, a bit of disappointment clear in his voice.

"Surprise me."

"I can do that." He walks out.

Rosaleen lets out a deep sigh. *Finally, I can breathe without him hovering over me.*

She barely has time to sit at her desk when the door opens. *Ugh.* "Easton—" Rosaleen stops speaking when Dixie walks in. "Oh, is there something you need?"

"Someone here's to see you."

"Me?" *I never have people come to see me.*

"Yep. Asked for you."

"Well, who is it?"

Dixie shrugs her shoulders, pointing behind her, "He's a looker," she mouths.

Strange. "Thanks. You can let them in."

Dixie walks out.

Rosaleen sits tall in her chair, trying to look professional. She is excited that she has a visitor. Her position at work doesn't include people having to meet with her.

Todd walks in and shuts the door behind him.

Rosaleen doesn't know whether to scream or quietly try to get out. *I'd hate to set him off if he's brave enough to walk into my job in broad daylight.* She shifts in her chair, looking for a way around him. "Todd . . . what are you doing here?" She can't hide the terror in her voice.

"Surprised to see me?" He takes a step toward her.

"I . . . just." She shakes her head in disbelief. "Is there something you need?"

"I was thinking this would be a perfect place to have a little chat, since you keep blocking my calls."

Rosaleen goes to slowly stand, trying not to panic. *I've got to get out!*

Todd walks up behind her chair and places his hands on her shoulders, forcing her to sit back down.

"Todd, please." Rosaleen knows there's no use pleading, but she tries anyway. He's never shown any remorse when she's cried in front of him.

Todd jerks her around, almost tipping her chair over.

She tries to lean back, and he grabs her face. A single tear runs down her cheek, and she's sure her jaw will snap under Todd's tight grip. *It doesn't last long. If I let him hurt me, then everyone will see how he really is.* She clenches her eyes shut, waiting for the blow to the face.

Her sweaty hands clutch the arms of her chair. *Breathe through it.* She tries to take a deep breath as he digs his fingers further into her cheeks. *Please just get this over with.* Unable to bear the pain, she tries to twist out of his grip. "Please."

He leans into her and places his other hand on the desk, making it impossible for her to escape his hold. He's so close that Rosaleen is sure he is going to kiss her. "Listen here. You're my wife. Do you hear me?" He speaks in a dangerously low tone. "You're getting out of control, and you will learn your place."

I'm no one's belonging. Anger rises inside her. She jerks her head back and pushes his hand from the desk. "Get your disgusting hands off me."

Todd straightens and adjusts his shirt.

I shouldn't have done that. She sits and waits for him to back-hand her.

He smirks smugly, turns around, and walks out.

What was that? Too afraid to move, she waits a few moments for him to walk back in. *Surely that's not all?* He's never just walked away from her like that. There is always a consequence. *Why didn't he hit me?* The unnerving feeling he left her with is more than she can bear. *What was that smirk for?*

When she realizes Todd isn't going to return, she lets her guard down and buries her head into her arms on her desk. *I can't take this anymore.* She muffles her crying so no one outside her office can hear.

Rosaleen leans back in her chair, trying to breathe through her shallow breaths. *I'm never going to be able to escape him.* She rubs her throbbing cheeks, trying to clear her thoughts. *Why did I stand up to him like that? I know better than that. Stupid.*

The office door swings open, and her heart nearly falls out of her chest. The color quickly drains from her face. *He's back!*

"I got your coffee." Easton walks in as cheerfully as he'd walked out earlier. He sets the coffee down in front of her, bending down and looks at her. "What happened to your face? It's all red." He hands her the napkin that is wrapped around the cold coffee. "Here, wipe your face with this. It's wet from the ice in the cup."

She dabs her eyes and wipes her face. The coolness feels good on her throbbing cheeks.

Easton reaches to touch her face, and she turns her head away, trying to hide the marks. *Don't touch me.* Embarrassed, she tries to come up with a lie. "I get like this when I'm stressed. I'm fine."

"Rosaleen." He kneels next to her chair. "Look at me, please."

Shamefully, she turns toward him without making eye contact.

"I'm so sorry I upset you. I shouldn't have kept on when you said no the first time."

It's not even about him, and he's apologizing to me for something he thinks he did. Todd would just keep forcing me without caring if I didn't want to.

"Please, at least look at me." He takes her hand into his. It is much softer and more caring than Todd's was a few moments ago. "I'm still so sorry. I thought that if I kept trying, you'd eventually see how much I care about you."

In that brief moment, Rosaleen wants to feel loved and wanted. She wants someone who respects her decisions. "Actually, Easton. I was going to tell you I do want to go out with you."

TWENTY-TWO

Rosaleen sees Patsy walking over with the tools to pry the old board off the windows. It is finally Saturday morning, and the new windows will be delivered later in the day. *I need to tell her about Todd coming to my office before we get started.*

"Hey there!" Patsy greets her cheerfully. "Let's get to work." She hands Rosaleen a hammer. "This is the fun part."

"We can't work past 5:00. I have somewhere to go this evening."

"You've got a hot date or something?" Patsy teases.

"Well, actually yeah." *Ugh. Just tell her.* "It's with Easton. Just as friends." *Liar. I acted out of impulse.*

"Easton! Oh, no, ma'am. I can't stand what you've told me about hat man. He is too persistent with you." Patsy puts her hands on her hips. "You should be focusing on bigger and better things than that sack of horse grits."

"But he's so sweet and actually wants to be around me."

"I'm only calling it like I see it." Patsy pulls out a pocket knife and grabs a stick from the ground. "That boy tries to harm you in any way . . ." She chips off a piece of bark with her knife. "Look, I don't need any repeats."

"Repeats of what?" Rosaleen's confused.

"Let's get to work." She closes the knife and puts it back in her pocket.

Yeah, there's no way I'm telling her about Todd if she's this mad over Easton. She'll kill him.

Rosaleen walks to the side and climbs a ladder that came with the house. While Patsy works on the first floor, Rosaleen works on the second story.

The secondary story windows are the tricky ones because she has to watch where she steps to avoid falling through the roof. The shingle repairs are next on her list.

"You lost up there?" Patsy yells from below. "Windows just arrived!" Patsy puts her hands on her hips. "By the time you climb down, it'll be next year."

"Okay, okay. I'm coming. Give me time to breathe." By the time she descends, Patsy is already in front of the house. *She sure doesn't play around when it comes to repairing things.*

Following, she sees a man walk up to Patsy and say something. He glances over at Rosaleen and starts making his way toward her.

He approaches her. "Hello. Rosaleen Hart?"

The use of her full name throws her off, leaving her unable to say anything back.

"That's your name, right?" He looks puzzled.

"Yes? How do you know my name?"

"That sweet lady told me." He points at Patsy and laughs.

Sweet? More like rambunctious. Something about this man draws Rosaleen's attention. *Do I know him?*

"You got here pretty quickly. Normally, windows can't be installed for a few days after delivery."

"Actually, I live a couple of houses down that way." He points toward a small cottage down the road to the right.

"How convenient."

He steps closer. "My name is Gareth, by the way."

He sticks his hand out toward Rosaleen.

She extends hers and shakes it.

His hands are clammy and cold.

Rosaleen pulls her hand back. "That's a unique name, Gareth," she says, wiping her hand on her shorts.

"It's Latin." He smiles.

"Well, this is all lovely, but we really need to get the old windows out before the heat of the day." Patsy walks up, interrupting their conversation. "The high is 107 °F today, and I'm not about get roasted like a chicken out here."

As Gareth walks off, Patsy nudges Rosaleen. "Not much to look at, is there?"

Rosaleen laughs. "Patsy! He's going to hear you."

"Man bun."

"Huh? Man bun?"

"Yeah, that's gonna be his name. He could use a good hair wash too. I could cook a pound of bacon with all that oil."

"I think his hair is just really dark. I can't tell if it's dark brown or black." Rosaleen looks at Gareth just in time to see him throw the end of a cigarette on the ground and put it out with his shoe. "All I know is he better not leave a bunch of cigarette butts laying around my yard. I have enough to clean up as it is."

They watch Gareth struggle as he starts to put a new window in. "It looks like that window could snap him in half if it fell on him," Patsy jokes.

Rosaleen gasps as she watches him almost drop the window. "He may need some help."

Patsy ignores her. "It seems pretty odd that he doesn't have helpers with him." She crosses her arms. "He's strange."

"You think everyone is strange." She watches Gareth. "Well, I'm not gonna let the poor man suffer. He probably couldn't find extra workers." Rosaleen leaves Patsy to ponder her thoughts. She walks over to Gareth. "Do you need any help?"

"Sure. Grab the other end, and we can put it in together."

Rosaleen holds the window at the top while Gareth tries to push the bottom into the frame. She can feel the window slipping from her hands just as Gareth backs up. It falls on the ground, and one of the frames cracks.

"Oh, no!" Rosaleen's eyes widen and she backs away from Gareth. "I'm so sorry." *He's going to be livid.*

She waits for him to start yelling. Instead, he places his hand on her shoulder.

She scrunches her face, expecting him to squeeze her.

"Hey, it's okay." Gareth's tone is soft and grounding. "Did it hurt you when it fell?"

"Huh?" She looks at him, then the window, and sees it's cracked in the corner. "I broke it. Again, I'm so sorry."

He looks at her with a concerned expression. "Did you get cut or anything?" He grabs her arm and looks it over. "Are you okay?"

"Oh, umm . . . yeah. I'm not hurt." *I'm okay.*

"Good. I was worried the glass had cut you." He sits the window up. propping it against the house.

Rosaleen looks away. "I should have held it tighter." *He's too calm about this. There's no way he's not mad.*

He leans down, getting her attention as he straightens back up. "Look, it's only a panel. It can easily be replaced." His nerdy smile settles her. "Plus, I let it go. I was worried I'd hurt you."

Worried about me? Todd would have yelled and thrown the whole window at me. He would have never owned up to his mistake.

"Come on. We can start on the next one."

"What if we break that one?"

"Then it breaks, and we get that one fixed too." Gareth shrugs it off.

Well, that's not what I was expecting. "Very well, then." She follows him to the next window with more confidence than before.

The next couple of windows went in with no issues.

Patsy walks over from the back of the house. "Got the old back windows out. I just need to get that side one." She points toward it. "Sure is hot out." She wipes her arm across her sweaty forehead. "Rosaleen, how about some water?"

"Sure." Rosaleen turns to Gareth. "Would you like some too?"

Patsy cuts in, "Of course he would. It's 500 degrees out here."

Rosaleen goes inside, coming back out with water. She hands Patsy hers, and she goes back to finish pulling the plywood off the side window.

Gareth sits on the edge of the porch. "Patsy sure has a take-charge personality."

"Yeah, she can be like that sometimes, but she really means no harm." She grabs for the pitcher and knocks it over. Water soaks into Gareth's pants. "Oops." She gives him an apologetic look when he pulls his soaking pack of cigarettes out of his back pocket.

"I really need to quit anyway." He tosses them into the trash pile next to him. "That actually felt good." He stands up and pours his glass of water on the top of Rosaleen's head.

"Hey!" She throws the rest of her water back at him.

They set their glasses down, laughing.

Gareth lets his hair down and runs his fingers through it. His hair falls just below his shoulders in ringlets. "You know, whatever happened, it's going to be okay." He twists his hair back up into a bun.

"What do you mean?" She knows exactly what he means. It isn't hard to detect her nervousness.

"Just that whatever happened to you—it gets better, is all." He dusts off his pants. "I shouldn't need help on this last window, but it looks like Patsy may need your help." He points at Patsy, who waves Rosaleen over.

Gareth walks over to them after a while. "Sorry to interrupt, but I must be off. The first floor is almost complete."

Rosaleen and Gareth look at each other and smile.

"Perhaps we can talk about the windows over some coffee soon?"

Rosaleen stares at him for a moment, "I'm pretty busy for the next few weeks. I'm sorry . . ."

Before she can finish answering, Patsy cuts in. "I'm sure you two will run into each other before you come back. Let's go finish getting some of that broken glass off the ground, Rosaleen." She glares at Rosaleen.

Rosaleen rolls her eyes at her. *I didn't need Patsy to save me. I was already telling him no.*

He bows slightly, his head toward Rosaleen. "Have a lovely evening." He gets into his truck and lights another cigarette before driving off.

TWENTY-THREE

Later that evening, Easton arrives at 7:00 p.m., just as he promised. "I have a fun and relaxed night planned for us!"

"Well, let's head out." She grabs her sweater and locks the door behind her.

"You got some sun today," Easton says, referring to the sunburns on her face and arms.

"Patsy and I have been in the sun all day. We got a lot of old tree limbs cut down and replaced windows."

"You and your friend replaced these windows?" Easton arches his eyebrows, impressed.

"Well, we had a little help. An installer came and put them in."

"Just one?" Easton walks over to a window and inspects it. "Not very professional work."

"I think he did a great job."

"You should have called me. I would have hired a more experienced company to do this. Still would have been free for you."

"That's okay. I think Gareth did a fine job."

"Gareth huh? Who's this Gareth guy?" Easton sounds defensive.

Rosaleen is surprised. *Surely he's not jealous.* Todd started getting jealous early on, but he tore Rosaleen down, saying no other guy would want her. Rosaleen stops herself from comparing Easton to Todd. *There's no way they are the same. Easton is such a gentleman. He's just looking out for me.*

"Are you ready?" Easton asks.

Rosaleen is relieved that Easton changes the subject. "Sure."

"I have a surprise for you tonight."

It's probably some cheesy restaurant, and I'll have to hear his boring jokes again. I can't believe I agreed to this. "Really? What's my surprise?" Rosaleen asks, trying to sound excited.

"You'll see when we get there," he teases.

As the ride continues, Rosaleen starts to get antsy. "We've been driving for an hour now. Are we almost there?"

"You could at least act like you enjoy being around me," he snaps.

What did I do to offend him? "Sorry, I've just got a lot on my mind."

"Okay, but just wait. You'll be glad you came." Easton pulls into Play N Putt. It's the one Rosaleen went to as a child. "We're here. What do you think?"

Wait? He's not mad? He was probably nervous, thinking I wouldn't like this place. She feels bad for being so impatient after seeing him go out of his way for her. "You remembered me talking about this place?"

"See, aren't you glad you came?"

"I am! This is really exciting."

"Let's go inside." Easton opens the truck door for her, and she notices that he still doesn't look too happy with her.

This isn't Todd. I just hurt his feelings. Of course he's not gonna be happy right now. He'll lighten up when we get in there.

After Easton pays for their rounds, Rosaleen grabs a club and walks over to the first hole.

Easton comes up behind her and wraps his arms around her waist.

"Easton, how am I going to swing with you wrapped around me?"

"Maybe I can help you?" He nuzzles her neck.

Rosaleen politely squirms her way out of his embrace, trying not to upset him again. She swings the club, sending the ball flying towards the bumpers and over-shooting the hole.

"See, if I'd been holding you, then you would have made it."

"I've never had a man help me putt before, and I sure don't need one now."

Easton drops his club and rubs his forehead for a moment, then looks up at her, grimacing. "You sure are starting to sound like that crazy friend you've told me about. What's her name again? Patti?"

"It's Patsy, and I take that as a compliment." Rosaleen tries to tease Easton, but his facial expression tells her that he doesn't take it as well as she thought he would.

"Your turn." She playfully pokes him in the side with the handle of her club.

Easton jerks the club out of her hand. "I don't like that," he snaps.

She steps back. "Sorry." She thinks he is talking about poking him.

"Patsy needs to stop filling your head with all that nonsense." Easton is starting to act more like Todd and less like the man she thought he was.

Why did he snap so easily over my friend? What's his deal? She knows Easton and Patsy don't really see eye-to-eye, but she can now see that Easton doesn't like her so much. It's almost like he's threatened by her.

But really, what 'nonsense' is he talking about?

Rosaleen keeps her distance as she watches Easton's grip tighten around the club. She can tell he's still aggravated as he hits the ball well over its target and into the next round's lane.

"Looks like we're done here." His tone instantly changes back to the nice, sweet Easton she knows him to be. He swings his club over his shoulder and casually asks Rosaleen, "Would you like to come back to my place and watch a movie after this?"

Not with how you've been acting. But he did take the time to surprise me with one of my favorite childhood memories. "I guess I can watch one movie before I go home." She doesn't want to make him feel like she isn't grateful.

Back at Easton's house, he makes them both hot cocoa. He adds the big marshmallows, then sprinkles the top with cinnamon. He places the mugs on the coffee table and lights the fireplace.

He grabs a fuzzy, gray throw blanket, lays it on Rosaleen, and sits on the couch further from her than she's expecting.

He looks upset and lonely. I better make it right with him. He just wanted me to have a good time. Rosaleen moves closer to Easton, laying her head on his shoulder.

After a moment, he wraps his arm around her, rubbing her shoulder with his fingertips. "Did you have fun tonight?" His voice is subtle and sincere.

Chills instantly run up her body. She looks up at Easton. "I did." Her golden-brown eyes fall into his soft blue eyes.

He leans in and kisses her lips and runs his hand up her back, tracing her neck with his lips.

Rosaleen lets out a soft sigh. She can't resist him as he kisses her.

Easton trails his hand down to her thigh and kisses her neck to her chest. "Rosaleen, I love you," Easton whispers. Her heart skips a beat when she sees he's serious.

Is this what love feels like? Rosaleen never says it back. Instead, they lie on the couch, listening to the fire crackle while he holds her.

TWENTY-FOUR

The next morning, Rosaleen wakes to find Easton searching frantically under the couch.

"Everything okay?" Rosaleen grips the blanket tightly.

"Yeah, I lost my flash drive." Easton lifts a couch cushion. "I can't find it anywhere. There's a lot of client information on there." He pulls the blanket off Rosaleen.

I better move. Remembering how Todd reacted when he lost something, she quickly gets out of his way.

"You didn't have to get up. It's probably in my truck or somewhere close by."

"I can call Patsy to come get me. I really should be heading home now." Rosaleen's hand trembles as she pulls her phone from her pants pocket.

"I don't understand. Why are you shaking?"

"It's nothing." *I want out of here.*

"Come on, Rosaleen. I can tell something is wrong."

"I'm sorry. I'm so used to Todd lashing out at me when he couldn't find something." The words pour out, and she hopes they don't agitate Easton further.

"Rosaleen, you know I'd never . . ." Easton's voice trails off as he sits on the edge of the couch. "You think I'm a monster like Todd."

I have to make this right. I should have been more understanding. Why do I keep upsetting him? I should be more gracious. He's been nothing but good to me.

Feeling obligated to comfort him, she sits next to Easton and puts her hand on his leg. "I know. It's instinctive. It's nothing against you." Wanting him to feel better after upsetting him again, Rosaleen says those four words she knows aren't true. "I love you, too." *I shouldn't have said it. This isn't love; it's obligation.*

He looks at her. "What?"

"Last night. You said you loved me, and I never said it back." She grabs his hand. "I love you, too." She instantly feels guilty, knowing there will probably never be anything between them. *How will I ever get out of this mistake?*

TWENTY-FIVE

Easton brings Rosaleen home and walks her to her fence, lightly kissing her goodbye. She holds her hand up to her cheek, where he kissed her. If it had been a kiss from Todd, she would have viciously scrubbed her face wherever his lips had touched. Easton's kiss had been soft and light.

Why can't I just let myself fall in love with this man?

Rosaleen starts walking inside, but stops when she sees Patsy quickly running over.

"I wanted to catch you before you got too busy to talk to me."

"What is it, Patsy? What's wrong?"

"Last night, I saw a truck lurking around while you were with Easton. I didn't want to alarm you and ruin your night. I called the police, and they were able to stop him and see what he was hanging 'round for. They said the man claimed he was lost and looking for his cousin's house. Said he was down the wrong road."

"What did they say his name was?"

"They wouldn't give his name to me. All they said was that it was a male, but they assured me that he wasn't any kind of threat. He left as soon as they talked to him. If he does come back, I've got ole Sally here to protect us." Patsy pats her chest.

Rosaleen tilts her head to the side, confused. "Um, what is ole Sally, and why is it in your chest?"

"My gun. She's a beauty. Wanna see?" Patsy reaches down through the collar of her shirt.

Rosaleen laughs. "No! Please, no. Maybe when Sally isn't in your shirt. That's a little weird."

"Weird? Why, I've got the best holsters 'round here. We are going to get you one soon. No question about it." Patsy sits on Rosaleen's porch swing. "So, how was it?"

"How was what?" Rosaleen tries to act like she doesn't know what Patsy is talking about.

"Don't think I don't know that you are now just rolling in. I saw you leave yesterday with that man and pull up with him a second ago."

"It was okay." She sits next to Patsy. Some rust falls onto Rosaleen.

"This old swing cracks me up." Patsy flicks the debris off Rosaleen's arm. "Wait. Hold on? Just okay?"

"Well, I didn't really want to go, but I kind of felt bad for him. He went out of his way for me all evening."

"So? That don't mean you have to stay somewhere you don't wanna be."

"I know, but . . ."

"No, Rosaleen."

"I just felt like I owed him that much."

"Rosaleen, stop." Patsy puts her hand on Rosaleen's shoulder. "You don't owe that man anything."

"Well, I did upset him a little. I had to make it right with him."

Patsy stares at her, incredulous.

"There is one more teensy detail I left out..."

Patsy squinches her eyes up. "Just say it."

"I may have told him I loved him." Rosaleen face-palms herself.

"Now, you wait one damn minute! I think my ears are clogged." She twists her fingers in her ears. "Repeat that."

"But, I don't—I just felt so bad for him."

Patsy stands. "I can't listen to this anymore. He's just like Todd, and you don't even see it!"

Rosaleen jumps up, "Wait, Patsy! Just hear me out."

Patsy turns and grabs Rosaleen by her arms, shaking her aggressively. "You listen to me right now!"

"Patsy!" Rosaleen starts laughing. "Why are you shaking me?"

"It's not funny! You do not owe no one anything! You hear me?"

"Loud and clear. Jeez." Rosaleen sits back down after Patsy releases her grip. *She's right.* She knows Patsy is serious.

"You can laugh, but there's just something about him. You better watch him, Rosaleen." Patsy walks off without so much as a goodbye.

Well, that was a good friendship while it lasted. Rosaleen lets out a defeated sigh. "Now she'll never talk to me again." She slumps down in her swing.

TWENTY-SIX

With Patsy not around, Rosaleen lies on the couch with nothing to do. *Patsy hasn't even called me today.* She picks up her phone and looks at the blank screen. *Maybe I'll go put my new kitchen stuff up.* She had gone shopping a few days before, after she realized she couldn't get by with only a few things in her kitchen. She needed more.

As she's approaching the kitchen door, she hears the creaking noise from upstairs again.

She follows the sound as it gets a little louder and louder the further up she goes. *It's still in the attic.* More curious and frustrated than scared, she tugs the string hanging from the ceiling door. A ladder slowly trickles down until the bottom touches the floor.

Rosaleen hasn't stepped foot in the attic since she bought the place. Attics always give her the creeps. With all the true crime she watches, she knows nothing good has come from an attic. *I'll be the next victim on America's Most Wanted if I'm not careful.* Still, her interest gets the best of her as she looks up into the dark space, and she proceeds up the ladder.

She shines her phone light around the attic and spots a wall where boxes are neatly stacked. She attempts to pick up a box, but it's too heavy, so she slides it down instead. She opens it, but nothing inside piques her interest. It's just a bunch of newspapers and magazines. *Probably saved from important dates.* She opens a few more boxes, finding scraps of cloth and more magazines.

She hears the tapping sound again, louder now, and she loses interest in the boxes. *That's weird; the sound is coming from the wall.*

She scoots a few more boxes out of the way and puts her ear up to the wall. *Weird.* She knocks on it, hoping that if it's an animal it'll be enough to scare it off. *Probably a squirrel.*

The sound continues.

Rosaleen knocks again in a different spot. *Why does this wall sound hollow?* She feels along the wallpaper until her hands meet a small bump. *What's that?* She presses her finger hard into the wallpaper until a small part rips. *Is that a metal hinge?* She traces her hand further down until she comes in contact with another. *There's no way this is a door.*

She begins to rip more wallpaper off, revealing an old wooden door barely as tall as she is. "No door knob?" There's a keyhole where the knob should be.

She tries pushing it open, but it doesn't budge. "But what if...?" She runs down-stairs, opening the junk drawer in the kitchen and pulling out the third key that didn't belong anywhere. "Could it be?"

Back at the door, she slips the key into the hole. *It fits.*

She hesitates as she slowly turns the key. The door gives way and creaks open. Frightened, Rosaleen slams it back shut. *Stop being such a wimp.* She pushes it back open, and the smell of musk and mothballs hits her. Unable to see inside, she shines her phone light inside.

"Why is there a hidden room?"

Cautiously, She takes a step inside, following the sound.

She stops dead in her tracks when she sees a white figure dancing around, creaking sound coming from behind her. Goosebumps cover her arms. *Beware, your house is haunted*, Rosaleen recalls one of Patsy's twins saying the first day she met them. *Maybe the twins are right.* She shakes her head. *No. There's no way!*

She turns around, and the door is already shut behind her.

Rosaleen starts hysterically banging on it. "HELP! HELP!"

She hears the sound again and turns, letting her eyes adjust to the darkened room. She sees a brown baseboard below the sheet. *That's not a person.* She continues absorbing the room as she calms down. *Books?* Lots of book-filled shelves make up the wall.

She hears the creaking again and swings around so see a beautiful stained-glass window. A red rose with a green stem sits amid the blue and yellow frames, and a loose board sits behind the glass. *That's the sound!*

The loose board slowly creaks back and forth from what seems to be a small draft coming through it. She shines her flashlight from her phone over the fixture sitting above a little reading nook. The light beams off, reflecting the many colors. *How did we not see this from outside?*

She climbs onto the soft quilts and pillows, and dust sprawls up around her, sending her into a sneezing fit. "Yuck!" She wipes her nose on the bottom of her shirt. It is obvious to Rosaleen that no one has been up here for years.

A little crank handle sits just below the window. She rotates it until the window opens toward her. Pressing hard on the rotten board, she shoves it off. She looks at the dust sparkling around the room. It almost looks magical.

Is this Heaven? She runs her hand across some books, imagining herself sitting in the room and reading all day. She walks up to a small dresser in the corner with a picture above it. In it, a woman holding up an infant, no older than a few months old, in the air above her head. It's a beautiful, sunny day, and from the picture, you can tell that the pair share a close bond. Their eyes are locked, and the trusting smile from the baby says it all. The mother wears a yellow sundress with a pin of a butterfly with wings. Her long, untamed black hair blows in the wind.

"She's so beautiful." Rosaleen runs her hand across the picture. Emotions flood through her. She wants a baby and to have the same motherly look in her eyes. *Why can't this be me?*

Rosaleen's attention moves to the dresser below her. She opens it. A journal with the pin from the photo is wrapped together with some torn yellow fabric. *This must be from her dress.*

Picking up the journal, she unwraps the fabric and puts the pin on her dress. When she turns, the pin reflects the sunlight. *Stunning.*

Moving back to the nook, she sits and opens the journal. A small piece of paper falls out.

Rosaleen carefully unfolds it. She realizes the letter is bittersweet as she reads:

My baby boy, I hope this finds you one day. Love you forever, Mom.

By the time you read this, I will be in Heaven watching down on you. I hope you know how much I love you. I'm sorry I had to leave you when I did. If I had a chance to go back and redo anything, I'd choose to have you all over again. I knew you were perfect from the instant I felt your little flutters.

Rosaleen feels a tear trickling down her cheek. She closes the journal and wraps the yellow cloth back around it, sitting it down on the pillows. She'll wait for a better day to finish reading that. Her heart can't take any more pain at that moment.

She locks the door back up and proceeds downstairs.

TWENTY-SEVEN

Rosaleen hears a soft knock at the door while walking to the kitchen. *Patsy!* She heads over and swings the door open, ready to apologize to her. "Patsy, I just want to tell you how sorry I am—" She stops mid-sentence. "Gareth?"

Gareth looks amused. "Well, I'd accept your apology if I was her."

"How can I help you?"

"I actually came back to finish installing the windows." He holds up his tool bag.

"Oh. I thought . . . Okay. I can help you. Let me put on some shoes." Rosaleen shuts the door and throws a pair of old flip-flops on. *Not really the safest choice when handling so much glass.*

She walks around the house and up to Gareth, who already has an old window halfway out of the frame. "I figured that since it was such a pretty day, I might as well finish up the job."

"You don't have any hired helpers?" She still finds it odd that he works alone.

"Workers are hard to find around town. With it being small and all." He looks at Rosaleen's shirt and freezes before setting everything in his hands down.

"What?" Rosaleen is uncomfortable with the way Gareth is looking at her.

He reaches out and tugs at the pin Rosaleen is wearing. "Where'd you get that?"

Rosaleen slaps his hand away. "Stop that!" *Todd always took up my space like this.* Gareth isn't much bigger than her, so she feels like she can take him if he tries anything.

"Can I just look at the pin?" He reaches toward her again.

Why do the men I meet never realize what personal space is?

Rosaleen shoves Gareth back, causing him to stumble and fall to the ground. She grabs the hammer next to her and raises it at him. "Don't put your hands on me, or I'll hit you!" *I've had enough!*

"Wait!" He holds his hands above his head. "Please don't hit me," he pleads.

Rosaleen lowers the hammer, still gripping it firmly. "Well, stop coming at me like that."

Gareth must've realized how intrusive he was being. "I'm sorry, but I think that's mine." He points back at the pin.

She holds the hammer under her arm and takes the brooch off. "This?" She waves it above him. "So, you mean to tell me that a man like you prances around with a butterfly brooch on your shirt?" She places it in her pocket and points towards his truck with the hammer. "Leave!" she demands.

"But I—" He stands and rubs his arm, now covered in scratches.

"Get off my property. Now! I'll be sure to let the company know just how creepy their installers are."

"Just let me show you." He reaches into his pocket, leaving his other hand in the air. "Please." His voice cracks and his eyes water up as he puts his other hand down and pulls something out of his wallet. "I think that's my mom's." He holds up a photo and shows it to Rosaleen. "Please, just look at it."

Her eyes widen in amazement. "That's the same picture hanging on the wall in my attic. But how . . .?" Rosaleen drops the hammer to the ground.

"I'm not really an installer." Gareth hangs his head down, looking ashamed.

"So, you lied?" She puts her hand on her hip and glares at him. *Me and Patsy knew something was off with the repairs.*

"Kind of. When I came over to meet you, Patsy assumed I was here to put the windows in. I just went with it."

"But you're not who I bought the house from."

"Right. That's my father. I stopped talking to him years ago. I didn't even know he was selling the house until I saw Barbara in town, and she mentioned it to me. I knew I needed to meet you because there's one thing I wanted to check before someone moved in."

"Why didn't you check while it was vacant?" Rosaleen has a hard time trying to understand his story. *Is he telling the truth this time?*

"Because I had moved up north for college years ago. I came back a few weeks ago, and by that time it was too late. You had already bought the house."

"You mean to tell me that you haven't come back since you left? Why should I believe you?"

"Honestly. I didn't even know my father wasn't living here anymore."

"So, what did you want to check?" She pulls the pin back out of her pocket and holds it in her hand.

Gareth looks at the pin. "Please. Can I hold it?"

"Answer my question first."

"My father never allowed me in the attic. He said it was strictly forbidden. The one time I went up there, I had enough time to see a bunch of boxes and what I think was a tiny door. I never got to see past it. He yanked me up and yelled at me. We haven't been close since." He held out his hand. "Please, Rosaleen."

The picture is enough proof for her, and his story seems real. Gareth looks desperate to have something that belonged to his mother.

She hands the pin over, to him and he holds it tightly to his chest. "I've never seen this pin anywhere. Only in the photo." He wipes a tear from his cheek. "Can I please keep it? Besides the picture, it's all I have of hers."

It's the right thing to do. Everything matches, down to the picture he has of his mom wearing it. "Of course."

"Thank you, Rosaleen! This means everything to me." He pins the brooch on his shirt.

After seeing the joy it brings Gareth, she knows she needs to tell him about the rest of the stuff from the attic.

It would have been nice keep it for herself, but she can fill the secret room with her own keepsakes one day. "Would you like to see everything else?"

"What do you mean?" He looks up, hope lighting his face.

"There's boxes of fabric and magazines. Some newspapers." She puts her hand on his shoulder. "Gareth, there's even a journal she wrote to a baby boy. I think that may be for you, too."

"I'd love to see! I can't thank you enough!"

Rosaleen quickly forgives Gareth for lying to her. She would have done the same thing if she'd been in his shoes.

Rosaleen helps Gareth load the boxes and dresser from the attic into his truck, and they agree that he'll come back in a few days with some empty boxes to get his mom's books.

TWENTY-EIGHT

On Monday morning, Patsy comes rushing through the door. "PHEW! I thought I'd never get them little turds off to daycare."

Confused, Rosaleen stares blankly at Patsy.

"What?"

"I thought you didn't want to be my friend anymore."

"You aren't making any sense. What are you talking about?"

"You aren't mad at me for the other day?"

"Mad?" Patsy leans against the wall and sighs. "One thing you must learn is that I ain't going anywhere. You're stuck with me now. No matter how tough things get between us. We will just have to get over it and carry on. Now how about we go gun shopping?"

"I'll go get dressed." Rosaleen gets up without saying more, grateful Patsy is still her friend and she didn't run her off.

On the ride to the shop, Rosaleen wonders if she will have to use the gun. Just the thought of holding one with Todd around makes her anxious. "Patsy, maybe it's not a good idea to get a gun."

"Look, just look at it like this. You may never even have to use it, but if you're in danger, you will be able to defend yourself."

"What if I kill someone?"

"Then we will address that in the moment. You're no match for Todd, and he can seriously hurt you." Patsy makes a left turn. "He'll probably kill you . . ."

Rosaleen knows Patsy is right. Todd is too strong for her to fight off alone.

In the store, the women look at the guns, including many types of luger. Finally, Rosaleen finds a blue M&P 2.0 Shield. She gets the man behind the counter to take it out so she can hold it. It fits perfectly into her hands, and it is also small enough to conceal it.

She turns toward Patsy. "Hey, what do you think of this one here? It's even cute and blue!"

Patsy laughs and says, "I think that one would be the perfect size for you."

Rosaleen hands her license to the man, and he runs a background check on her.

Once she's cleared, she does the paperwork and purchases the gun.

As they walk to her car, Patsy says, "I hope you never have to use it on anyone."

Rosaleen's stomach drops. *Would I actually be able to use this on Todd if he ever tried attacking me again?* Just the thought of it makes her sick.

Rosaleen spends the rest of her day doing yard work around her house. She rakes leaves and the discarded shingles up, pulls weeds out of her flower garden, and waters her plants.

Rosaleen notices a body-shaped shadow approaching her from the side. *It's Todd!* She braces herself, waiting for a kick.

The shadow gets smaller the closer it gets to Rosaleen. *Huh.* She turns around and sees the elderly neighbor from next door approaching her.

"Well, hello there. It's nice to see that pretty face close up. My name is Esther."

Rosaleen stands and dusts off her knees. "Hi! Nice to finally meet you too." She sticks out her dirt-covered hand. "Sorry."

"There's nothing better than a dirt handshake." Her eyes wrinkle up as she smiles in understanding. "You remind me of myself when I was about your age."

"Thank you?" Rosaleen isn't sure where Esther is going with that. "Can I ask how so?"

"From the instant you pulled up to look at this house, I could see the hurt and exhaustion in your eyes. I just knew you were going to buy it because you also carried yourself with determination."

It's like she can see straight through me. She gets me. Rosaleen smiles at her with tears in her eyes. "You're so kind."

"I see a lot of courage in you. It took me years to realize I have it too. You'll make it through stronger, despite who's hurt you. Just look at Patsy over there." Esther gives Rosaleen a hug. She didn't realize how much she needed a hug as caring and comforting as Esther's.

"You know Patsy?"

"I do. She looked just like you when she moved out here. She's a tough one, but she made it through." Esther chuckles. "Still making it."

"She's amazing. I don't know what I'd do without her."

"She sure is amazing. Why don't you come on over for a nice homemade meal tonight? I'm cooking some buttermilk puffs made from scratch. They taste delightful dipped in good ole Steen's syrup."

"I would love to, but I'd hate to intrude."

"I'm the one who invited you, dear. You don't have to be so insecure around here. We will see you tonight." Esther walks off while humming "Go Tell It on The Mountains," a little tune Rosaleen used to hear in church.

Rosaleen walks next door to Patsy's and finds her on her porch.

"You met Esther, I see."

"She said she knows you?" Rosaleen sits next to Patsy.

"Yeah, she's the reason why I'm the way I am today. When I first moved out here, I was a hot mess. She dragged me outside and refused to let me give up. When we noticed you moving in, she told me it was my turn to help someone. Said I needed to pay it forward."

"You know you got on my nerves when we first met, right?"

"I know. I know. But Esther said to keep pushing you. I told her you were too stubborn, and I wanted to give up. Then she told me how hard-headed I was and that she never thought I'd come around."

"You bugged me so much; I was practically forced into being your best friend." Rosaleen laughs.

Patsy shrugs. "Hey, what else are friends for?" She playfully nudges Rosaleen in the arm.

TWENTY-NINE

Rosaleen takes a long, relaxing bubble bath with her favorite lavender suds. She dozes off in the tub and wakes up two hours later, the water so cold that she's shivering and covered with goosebumps. She looks over at her clock on the bathroom wall. 6:57 p.m.

Oh no! Esther is going to think I forgot to go! She hurries out the tub and quickly throws on some clothes.

Harrison, Esther's husband, is sitting in an old rocker on their front porch. As Rosaleen walks up, he says, "Go on and walk on in. No need for knocking around here."

She walks in and smells her way to the kitchen. As she passes through the hall between the living room and kitchen, she notices cuckoo clocks. Lots of them. Hanging on the wall from one end of the hall to the other. *Cute!*

She walks into the kitchen, where Esther is still frying her buttermilk puffs.

Esther turns around and faces Rosaleen. "Well, hello, dear. Go on and have a seat. Would you like a glass of milk for your puffs? That's the best way to eat them."

"Sure. It smells so good in here, Esther!"

"You'll love these." Esther walks over to the cupboard and grabs an old vintage glass with diamond-shaped imprints. They're just like the ones her grandma had when she was a child. Esther fills the glass up to the top with ice-cold milk.

"Thank you."

Esther walks over to the counter and grabs a few puffs from a plate covered with paper towels to absorb the grease.

Walking the plate over to Rosaleen, Esther grabs a bottle of Steen's syrup and pours some into a little saucer, setting them down in front of her. "Eat up, dear. I made plenty. Fill that belly up."

Rosaleen grabs a puff, dips it in the syrup, and takes a bite. She's never had puffs before. "Wow, these are good," she tells Esther with a stuffed mouth.

"Harrison! Super is ready, dear," Esther calls out.

Moments later, he walks into the kitchen and sits to Rosaleen's right. He pats his stomach. "I'm starved. What's the prize dish tonight?"

Esther walks his plate over and sits it down in front of him. "Your favorite." She kisses his cheek. "Milk, dear?"

"Wouldn't have it any other way."

Esther tops a glass of milk and hands it to him.

"Thank you, love." He takes a sip from his glass. "Come sit and eat. You've been standing all day. You should rest."

"If I stand and eat, the food will go to my toes instead of my hips." She sits next to Harrison.

Rosaleen can't help but admire the love and patience they have for each other.

After they finish eating, Rosaleen thanks Esther for supper and starts heading back to the house. It is dark outside, being past 8:30 p.m. Rosaleen pauses and looks around, listening carefully. She's unsure if she hears leaves rustling toward the back of the house.

She hears the sound again, confirming that she isn't imagining things. *Could it be Todd?* Starting to panic, Rosaleen grabs a stick off the ground and starts walking toward the sound. She hears the rustling again, but this time it almost sounds like footsteps. *He's about to kill me!* She raises the stick, getting ready to hit him.

Out of nowhere, a beam of light hits her, and she starts swinging the stick around her.

She sees a deer take off, running towards the trees when she hears a voice. "Whatcha doing out here?"

It's Patsy. Out of embarrassment, Rosaleen throws the stick down. "I was walking home and heard something out here."

"Well, no little stick is gonna save you if you're swinging it around like that! Plus, you just scared away some good deer meat for the freezer." Patsy laughs.

Of course, she had to see me swinging like that. "Goodnight, Patsy." She finishes walking into her house while Patsy shines the light on the door for her.

THIRTY

Rosaleen is sitting outside enjoying her quiet Sunday when Patsy walks over.

"That cornflower blue paint sure looks pretty now that it's dry and set for a while." Patsy sits next to her on the swing, and rust falls from the chains. "It's gonna break one day with both of us sitting here."

"Hey, leave my rusty swing alone. I already let you paint my fence white," Rosaleen jokes.

With Patsy's help, her house is finally coming together, looking more like a home and less like a run-down shack.

Barbara was right—all her house needed was a little TLC.

"So, guess what today is?" Patsy turns toward Rosaleen.

"Mardi Gras?"

"Try again. It's October 29th."

"Your birthday! Patsy, I forgot all about your birthday!" Rosaleen sits forward quickly. *I can't believe I forgot her birthday!*

"Well, let's celebrate it by getting some coffee while the boys are at their cousin's house!"

On the way to The Hideout, Rosaleen notices a black truck coming alongside them. In the dark tint of the glass, she can see her reflection. She looks worn down and tired. *I don't even recognize myself anymore.* Rosaleen knows the woman she used to be is forever gone. *Will I ever get her back? I probably wouldn't even know the old me anymore.* The truck speeds past them, and she stares out at the sky, trying to find shapes in the clouds.

While sitting in the coffee shop sipping coffee, they watch people come and go as they talk and lose track of time.

Patsy stares hard out the window. "Hmm."

"What is it, Patsy?"

"I keep seeing the same truck pass by. Just weird, is all."

"Maybe they really like coffee," Rosaleen jokes.

"It just looks familiar." Patsy taps the table, "Well, this was a fun, relaxing birthday, but I think we should head back now."

"Yes, and we both have to work tomorrow." Rosaleen stands and brings her cup to the trash can.

Walking back to the car, Rosaleen points to the sky. "Look at that beautiful sunset."

"Pretty, ain't it?" Patsy stares off into the distance as she climbs into the car.

As Patsy is driving, she adjusts her rearview mirror. "Don't make it obvious, but I think someone is following us."

"What makes you think that?" Rosaleen looks in the rearview mirror and notices the truck again. "I saw that truck on the way to The Hideout!" *That can't be anyone I know. Todd? No, he doesn't drive a truck like this one.*

"Yeah, that's the same one I saw at the coffee shop. I'm going to make a few turns and see."

"Just don't do anything too irrational, Patsy. You know how you're driving freaks me out as it is."

"Easy now." Patsy takes a few turns and confirms that the truck is following them.

Rosaleen grabs onto the handle above the door as Patsy increases the speed. "Just stay on the road!"

"If you're going to backseat-drive, then go ahead and jump in the backseat."

"Now's not the time to joke, Patsy. What if they run us off the road?"

Suddenly, the truck speeds up, shining their bright lights into her car and, blinding them in the side mirrors.

Patsy struggles to stay in her lane.

The driver rams into the rear-end of Patsy's car, causing her car to swerve. She gains control back quickly, speeding up more in her attempt to get away from the truck.

Finally, the truck backs off, and they can get away and lose him.

"I just know that was Todd. I can feel it deep down. I'm afraid he is going to find out where I live." Rosaleen rocks back and forth in her seat, panicking." It won't be good if he gets to me while I'm alone. I can't think straight. What am I going to do? I've got to do something to protect myself."

"Rosaleen, shut up!" Patsy yells. "Calm down. You're rambling. You won't be able to think straight if you don't calm yourself down." Patsy slows her speed and lowers her tone. "I'm sorry, I didn't mean to be so rude."

"No, I'm sorry, I was just freaking out." Rosaleen runs her hand through her hair. "I don't know what to do anymore."

Patsy pulls her gun from her bra. "You see this, darling?"

Rosaleen feels the color drain from her face. "You had that in there the whole time? Patsy!"

"Hold on. Chill out. It's not like I'm gonna use ole Sally on you."

"Who just carries a gun around in their bra like a crazy person?" *Well, it is Patsy I'm asking.*

"I do. And you need to start carrying yours. I'll even teach you to aim and shoot like me. Heck, I can shoot an acorn off a tree."

Rosaleen laughs, but she knows that Patsy isn't a woman to mess with.

"Let's go file a report at the police station." Patsy's voice cuts through Rosaleen's lingering thoughts.

"There's no use. They will just blow us off. Two women driving from a coffee shop? With no physical description other than a black truck? We didn't even see the driver. I'm sure they'll laugh and tell us to go home."

"Yeah, I guess I can see it from your point of view. You don't need to be the talk of the town, too. They'll call us the two crazies." Patsy chuckles as she continues driving down the road. "I just want to be certain that the truck isn't following us. We can still drive towards the police station and pass it. That might scare them off at least."

They ride in strained silence, and Rosaleen breaks the tension. "Patsy, why don't you talk to anyone in town? You're always to yourself."

"After *he* went missing, the town started referring to me as either the husband killer or the poor, battered woman with kids. The older women felt bad for me since I'm a somewhat older mom. I didn't have my kids 'til I was forty. I didn't need anyone feeling sorry for me, so I moved out of the city. I'm stronger than all that pity. You better be glad you don't have kids with that man."

"He wanted kids but . . . "Rosaleen grows silent.

"Well, what is it? You can tell me."

"I secretly took birth control to prevent it. I just couldn't put a child in my situation. I want kids one day, but I feel like my time is running out. I almost regret it."

"You say that, being as young as you are," Patsy teases. "Heck, if anyone's old, it's me. I just turned forty-five today." Patsy winks at Rosaleen as she drives past the police station.

"Ah, come on, you aren't old." Rosaleen nudges Patsy.

"Nah, you're right."

"Patsy."

"Yeah?"

"Aren't you wondering why I didn't leave him?"

Patsy looks at Rosaleen. "No, I'm not. Everyone asks abuse victims why they never left. Honestly, I want to knock them one in the head when they ask, but I just keep my mouth shut. They'll never understand the dangers. You don't have to explain yourself to me."

"Thank you." Always embarrassed and ashamed, Rosaleen has never felt so understood before. *It's not my fault that I was left with all this trauma to sort out on my own. I didn't take Todd's hand and make him hit me. It isn't that simple. They don't understand. They've never had to live in survival mode. They've never had to fight this emotional war going on in my own head. It's completely different when you are the one in the situation.* It feels good to have someone believe her and not ask questions.

"You can't just leave," Patsy says, almost as if she can hear what Rosaleen is thinking.

"You said 'he' earlier, instead of a name. 'He' as in your husband, right?"

"Yeah. I hate referring to him as that. *He* was no husband to me." Patsy turns down their street, and the rest of the ride is silent.

THIRTY-ONE

Rosaleen and Easton pull up to work at the same time. The night before, a storm blew in and it is still pouring outside this morning.

Easton looks through his car window, motioning for Rosaleen to stay in her car. He runs from his truck to her car, helping grab her belongings. With his free hand, he grabs her hand, and they take off running through the rain and into the office.

Setting their stuff down, Rosaleen bursts out laughing. Her laugh is contagious, sending Easton into a laughing fit.

Easton unbuttons his green and brown plaid shirt and lets it drop to the floor beside him, where a puddle of water is forming. "I better get my extra shirt before someone walks back here and sees me like this."

Rosaleen searches him over with her eyes, holding back every urge in her body. "I need to find some paper towels or something so I can dry off. I'm cold."

Pulling her into his body, Easton says. "I can warm you up." He wraps his arms around her and kisses her neck.

The act sends sensational chills up her spine. Rosaleen pulls away and puts her hand on his chest. She takes a step back, watching as Easton's eyes burn through her white blouse. She knows her nipples are piercing through the fabric of her cold, wet shirt. *I can't lead him on like this.* She quickly turns to go clean up.

She's still thinking of the incident when, later that day, Easton slips into Rosaleen's office. "You left so suddenly earlier. Did I do something wrong?" He sets a coffee down in front of her. "There's cinnamon in it, like you like."

"That was sweet of you. Thank you." She keeps her face serious and continues working. She can't help but lead him on sometimes. He is different, but a side of him she doesn't like keeps trying to surface.

"Your mood has changed since this morning." He stands behind her and kisses the side of her neck. "Maybe I can fix that for you."

Rosaleen spins around in her chair and faces him. "Look, about this morning. I'm sorry. We can't do that again. I have too much going on in my life right now."

"Well, if fixing your house is an issue, let me pay someone to fix it for you."

Rosaleen feels insulted but reminds herself that Easton was raised into wealth, and that's all he knows. "Money doesn't fix everything, and it's not even about my house. It's me I need to fix."

"Right, but money can fix your house, so you are free to fix yourself and spend more time with me outside of work. Let me help you."

"I'm not your charity case, and you can't buy me like that. Now, will you and your money please get out so I can do my work?" Rosaleen turns back towards her desk and starts typing on her computer.

Easton quietly starts to walk out. Before shutting the door, he turns and says, "Will you at least tell me if your coffee tastes good?"

Now I feel bad for being so hard on him. He did surprise me with a coffee from my favorite shop. Rosaleen sighs. "Yes, Easton. I will. I'm sorry." Rosaleen catches herself apologizing to him for the second time. *That's how it all started with Todd. I always apologized.* Although she feels like Easton is very different from Todd, she still doesn't want to pick up any of her old habits.

A few seconds after Easton walks out, her cell rings. She picks up her phone and sees it's an unknown number with a local area code.

Assuming it is an important call, she answers. "Hello? This is Rosaleen."

There's nothing but silence on the other end. "Hello?" She tries again.

"If you hang up, you'll regret it," a voice responds in a low tone that she can hardly hear.

Oh no! "Todd. What do you want?" She's too afraid to hang up.

"I've tried to play nice, but if you don't come home tonight, I will go to your mom's house and end her."

Mom! "Todd, she's been so kind to you all these years. Leave my mom alone!"

"If you even so much as call her, I will know. Now, you have until this evening to come home, or I will take further action."

"Please, Todd. Please don't do this to me. Can't we meet at a restaurant or something?"

"Do you really want to try me?"

Rosaleen knows there is no negotiating with Todd, so she agrees. "Okay. Can I at least finish out my work day?" She wants to postpone meeting up with him for as long as possible.

"Fine, but if you do anything suspicious, you know what will happen. Call me as soon as you get into your car—before you leave the parking lot. I have eyes on you, so no wrong moves." He hangs up on her.

Wanting to call her mom, Todd's words echo in her head. *I will go to your mom's house and end her.* She knows her mom will be fine if she obeys Todd.

The rest of the work day flies by much too quickly. Rosaleen gets into her car and calls Todd.

No answer.

She calls again.

Still no answer.

Finally, he answers on her third try.

"Hey, sweetie. You calling to beg me to take you back?" he says, smugly.

"NO! Todd, please meet me somewhere else," Rosaleen pleads.

"What are you scared of?"

"Please, Todd. You know what I'm scared of. Please don't do this to me." Tears sting her eyes as she tries to blink them away.

"Rosaleen, I'm sick of these games."

Rosaleen hears Todd slam his fist down on something. *Typical.*

"Stop being selfish and think of your mom." He hangs up on her.

Her phone starts ringing again almost immediately.

"You listen to me. If you agree to get back together with me and work this out, I will stop torturing you. You can also show me how sorry you are for leaving me for that guy you work with." Todd says, and Rosaleen can hear his anger rising.

"But Todd. It . . . it doesn't work like that. I have my own life now."

"DAMMIT, STOP BEING SO STUPID!"

I hate him so much.

He lowers his voice. "You know you can't make it without me. No one will love you the way I do. You are damaged goods, and it will always be like that. Just face it."

Rosaleen remains silent, feeling disgusted. Tears run down her face.

"Rosaleen, sweetie, you know it's all true."

She can feel herself starting to believe him again. She wants to give up and give in. *It would be easier. Maybe he would love me better if I went back to him.*

"Well? What are you going to do? We can even have a baby. You don't want to deny me a family, do you?"

"Yes, Todd. Okay." She agrees, just to get him off her back.

"I'll see you in a little bit, sweetie."

Rosaleen looks in the mirror and dries her eyes. She wipes her makeup off with her sleeve. *Todd doesn't like when I wear makeup.*

She leaves the parking lot and drives to Todd's house, wishing she could die instead. *I can drive off a bridge and end it all now. Then he can't hurt me or go after my mom. It would be an accident, after all.* She shakes her head in disbelief that she would even think such a thing.

I wish I had my gun with me.

THIRTY-TWO

After Rosaleen pulls into the driveway, Todd walks toward her.

This is it. He's about to make me pay for leaving.

He opens her door and puts his hand out.

She gasps, closing her eyes.

Todd laughs. "You overreact over everything." He grabs her hand. "Let's go inside."

Rosaleen walks with Todd to the door, and he opens it. "Ladies first." Todd gestures with his hand. "Take a seat in the kitchen."

Walking into the kitchen, she notices the hole in the wall above the cabinets. *That's where he threw the can of green beans at me one day while I was cooking.* Supper hadn't been ready by the time Todd had gotten home. Luckily, he had missed her head that time. Since he'd missed her, Todd had walked over and punched her in her back. He wasn't going to let her get away with not getting hit at all. That was her punishment.

Rosaleen is shocked that Todd has dinner cooked and waiting for her. *I bet my food is poisoned. There is no way he is just going to cook today without doing something to it.*

"Well, let's go ahead and sit in the dining room. Your coming home dinner is too special to eat here."

Rosaleen opens her mouth to say something but decides it's best not to.

She sits and starts twirling the ends of her hair as she glances over to the end of the table. *Yep, there's a chunk of wood still missing.*

After she didn't put enough ice in his tea one night, Todd had thrown a dining chair at her. When the chair flew across the room, it had hit the table, snapping the leg off and causing apiece of it to hit her eye. For the next couple of weeks, she had to wear sunglasses. Not even makeup would hide the bruise left behind.

In an effort to apologize, Todd took her on a three-day fishing trip. The fish bit every time the bait hit the water. Todd rejoiced and congratulated Rosaleen every time she reeled in a fish. Rosaleen knew he was just acting in front of the fishing guide.

That evening had been the most fun she had with Todd in years.

For a month after the incident, things got a little better. She became hopeful, thinking he was changing for the better. It never lasted long. He would always go back to his normal narcissistic self.

"Want me to go fix our plates?" Rosaleen almost chokes on her words.

"I got it." Todd places his hand on her shoulder. "You've worked all day. Just relax."

With a mixture of emotions, Rosaleen sits back down. "Thank you."

Todd carries their plates out and places them on the table. He serves baked fish with lemon pepper and garlic, broccoli and cheese, and mashed potatoes.

Did he take the time to remember my favorite dishes?

Once again, she half-wittedly feels like she is falling for his charming tricks. Only this time, she knows he is only trying to get the upper hand. She is just a possession to him. If she even offers the slightest opposition, he will go back to his normal abusive self almost immediately.

"I forgot the drinks. Let me go make something." Todd stands and goes to the kitchen.

Rosaleen quickly switches their plates, hearing him as he fills their cups with ice.

Todd walks back in and hands Rosaleen her glass. "I made some tea this morning." He takes a bite of the mashed potatoes.

Rosaleen watches all through dinner to see if he will fall over dead. *I guess he didn't poison me after all.*

After eating, they sit in the living room. "Feels good to have everything back to normal, huh?" Todd asks, kicking his feet back in the recliner.

"I'll be right back. I'm going to the bathroom."

"Use the guest room down the hall."

As Rosaleen walks out of the living room, she glances at the mirror in the hallway. Still shattered.

She ran her fingers through the back of her hair, feeling the scar. She'd gotten brave that night and mouthed off to Todd after he yelled at her. She left the emergency room with six stitches that night. She had told them that she and Todd had been wrestling, and she slipped backwards and hit the floor. The doctors couldn't understand why she had shards of glass in her scalp. They suspected abuse and, still, they let her go back to her hell of a home that night.

"Come for a walk outside with me," Todd says coldly when she gets back to the living room.

That didn't take long for him to return to normal.

Walking to the sidewalk, Rosaleen keeps a safe distance between herself and Todd. She knows if she gets too close, he will take advantage and grab her hand.

He grabs her hand anyway.

Figures. She tries to pull away, but Todd pulls her closer to his side.

It's no use fighting against him.

"When we wake up in the morning, we can go get you a new car. I don't know where you got that piece of junk, but I'll make sure you get something with good-sized back seats for the kids."

"Todd, I think you misunderstood me. I'm not having kids or getting back together with you."

"You listen to me." He squeezes her hand tightly and releases his grip, still holding her hand. "You are staying here with me. Don't you see? I'm changing for you."

How is he changing if he's still forcing me to stay? I've got to come up with something. Rosaleen thinks quickly.

"If I don't go to work tomorrow, my colleagues will come looking for me. That'll make you look bad."

Todd sighs in resignation. "Then you will go to work and come straight back." *If I don't come back, he will make sure to retrieve me.*

Dead or alive.

Rosaleen pushes his hand away from her. "Fine," she says coldly. She rages at how little control she has on her own life. "But I have to go back to my house tonight. I have to pack some clothes to bring back here."

"Don't try anything stupid. It won't end well."

Todd allows her to go back home with the mutual understanding that she better be back at his house after she gets off work the following evening.

The next morning, Rosaleen goes to the office to talk to Easton face-to-face.

Todd won't show up because it's midweek, which means a busy work day for him. He won't want to get behind on work.

Rosaleen explains the whole situation to Easton.

"Can I help? I'd really love to help make things easier for you." Easton looks sympathetic.

"I wish you could, but this is something I have to do on my own."

"Very well. Just don't shut me out. Please."

Rosaleen leaves work, refusing to go to Todd's house that evening. After seeing forty-seven missed calls, she can only imagine the fit he's having about it.

Todd's calls unanswered, he leaves her some disturbing texts.

You're going to regret this.

I can't wait to get my hands on you.
You're dead.

She knows if they run into each other, he'll probably kill her this time.

Out of options, she leaves town without telling anyone. Not even Patsy.

THIRTY-THREE

Rosaleen drives until she gets to the Mississippi River Bridge, outside of Vicksburg. She hasn't seen another car for over an hour, which isn't surprising for 2 a.m. The empty road makes her feel lonelier than ever. It doesn't help that no one has tried calling her yet.

"Not even Todd cares enough to call me." He stopped calling about an hour ago. *Patsy only became my friend because I'm her neighbor.* She drives slower as she gets further down the long bridge. *Easton gets so frustrated when he doesn't get his way with me.* The thoughts are so loud in her head, it's almost like someone is talking to her. *Am I going crazy?* She shakes her head, trying to dismiss the voice inside her. *Do I really have anyone on my side?*

"I have nothing to live for. I'm better off dead."

She slows to a stop in the middle of the bridge. "No one will even know I'm gone." She gets out before she can stop herself, listening to the locusts humming as she walks over to the railing. Looking down at the river rushing below her in the eerie moonlight, she looks up to the black sky. *Why me?* In the distance, she sees a flash of lightning. *I can easily climb over the fencing.* Thunder fills the air. "No one's gonna stop me."

"YOU TOOK EVERYTHING FROM ME!" she yells, cursing the sky. "I wish Todd could feel every ounce of darkness trapped inside me."

She takes her phone out of her pocket, checks it, and puts it back. Tears roll down her face. "Nobody loves me. Nobody." Her heart aches at the thought.

Mom hasn't called. "But she has another daughter to distract her."

Why hasn't Patsy called? "It won't take her long to find another friend."

"There's nothing left of me. I'm done." She puts a leg over the railing, straddling it. "This is it. He can't hurt me anymore if I'm gone." The thunder rolls through the air again, closer now.

The world stops as the night grows silent. *Everything is coming to an end.* She swings her other leg around, completely on the edge. *Maybe I should call Patsy and tell her goodbye.* "No." *She'll talk me out of it. I'm sick and tired of everyone controlling me. Todd. Mom. Easton. Even Patsy. They all think they know what's best for me.* "I have control of this. This is my decision!"

She stands and leans forward, holding onto the railing behind her back. "All I have to do is let go now." She rocks back and forth, getting ready to jump.

One.

Her phone buzzes. *It's too late now.*

Two.

What's it matter who it is? Her phone buzzes again.

Three.

Rosaleen hesitates. *Could Patsy be worried about me?*

She sits back on the railing and pulls the phone out of her pocket.

Patsy. She opens their thread and reads the messages.

Where on God's green earth are you!?
Are you still alive?

Another message pops up. *Todd!* She deletes the text without reading it. *He's always said that if he can't have me, then no one can. He isn't going to win!* "I'M NOT YOUR PROPERTY!" she yells over the rumbling of the storm coming in.

She grips her phone tightly and throws it as hard as she can, sending it flying into the water. "CONTROL ME FROM THERE, BASTARD!"

She turns around and climbs back over the railing, safely grounding herself on the center of the bridge. Lightning flashes across the sky, and thunder roars, shaking everything around her.

She looks up. *Thank you.* As she raises her arms toward the sky, rain comes pouring down, washing away all the darkness she's been holding inside. She wraps her arms around herself. *I'm alive.* She hugs herself tighter.

"I'm not battered. He is."

THIRTY-FOUR

Rosaleen arrives at a hotel in Vicksburg a little after 3:00 a.m. *I need some rest before I keep going.* She walks into the lobby to get a room. The lady behind the counter is sleeping, her head on a pile of hotel brochures.

"Ma'am," Rosaleen whispers.

The woman continues to sleep.

If this lady doesn't wake up . . . I'm so tired. "Ma'am," Rosaleen says with a little more force.

The lady jumps up. "Oh, I'm sorry. How can I help you?"

"I need a room for the rest of the night." Rosaleen stares at the lines the brochures left on the woman face.

After checking Rosaleen in and paying, the woman yawns. "You'll be on the fourth floor in Room 421. Have a nice stay."

Rosaleen walks away, and the lady lays her head back down, mumbling something under her breath.

Rosaleen pushes the up button on the elevator.

The button never lights up.

She presses it again.

Come on. I'm so tired.

Rosaleen walks back over to the lobby counter. *Of course, the lady is going to be gone now.*

"Elevators out."

Rosaleen turns to see a man in a worn blue jumpsuit holding a mop. *Must be the janitor.*

"Have to take the stairs." He points the top of the mop toward the back of the building. "That way." He looks away and continues mopping the floor.

"Thanks, sir."

"Floor is wet." He doesn't look back up.

Rosaleen climbs the four stories to her room. Each step feels like steel weights are tied to her feet.

As soon as she lays eyes on her bed. "I'm so exhausted." *I need to call Patsy before she thinks I'm dead. She did save my life.*

She grabs the hotel phone and tries to recall Patsy's phone number. Her number is easy to remember. "Come on, please be right." She dials a number.

Nine. Eight. Five. Zero. Zero. Zero. One.

But wait, what if the one is first? She puts the phone up to her ear.

"Where in the hell have you been? I thought you were dead!" Patsy doesn't give Rosaleen a chance to speak.

"How did you know it was me?"

"Because who else would be calling me at this time in the morning? Why does your area code say you're in Mississippi?"

"Well, I kinda am."

Rosaleen explains everything that happened with Todd yesterday.

"Why didn't you come to me about all this?"

"I didn't want to bother you with all my drama." Rosaleen pulls the covers back and crawls under them. *It's like heaven.*

"I'm coming. What's the address?"

Would she really come this far just for me? "But . . . I won't be here tomorrow. After I get some rest, I'm heading to Tennessee."

"Tennessee? I do need a good vacation. Where will you be? I can leave in the morning."

Someone really does care what happens to me. Maybe I'm not alone. "I think I need to do this on my own."

"Do what?"

"I'm going back home. I want to feel like my old self again."

"Running away from your problems isn't going to do anything. You need to man up and face them head on. Your home is here now." Patsy lets out a big yawn.

"I can't explain it. I need to find myself and start fresh."

"Well, I'm still coming, because I'm going to be a part of whatever you find. You're stuck with me."

Rosaleen swallows hard, trying to stop herself from crying. "Patsy, that would be amazing."

"That's more like it."

The two agree on a time and place to meet in Tennessee.

"Get some sleep. I'll bring you my old phone. You can put some minutes on it at one of them stores up there."

"Goodnight, Patsy."

"Love you, girl. I'll see you soon."

Patsy's words hurt, but not in a bad way. It's as if they were knocking down the hatred building in her heart. It's the first time in a long time that she feels like someone loves her.

THIRTY-FIVE

Rosaleen forces her eyes open, checking the time on the alarm clock next to her bed. *11:30. Woah! It's almost checkout.*

She climbs out of bed and brushes her teeth, thankful that the hotel supplied toothbrushes. She looks in the mirror at the clothes she's been wearing for the past twenty-four hours. *I feel so dirty.* She tugs at her stretched-out shirt.

Rosaleen continues her drive along the Mississippi River into Tree-Bird Village, Tennessee.

She drives around, looking for familiar places and trying to remember the fun times she had as a child. *Maybe if I look back on my life and rediscover who I am, the chaos will go away.*

As she passes the river, she remembers the peaceful feeling that accompanied those hot, July summer days when her dad would take her and her sisters swimming.

"Here, Adeline. Hop on so we can beat Aria and Rosaleen at chicken."

Adeline climbed onto her dad's shoulders, and Aria helped Rosaleen onto hers. They grabbed onto each other's arms, trying to knock each other over.

Their dad tickled Aria, causing her to drop Rosaleen and sending them both under water. They came up laughing, as they all three tried to jump onto their dad and pull him under. It never worked, no matter how hard they tried. He was much too strong.

When the sun went down, they laid out a blanket and watched as the firecrackers lit up the night sky above the water for the Fourth of July.

Rosaleen drives further down and passes a house. Oh, Patrick! I almost forgot about him. He reminds her of one of her favorite memories.

"Rosaleen, come see. I've come up with another song. This one's for you."

Rosaleen sat at the end of his bed, watching as Patrick's fingers ran gracefully over the keys.

It had been an innocent middle school crush. It ended with a few calls here and there until they just stopped talking and went their own ways.

Shaking off the memories, she drives a few blocks down the road, slamming on her brakes in front of a dilapidated house.

Connor's house. *It must have gotten hit by one of the tornadoes last year. I wonder how life is treating him.*

She stares at his old car in the drive that now has a tree on top of it.

Rosaleen was only a senior in high school, but she could never forget Conner.

"Dad, can Conner come visit?"

"You know how I am about boys in my house with all of you girls."

"But Dad!"

Her stepmom looked over at him and gave him that look. He agreed, "But the door has to stay open."

Later that evening, Rosaleen and Conner sat on the floor playing board games when Rosaleen jumped up and let out a huge shriek.

"What is it?" Conner jumped up too.

"A spider! On my window! Look how huge it is!"

"Awe, it's just a banana spider. It's harmless."

"I hate spiders. What if it gets me while I'm sleeping?" Rosaleen placed her hand on her chest dramatically.

"Well, we can't have that, now, can we?"

Conner walked out and, moments later, returned with a mason jar.

"Your dad said I could use this."

"For what?"

"Watch." He went over to the window, nudged the spider into the jar, and tightly closed the lid. "You have something with a sharp end?"

"Um, why?" Rosaleen was confused about what Conner's intentions were.

"He's got to breathe. I need to puncture holes in the lid."

"Oh, yeah. Hang on."

She rummaged around her room and found an old pen. "Here, use this."

Conner punched holes in the lid and raised the jar toward the light. "Look how beautiful his legs are."

"Kinda cute." She grabbed the jar from him purposely, swiping her hand across his.

He placed his hand on top of hers, holding the jar with her. "See? There isn't any reason to be afraid of this little guy."

That night sparked a summer romance she'd never forget.

The whole summer was magical. She remembers their first bittersweet kiss. They were sitting in a field on an old plaid blanket, watching the stars. He leaned in and sweetly touched his lips to her. She'll never forget the taste of his sweet peach wine kisses.

Her heart broke when she had to go back home after their summer together.

Rosaleen held onto the memory tightly. It was the first time someone she liked made her feel loved.

Wanting those innocent moments back more than ever, she wipes a tear away as she continues to drive down the road.

She takes a left turn toward her most painful memories. Her dad. *I wonder if his house is still standing.*

She pulls into the broken-up driveway. The house has taken a turn for the worse. Vines smother the outside structure. She can tell no one has lived there since that dreadful day.

If he were here, Rosaleen's dad would have the radio on the Cajun station. Anytime a Wayne Toups song played, he'd grab her hand, and they'd two-step until the song was over. That had always been Rosaleen's favorite memory of her dad. They shared a love for music that always kept them close.

On Sundays, they'd go to church. During song and worship hour, her dad would grab her hand and hold it as they sang "The Old Rugged Cross" together. She'll never forget how gentle his big, callused hands were. It never made sense to her why he moved to Tennessee from Louisiana. She hated living so far away.

Nothing can bring him back. *Why was he so selfish? Didn't he think about what he would be leaving behind?* Getting mad at the thought, she grips the steering wheel tightly, just as aggravated at herself. *We are not the same. I didn't go through with it like he did and leave children behind.*

Still, she backs out of the driveway smiling, even though she's hurting with the painful memories. She remembers how much he loved her.

Rosaleen's looks at the clock above the radio. *It won't be long until Patsy will be arriving at the park!* Driving away from the neighborhood stings. *Perhaps this is what I need in order to get back what I've lost with Todd.*

Rosaleen parks at the park and rests her head on the steering wheel. *What if I had jumped? Would my family have missed me? Patsy wouldn't be on her way right now. What would my mom have said when she found out?* Rosaleen shakes her head, dismissing all thoughts.

She gets out of her car and sits on a bench near a shaded tree. She shivers as she watches some kids running around with their coats on. It's been a long time since she's enjoyed this kind of cold weather. *I need to find a store and get some winter clothes later.* She doesn't need a coat in Louisiana. Tennessee is completely the opposite.

A young man and woman walk past her, laughing and talking. Their hands bump into each other. The man grabs the woman's hand, swings her around, and whispers something in her ear. She wraps his arm around his neck and kisses his forehead.

I kind of miss Easton. Even though she doesn't want to be in a serious relationship, she misses the feeling of being wanted. Is she in love with him, or is he just filling an empty hole in her life? *Why can't I just let him go?*

Rosaleen jumps as a car honks behind her. "Patsy! You're here!"

Patsy climbs out and stretches, grunting. "That was a long drive!"

"You act like you're old," Rosaleen jokes.

The back doors of Patsy's car fling open, and her wild twins dart out and head straight for the monkey bars.

Boy, aren't they wild? Rosaleen shakes her head, laughing.

Patsy walks over to Rosaleen and hugs her tightly.

Rosaleen breaks down, letting all her bottled emotions pour out. "I don't know if I can get through this."

"You have me here for the week, and I'm going to help you."

They watch the kids play for the next three hours as they talk. Rosaleen tells Patsy all about Tree-Bird Village and how she half-lived here with her dad.

After visiting, they all go back to the hotel Rosaleen reserved for the week.

Patsy and her kids stay in Rosaleen's room with her. Rosaleen wouldn't have it any other way.

She helps Patsy bathe and settle the twins into bed for the night. Even though they keep jumping on the beds and running around screaming, she can't help but regret not having any kids with Todd.

Hunter and Beaux fall fast asleep as soon as their little heads hit the pillow.

Using the hotel coffee maker, Patsy makes some much-needed caffeine.

As the coffee is brewing, the pot makes horrible gurgling and crackling sounds, causing them both to laugh.

"It sounds like death is soon." Patsy makes a gesture of cutting her throat.

Rosaleen laughs. "As long as it dies after our coffee is made."

The whole night, Rosaleen and Patsy sit outside on the balcony, drinking their coffee and talking.

The air is cool and fresh, and they can see their breath with each exhale. "It's definitely not like this in Louisiana. We never get cold weather in November," Patsy complains.

Rosaleen's stresses are put to the side as they talk about their childhood memories, laughing until their stomachs hurt.

THIRTY-SIX

Rosaleen and Patsy bake a casserole dish and a few sides at the hotel.

Rosaleen is excited to enjoy her first Thanksgiving without Todd in a long time.

Finally, she'll get the chance to relax instead of Todd yelling for her to fix his plate so he won't miss the game. He never even watched football. He just lay there napping all day. *I wonder if he's watching the game right now.*

One year, she didn't have the table cleared and leftovers put up by time he woke from his nap. Todd walked into the dining room and shoved everything off the table. Their fine china crashed and shattered everywhere.

She could feel green beans squish between her toes, sharp shards of glass cutting her feet. "Ouch!" She pulled a sliver from her heel.

"There's still turkey under the table." Todd sat watching her from the living room with his legs propped up, criticizing her as she cleaned up his mess.

Rosaleen could tell he found it amusing. She picked up the carving knife from the floor and glanced at the cranberry sauce running down the curtains. It reminded her of blood.

That could be Todd's blood, she thought, humoring herself.

He looked at her and squirmed in his chair, laughing nervously.

It was obvious to Rosaleen that seeing her with the knife made him nervous.

"Don't forget to wipe the pumpkin pie off the table legs." He pointed to a spot she hadn't had a chance to clean yet.

She grabbed the turkey dish and grasped it tightly in her hands. Or I could just smash this over his head. That might be satisfying.

Another year, some old friends spent Thanksgiving with them.

Todd had been rude to Rosaleen in front of their friends.

"I don't know why you don't just leave."

"I wish it was as easy as it sounded, Maddie." Rosaleen tried to change the subject, focusing on Maddie's round stomach. "So, are you ready for little Emery?"

"If you were truly miserable, you would not still live with him. I don't feel bad for you. You deserve what he does if you won't leave. You obviously enjoy it," Maddie remarked, ignoring Rosaleen's deflection.

"No one asked you to feel bad for me. This is why I never talk to you about Todd." Rosaleen wanted to tell her to leave, but didn't. There was no way she'd ever understand her life. Her husband was laid-back, and you could see how much he adored Maddie just by the way he looked at her. He planted little kisses on her cheek throughout the day. It was something Rosaleen craved.

Todd walked into the room as the women were exchanging awkward glances. "Is everything okay, dear?" He put his hand on Rosaleen's shoulder.

Maddie shoved her chair back and stood. "Let's go, Kevin. I can't stand to be around fake people."

Kevin looked confused, but did as his wife said.

Rosaleen hasn't seen Maddie since that night.

What Maddie would never understand is that it would have put her in more danger if she had left then and there. The kind of danger she's in at this very moment.

After Patsy helps her clean up the leftovers from their feast, Rosaleen walks out with a bottle of wine.

Patsy grabs it, looking at the label. "Proper peach wine? What's this for?"

"I just thought we might enjoy a glass. That is, if you don't drink the whole bottle." She laughs. Rosaleen doesn't tell her that she got the bottle to remind her of her first kiss with Conner.

Surely this will bring me back to the girl I once was.

"Well, you'll be drinking alone. I hate to leave you here, but I have a few things I need to get done at home." Patsy gathers up the boy and eventually leaves.

Rosaleen sits in silence and stares at the bottle of wine across the room from her. "What's one glass gonna hurt?" She opens it, pouring herself a small cup.

She feels disappointed when she takes the first sip and it doesn't taste like their first kiss. *Maybe a few more sips.*

One small cup turns into five, but the wine doesn't bring back any of the feelings from the first night she drank it with Conner. The only thing she feels now is a nagging buzz.

She lies on the bed and stares at the ceiling. She hears a few thumps from above her. *Sounds like a dance party on the floor above me.* She sits up abruptly and the room spins. "I'm so lonely."

Todd messes up everything.

She throws her hands down like a child throwing a tantrum. "I could always call Conner and see how he's doing." She grabs the hotel phone book and thumbs through the pages before closing it.

"I kind of have to know his last name." She scratches her head. *Hmm. What was it? Campbell? No. Oh, Roberts.* "Conner Roberts." *No. Why can't I remember his last name? CC.*

Those were his initials. "Conner Cunningham! That's it."

She opens the book back up and turns to the C's. Running her finger down the alphabet, she stops at his name. "It's him! He doesn't live far from my hotel." She grabs the hotel phone and hesitates. *I shouldn't do this. I've been drinking too much.*

Nah, what the heck. She dials the number.

"Hello?" a woman answers, her voice groggy.

Rosaleen looks at the time. It's half past midnight. *Oops.*

She hears a man's voice. "Who is it, dear?" *Conner.* She'd recognize that voice anywhere.

"I'm not sure. No one is talking." A baby starts crying, and she can tell that the woman set down the phone.

"They woke up the baby. I just got her back to sleep." The lady starts quietly sobbing.

"It's okay. I'll rock her. You get some rest," Conner consoles her, then Rosaleen hears what sounds like a kiss. *Maybe the woman thought she hung up?*

"Thanks, babe. I couldn't do it without you." The woman sounds like she's falling asleep.

Rosaleen quickly hangs up the phone. "What was I thinking?" She slaps her forehead and grabs the half-finished bottle of wine. "No more of you." She walks over to the bathroom sink and pours the rest out.

Hearing Conner's voice didn't quite do what she thought it would. *That could have been me with the baby and the reassuring, caring husband.* Instead of reigniting her old self, it only makes her feel more lost.

She thinks back to her attic. *Maybe I let something out that has been causing me to have all this bad luck. People do say my place is haunted.*

Maybe I should have jumped the other night. She shakes the thought out of her head. *That's just the wine talking.*

She lies down to sleep the buzz off.

THIRTY-SEVEN

I wonder if Patsy made it home safe. I already miss her. Rosaleen calls her.

"Well, hello stranger."

"Hey! I was just calling to see if you made it back yet."

"We only just got back. I made a couple of extra stops on the way."

Had to let these boys burn off some energy."

"I was wondering if you knew of any good lawyers around town. I really need to divorce Todd. The sooner I get things going, the better. I already know he's going to fight me on it." *Or kill me. He isn't going to allow me to officially leave him. Ever.*

"Let me give someone a call, and I'll call you right back."

They let each other go. After about thirty minutes, Rosaleen figures she's forgotten to call her back. *The twins probably went crazy and distracted her.* She starts picking things up around the hotel when her phone rings. "Hello."

"Sorry about that. Mr. Walters gets to talking, and he never shuts up."

I guarantee you Patsy did all the talking.

"I've worked with Mr. Walters before, and he said he'd love to be your lawyer."

"But how much does he cost? That's my only problem."

"Oh, he's not gonna charge you. He owes me a favor from years back."

I'm not even gonna ask. Although I could use some humor.

"He's straight forward with his clients. He'll get the job done."

Rosaleen calls Mr. Walters a few moments later.

He answers almost immediately. "Patsy told me you'd be calling sometime today. That crazy woman." He laughs. "I do owe her though."

I'm not even going to ask. Rosaleen doesn't want to know what he owes Patsy for.

After explaining her situation, Mr. Walters suggests a restraining order. Rosaleen couldn't agree more.

Mr. Walters gives her details on the protective order and the charges that are going to take place. "This order isn't going to stop Todd from going after you. You must still be careful. If anything, this might provoke him further."

"He's going to kill me after all this, isn't he?"

"It's happened before. Please understand. I know this is a lot of information to process. It's not going to be easy."

Rosaleen knows the risks once she makes it back to Louisiana. She can only imagine what Todd will do at this point. She picks up her phone and dials the number she's been avoiding since she arrived in Tree-Bird Village. *Might as well see her before Todd kills me.*

Hoping she still has the same phone number after all these years, Rosaleen waits as the phone starts to ring.

"Hello?"

My sister's voice. She sounds so grown up now. Rosaleen can feel a lump in her throat as she swallows and tries to get words out.

"Hello?" This time Aria sounds a little testy.

"Aria?"

"Kiddo—Rosaleen?" Aria always called her kiddo growing up.

"Yes! I was hoping this was still your number."

"I haven't heard from you in years! How are you?" Aria yells excitedly.

Rosaleen lost contact with her sister after their dad died. Eventually, they stopped talking altogether. "I wanted to see you. As weird as it sounds, I'm actually in Tree-Bird Village." Rosaleen stumbles over her words.

"What! Why? Are you serious? Wait . . . what's wrong?"

"Never mind all that. I just really want to see you."

"I'd love to see you. You can come over now! Please tell me I'm not imagining things?"

"It's really me. I'm really coming."

Aria explains how to get to her house, and Rosaleen can't get there fast enough.

She pulls up to Aria's two-story, vintage yellow house. She already has her Christmas lights hanging outside. She's always liked to decorate early. She and Rosaleen have that in common. Christmas is their favorite holiday. On her front door, there's a big Christmas wreath with pinecones around it, smelling of cinnamon. It is a cold morning, and her windows are frosted with warm light glowing through.

Rosaleen rings the doorbell.

A few moments later, Aria opens the door with her housecoat wrapped around her.

She excitedly puts out her arms and embraces Rosaleen. "I've missed you so much!" Tears stream down her face.

"I'm sorry I haven't called. So much has happened."

"Come on in. It's cold out here. Plus, I'm dying to know why you're here."

They go inside and sit at the dining room table, and Rosaleen explains her situation to Aria.

"I'm so sorry, Rosaleen. I had no clue!" Aria sounds hurt and shocked at the same time.

"You wouldn't have believed me."

"Don't say that. I would have believed you. I would be sitting in prison right now if I'd known."

"I should have trusted you more and told you. I just hated the idea of calling you out of the blue and dropping that kind of load on you." *Technically, that's what I'm doing now.* "I'll be in Tree-Bird Village for a few more days if you want to catch up."

"Say, why don't you stay here with me instead of at a hotel. Please, Kiddo?!" Aria put her hands together, pleading.

This could be just what I need. A dose of the good ole days to spark the old me back up! "I'd love to. I'll pack everything up tonight and come in the morning."

"This is going to be so much fun! I can't wait."

Rosaleen visits for a little while before she goes back to the hotel to take a shower and pack. Packing and leaving feels like her new way of life.

The next morning, Rosaleen loads her belongings into the car and sets out for Aria's house.

Aria is at the door, waiting for her.

She helps Rosaleen unload her stuff and shows her the guest room. "It's not much, but I went to Walmart last night and got stuff to make you your own room here. I want you to come anytime you'd like. My home is your home. Never forget that."

That night, Aria whips up some pancakes, bacon, sunny side up eggs, and hash browns topped with cheese for supper.

"I remember breakfast was always your favorite thing to eat for supper. You always liked to be different."

"Being different is way more fun than being the same as everyone else."

As they sit at the table eating, they joke around and remember the trouble they caused growing up.

"Let's go make some hot cocoa." Aria pushes her chair back and stands.

"Only if you have marshmallows and cinnamon!"

"Do I look like an ax murderer? Of course I have that!"

Aria makes some hot cocoa, lights her fireplace, and grabs two fleece blankets. They sit on the opposite ends of the couch, their feet facing one another as they watch the ID Channel and doze off. Just like when they were kids.

The next morning, Rosaleen wakes up to Aria standing over her, poking her arm.

"Huh? What is it?" She's barely awake, and it takes her a moment to remember where she is.

"IT'S SNOWING! IT'S SNOWING!" she yells at Rosaleen.

Rosaleen jumps up. "Well, what are we waiting for?"

They bundle up and run outside like two kids seeing snow for the first time.

Rosaleen lies in the snow, moving her arms and legs up and down to make a snow angel.

Aria balls up two handfuls of snow and chunks it at Rosaleen, hitting her in the arm.

"I'll get ya back for that!" She jumps up, scooping snow along the way.

After their snowball fight, Aria starts rolling the snow into a huge ball on the ground. "Come on! Let's build a snowman."

Shortly after, Rosaleen pitches in, and within no time they have a six-foot snowman.

"This sure beats the ones we made as kids. I wish Adeline was here. I haven't seen her in a while either." Rosaleen packs the final touch of snow on the snowman's head.

"She would love this. We were lucky if we could even build one knee high. It hasn't snowed this much since . . ." Aria's voice trails off.

Rosaleen knows she's thinking about their dad. "I wish he was here to see us now. I'm sure he's very proud of all of us."

"I think we are still missing something for the snowman!" Aria says quickly changing the subject. She jogs inside, returning moments later. "These were the first decorations I could find," she says, carrying out an old hat, scarf, and a box of raisins.

She sets the items down and grabs two sticks that had recently fallen from a tree.

She shoves the sticks on each side of the snowman, forming arms. Then, she makes eyes and a mouth with the raisins. After that, she places the hat on its head, and wraps the scarf around the snowman's neck.

"It's the nose-less snowman!" Rosaleen laughs.

"Hmm, I'm all out of carrots." Aria looks around and finds a small clay rock on the ground. "This will have to do."

Rosaleen grabs her phone and yells, "picture time!" They huddle up around the snowman, and Rosaleen stretches out her arm to snap the picture.

"A moment to remember forever." Aria smiles at Rosaleen as she wraps her arm around her shoulders. They walk off to the porch together, and Rosaleen realizes something. *I can never have the old me back. She's gone. It's never going to be the same, but I'm building new memories with the ones I love. I don't need to go looking for me anymore. It's back at home, where I belong.*

Rosaleen turns to Aria and hugs her. "It's time for me to go home now."

THIRTY-EIGHT

Patsy rushes over before Rosaleen has time to grab her belongings out of the car. "Get inside. Now." She shoves her toward the house.

"Hey! Stop that! You're scaring me."

"Todd's been here every day since you called Mr. Walters. That black truck? Yeah, that's him. Apparently, he got another vehicle after you left him so he could follow you around without you knowing."

"How do you know all of this?"

"Never mind that. Get inside. That man is mad, I tell ya." She pulls her into the house and locks the door behind them. "I saw him get out of the truck a few days ago and walk up to your door. He had a baseball bat."

"This is terrible!"

"That's not all of it. He walked around to the back. Next thing I know, I hear glass shattering."

"Patsy, you didn't go out there, did you?"

"Oh no. What do I look like? Stupid?" Patsy put her hands on her hips. "This is getting way out of hand. I like taking things into my own hands, but I was tempted to call the cops."

"It's pointless. That will only set him off. It's not safe to call them."

"Your point is justified. I get it." Patsy sighs. "On the plus side, after he sped off, Mr. Harrison came outside. We measured your window a few days later, and he helped me replace it. I went inside and cleaned up the glass."

"Oh, thank you so much, Patsy. How much do I owe y'all?"

"Nothing. Mr. Harrison apparently has ties with the hardware store in town. He used to own it, and the new owner gives him whatever he needs."

"Oh! That's so kind. I'll have to thank him later. When was the last time Todd came by my house?"

"This morning. You literally just missed him. It's not safe for you here."

"I really have no choice but to stay here. Can you come with me to the lawyer's office?"

"Well, of course. The sooner the better."

"I'll wait in the car while you go in," Patsy tells Rosaleen as they find a parking space.

Rosaleen gets out of the car, leaning back inside. "Sure you don't want to come in?"

"As much as I'd like to be there for you, this is something you have to do on your own."

"I understand." Rosaleen motions to Patsy to lock the door, walking into the office.

A woman sits at the reception desk, filing her nails and talking on her phone.

Rosaleen walks up to the counter and clears her throat.

"Hold on," she says to the person on the phone, rolling her eyes.

Rosaleen forces herself to smile.

"Can I help you?" The receptionist acts as though she interrupted an important conversation.

"I have an appointment to sign papers with Mr. Walters."

"That way." The woman points toward a door. She picks her phone back up and resumes talking and filing her nails.

The door to her lawyer's office is heavy and wooden, with a small tinted window Rosaleen can't see through. Above the door is a gold and black metal plate that reads EDDISON WALTERS.

She taps on the door.

"Come on in. It's open."

Rosaleen walks in. Mr. Walters looks nothing like he sounds on the phone. He's short and plump, resembling a peach.

"You must be Ms. Hart." He stands and extends his stubby hand for her to shake. His shirt is wrinkled and partially untucked.

I hope he works better than he looks. "Yes, sir." She shakes his hand and sits in the chair in front of his desk without invitation. She is ready to sign the papers so the legal actions can start taking place.

"I'm going to ask you one last time. Are you sure you want to proceed? Once the papers are signed there is no backing out," he asks, stroking his mustache.

"Yes," Rosaleen says firmly, trying not to focus on the light reflecting off his gleaming, wrinkled head.

Mr. Walters hands her the legal documents.

She reads and signs them without hesitation.

"I'll be in touch," Mr. Walters says.

Walking out of his office, she sees Todd's truck pass in front of the building. She quickly steps back inside and moves away from the door, not wanting him to see her. She tries to motion to Patsy for help, but she is too busy singing in the car to notice her.

Ugh! Come on Patsy!

The lady behind the counter sets her phone down. "Ma'am? Everything okay?" She sounds less annoyed than she had when she greeted Rosaleen, and there's concern in her voice.

"Actually, no. My ex is driving down the street, watching my car. I can't go outside or he will see me."

"Men like that have a special place in hell. Hang on, and I'll ring the police to escort you out."

"Oh no thanks. I don't want to cause a scene. I'll just wait until I can't see his truck anymore. Thank you, though."

The woman picks up her phone and tells whoever is on the other side that she has to go. She watches Rosaleen.

Rosaleen waits until she can't see Todd's truck circling anymore. She slips out the doors and runs to her car, jumping in.

"What's your hurry?" Patsy asks.

"While you were in here having a concert, Todd passed by the car." Rosaleen speeds off, leaving black tire marks behind.

Rosaleen and Patsy arrive back at Rosaleen's house.

"Let me go grab some iced tea from next door, and then I'll come sit with you."

Rosaleen stops patsy before she walks away.

"Maybe we should sit inside?"

"Heck no. It feels too good outside today to be stuck inside."

"But what if Todd is around?"

"Yeah, what if he is?" Patsy walks over to her house, mumbling something under her breath.

When she gets back, Patsy sits next to Rosaleen on the porch swing. Rust falls from the chains and into Patsy's glass of tea.

"It's almost time to retire this swing to the burn pile," Patsy jokes, getting up to pour her drink in the grass.

"Believe it or not, I can actually say I missed this old rust bucket."

Patsy laughs, grabbing the pitcher from the porch railing and refilling her glass.

"What do I do now, Patsy?" Rosaleen asks, breaking their silence.

"You just live day by day."

"I don't know how much more stress I can take."

They sit in silence for a while longer, finishing up their tea.

THIRTY-NINE

On Monday morning, Rosaleen can feel the cold stares of her coworkers as she walks into the front office.

"Good morning, Dixie," Rosaleen says, trying to spark a conversation as they pass each other in the hall.

Dixie nods but keeps walking.

Even sweet Dixie is mad at me. Rosaleen sighs. *I let my coworkers down by not showing up to work.*

She pauses outside of Easton's office, taking a deep breath before walking in.

Easton lifts his head only long enough to see that it's her, then gets straight back to work.

Trying to gauge if he's upset with her, she sits in front of him and reaches out for his hand. "Easton I—"

Easton jerks his hand away. "Ms. Hart, it's tough to meet deadlines when people don't show up to work."

Ms. Hart? He called me by my last name. "Easton, just let me explain."

"I'm busy," he says coldly, not looking at her.

Rosaleen walks out, feeling guilty and disappointed.

She sits at her desk and pushes the mountain of paperwork to the side. *I'm already behind. What does it matter if I take a little longer?*

The guilt of hurting Easton eats her alive. *Why didn't I call him? Heck, or send him one little text? Why'd I have to push away the one man who loves me? I don't even really love him. Why am I such a people pleaser?*

In the back of her mind, she can hear Patsy's voice. "You can't let no one love you until you love yourself first."

Rosaleen knows she's right.

For the next few hours, Rosaleen does little work. When lunch rolls around, she wonders if now might be a good time to talk to Easton. She walks past his office and sees him still hard at work. He looks up, and they make eye contact briefly before Rosaleen quickly walks away.

She walks down to The Hideout for some much-needed coffee. She orders and sits at the patio table closest to the doorway. The barista walks out and pins a note to the sign board.

Help Wanted.

The Barista looks over to Rosaleen and jokes, "You're not looking for a job, are you?"

Actually, it would be perfect. I'd be doing this for me. The thought of starting over fresh thrills her. *The pay will be less, but I can manage. Plus, I love coffee.*

The barista starts walking back inside, and Rosaleen stops her. "Miss. If you're serious, so am I."

"I'm Belle." A warm smile spreads across her face. "Come on in, and we'll talk."

After talking with Belle, Rosaleen walks back to the office giddily. When she enters the building, she realizes she has to end it with Easton completely. *This is it. This is for me.*

When she walks into his office, he acts like he's expecting her. "Rosaleen. Sit down, please." He gestures toward the seat next to him.

At least he isn't still calling me by my last name. She sits down.

Her eyes shift toward the door, naturally looking for an escape in case she feels the need to run. When Todd would tell her to sit like this, she knew it wasn't going to be good. The seriousness in Easton's tone makes her want to vomit.

"Why did you leave me like that?" Easton cuts straight to the point.

"Easton, I'm so sorry. I had to get away from Todd. It was my only option."

Easton looks both hurt and aggravated. She knows that look too well. *Now I'm the bad guy.*

"Easton, please don't take it personally. This has nothing to do with you."

Easton leans forward and slams his fist on his desk. "Nothing to do with me? Rosaleen, listen to yourself. You're so selfish."

Rosaleen jumps back. *When Todd slammed his fist down, usually she was the next thing to get hit.*

She's never seen Easton mad like this before. "Easton, you're scaring me. I said I'm sorry. I really am."

"Rosaleen, I'd never hurt you. You should know this by now. I've put up with you acting weak far too long."

Rosaleen jumps to her feet, knocking the chair back. "How dare you say that to me!"

Easton looks away, not looking the least bit phased. "You're confusing me, Rosaleen. What do I have to do to keep you?"

"Quit making me out to be some kind of object you own!"

"Don't put words in my mouth!"

"I want to feel free for once in my life." Rosaleen sits back down.

"What do you mean you want to feel free? I give you all the freedom you want." Easton has tears in his eyes.

"Easton, stop. Listen to me." Rosaleen grabs his hands in hers. "Todd has taken everything from me. I need to get my life together and focus on myself."

Easton stands and pulls her into his arms. "Don't walk out on me."

He presses his lips against hers, and she fights him off, shoving him back. "I don't want you to kiss me!" It reminds her of Todd's kisses, in that it isn't a kiss of love. "Today's my last day."

"You'll be back. You won't be able to get by without a job."

He doesn't deserve to know I already have a new job! "Goodbye, Easton." She turns and walks out, feeling her coworkers' stares. *I need to get out of here!*

The Louisiana heat adds to the suffocating sensation building in her throat.

That felt good. She starts gasping for air. *Why did I do that? What if he's right?* She walks a little further down the street and jerks off her jacket, breathing shallowly. *I can't believe I did that.*

Should I apologize to him?

No, I actually stood up to him.

Trying to gain control of her shaky legs, she slumps onto a nearby bench and takes a deep breath. She starts to doubt herself. *Maybe I was too harsh on him.*

I feel horrible.

No, that's what he wants.

No one said this was going to be easy.

FORTY

Rosaleen tosses and turns all night. She can't sleep, too busy thinking about how she left things with Easton. She looks at her phone. 1:30 a.m. Rosaleen crawls out of bed to sit on her porch swing.

Patsy's front light is on. She sees her sitting on her porch too. *What on earth is she up to?*

Patsy yells over to Rosaleen, "Hey girl, what the heck are you doing up this time of night?"

"I can't sleep. I'm wondering the same about you," Rosaleen yells back.

Patsy grabs a red solo cup and staggers over to Rosaleen's porch. She sits next to Rosaleen on the swing, almost missing it.

Rosaleen can smell the strawberry wine on her breath. *Only Patsy would drink wine from a solo cup.* Rosaleen chuckles. "Patsy. On a weeknight? What's gotten into you?"

"Just because I have my life together now doesn't mean I still don't have problems." Patsy laughs. "I've got a lot on my mind tonight. What seems to be your problem, young lady?"

Rosaleen sighs. "I quit my job, got a new job, and told Easton we'd never be together all in one day."

"YUP! That's a lot for one day." Patsy laughs. "You'll be okay, though. See I'm okay, aren't I?"

Besides being drunk in the middle of the night on a weekday. "Yeah, you're okay." Rosaleen rolls her eyes.

Patsy raises her cup in the air. "Cheers!" Some wine splashes out as she brings it to her lips. "Taught that old bastard a lesson, too."

What is she hiding? Rosaleen can only assume Patsy's referring to her husband. *He must've really hurt her.*

Patsy leans forward, closer to Rosaleen's face. She slurs, "Rosaleen Hart, you do not need a man to get by in your life. You seemed to be in a good place the other day. You knew you wanted to be independent."

Even though she's drunk, she has a point.

"Y'all weren't even together. A few dates don't mean anything."

Once again, another good point. Rosaleen knows it's the wine talking, but she also knows Patsy's blunt regardless of the situation.

"Dangit, girl! Pull your head out of your ass and get your life together! There ain't no use wasting your life away feeling guilty over some man like that."

"I think he really loves me, Patsy."

"Yes, I know you think he loves you and all that other sappy stuff, but you can't love him the way he needs to be loved until you can love yourself. You said so yourself." Patsy takes another sip from her cup.

Rosaleen slowly reaches for the glass. "Maybe you've had enough for tonight."

"Don't." She pulls back, not letting her grab the cup. "I've seen some things I wish I never had."

Rosaleen is taken back by the abrupt change in Patsy's tone. *What is she not telling me?* "It's not okay that we've had to suffer like we did."

Patsy starts rocking back and forth. "I can't close my eyes at night sometimes!"

Patsy's losing it! She pats Patsy on the shoulder, trying to reassure her.

Patsy jumps, looking Rosaleen directly in the eyes. "Make it all go away. Please, Rosaleen!" she pleads desperately.

"I don't know how to help you if you don't tell me what happened." Rosaleen grabs Patsy's hands. "I want to help you. I really do!"

A small figure creeps onto the porch. "I can't let you two out of my sight, can I?"

"Esther, I think Patsy needs help." Rosaleen panics at the sight of Patsy losing it.

"No, no, dear. She'll be fine." She grabs Pasty's cup and throws it off the porch.

"That was mine!" Patsy takes a deep breath.

Esther laughs. "Do you think that wimpy wine is going to help with anything? Now you look at me, Patsy."

"I can't."

"I'm telling you one last time before I throw cold water on you. Look me in the eyes, Patsy."

So that's why Patsy told me she was going to throw cold water on me. Esther must've done it to her before.

Rosaleen watches as Patsy looks at Esther.

"Now, breathe with me, Patsy. Keep looking at me." Esther takes deep breaths, and Patsy breathes with her. "You too, Rosaleen. Breathe with us."

"But I'm fine," Rosaleen tries to argue.

"No, you're not. You were consorting with a frantic drunk woman," Esther says firmly. "You're not okay. So, let's breathe through this." Esther sits in the middle of the two and grabs their hands.

Minutes later, Patsy breaks the silence, "Welp, I guess I better go off to bed now. Try to get some rest y'all." Patsy walks over to her porch and goes into her house.

Rosaleen turns to Esther. "You fixed her. I've never seen her like this."

"Dear, no one thing is going to magically and completely fix a person. It is a lot of work, and it doesn't happen in one night." She stands, slowly climbing down the steps. "What would you two do without me? Now go on inside and get to bed so I can rest easy."

Rosaleen goes inside, pouring herself a glass of milk before lying back down and falling fast asleep.

FORTY-ONE

The following weekend, Rosaleen receives a call from her lawyer, Mr. Walters. "Ms. Hart, we finally have a court date set to sign the divorce papers. The signing will take place next week on Wednesday morning. You will have to face Todd, as you will be in the same room together. There will be security everywhere in the building."

"Thank you so much, Mr. Walters."

"I hope you're ready for this."

"I'm ready to get this over with."

That's an understatement. Rosaleen is more than ready to be free of Todd. *Will I even be free?* She's thankful she doesn't have any kids to tie them together for the rest of their lives. Still, she feels guilty for thinking such a thing when she's wanted kids for as long as she can remember.

She arrives at the courthouse and looks up as the building's bell chime above her. *I wonder what it's like way up there.*

Walking inside, she passes through the metal detectors stationed at the entrance.

The alarm goes off, and one of the security guards stops her. "Ma'am, your bracelet, please."

"Oh." She is so lost in her own thoughts, that she didn't even notice. She slides the bracelet off and drops it in the basket.

After she slips through, she grabs the piece of jewelry and puts it back on. It was a gift from her mom, congratulating her for leaving Todd.

She passes a few people and heads over to an old wooden bench to wait for her case to be called. From the corner of her eye, she sees someone sit nearby.

Todd?

He looks sickly. He's lost weight, bonier and paler than Rosaleen has ever seen him. *Is he...nervous? That would be a first.*

She doesn't dare turn her head to face him completely.

She tries to hide the fact that she's shaking by putting her hands flat on her legs. *No. He's not going to take over my mind like this.* She sits up tall with her shoulders back and swallows, but it feels like she has cotton stuck in her throat. *I need some water.*

Todd scoots closer to Rosaleen and places his hand lightly on Rosaleen's leg.

Rosaleen flinches.

"I see I still have my magic touch. You've always been a little coward," Todd whispers.

She grabs his hand and flings it off. "Don't you dare talk to me like that."

"Now is your chance to back down. You don't know what line you're crossing."

Rosaleen turns her head and looks him square in the eyes. "It's you who needs to be afraid, Todd. I'm about to cross you like you've never been crossed before."

"Getting a little brave, aren't you?"

"You won't know what hit you when I'm finished with you. Now get away from me." Rosaleen raises her voice higher than his whisper.

Todd looks around and moves over to the other side of the bench, not saying anything else to her as they wait. Occasionally, he glances over and cuts her a death stare.

Rosaleen has never spoken to Todd that way before. She feels a sense of satisfaction for standing up to him like that. She doesn't know if being around people makes her feel safe or if she is just tired of being afraid of him. *Maybe it's both.* That said, Todd will more than likely try to put her back in her place. He won't let her slide away that easily.

After sitting for nearly an hour, their case is finally called.

They walk into the room, and their lawyers are waiting for them on opposite sides of a large table. After signing the divorce papers, they are dismissed.

Rosaleen takes the opportunity to leave the building while Todd is still talking to his lawyer.

Still, Todd catches her eye. He tries walking behind Rosaleen, but his lawyer places his hand on Todd's shoulder, stopping him.

She hears his lawyer whisper to him. "Let her go, man."

Rosaleen hurries out the building, gets into her car, and locks it.

She sees Todd walking briskly down the steps as she drives off.

Patsy storms through Rosaleen's bedroom door a little past 3:00 p.m. "Get up!"

"Sometimes I regret giving you a house key," Rosaleen grumbles.

"I don't wanna hear it."

"Please just go, Patsy. I just want to sleep."

"Yeah, that's not happening on my watch. I haven't seen you outside all day. GET UP!" Patsy puts her hands on her hips and shakes her head. "Pathetic."

"I'm so stressed after seeing Todd today. Go away."

"You're not wasting this beautiful sunny day away crying in bed over some idiot who probably can't even spell his own name. I'm not having it." She yanks the comforter off Rosaleen and pulls on her arm.

"Alright, alright. I'm getting up."

"Get dressed. We are going into town to get some coffee. Lord knows you need some. You look awful." Patsy walks over to her closet and pulls out an old dress, handing it to Rosaleen. "Here, put this on. You aren't going into town looking like that."

Rosaleen slips the dress on and throws her hair into a messy bun. "How's that? Now I look even more awful. I can't go to The Hideout looking like this. Especially since I'm about to start working there soon!"

"Oh hush. The car is running downstairs. I'll be driving today."

Rosaleen leans the seat back as far as it will go, watching the sun flicker between trees. She lies there in silence as Patsy drives into town.

Patsy pulls up to the drive-through.

"What? You can't be seen with me in public?"

"No. We are going to sit at the park instead of inside a building. You need air. What do you want?"

"Coffee. Black."

Patsy ignores her coffee selection and orders her a seasonal flavor.

Rosaleen perks up a bit when she smells the cinnamon coming from her cup. Patsy always knows how to cheer her up.

"I'm not handing this to you until you sit up."

"Patsy. You know you get on my nerves, right?"

"Yeah, well, you're about to hate me after I throw this whole cup out the window."

"Okay, okay." Rosaleen pulls the seat up. "You know you're a little crazy sometimes?"

"Hey, whatever it takes." Patsy winks at Rosaleen jokingly.

Patsy drives to the park. "Look, there's an empty bench."

"But that's in the middle of the park. There are too many people around. There's a bench over there by the trees."

"Nope. I'm picking today. Now get out."

Rosaleen climbs out of the car, and they both walk to the bench.

A small pond sits to the side of them, and they watch ducks play in the water.

"Just what you need. Some fresh air and silly ducks. I already told you that I'm not going to let you steep in self-loathing. You're gonna come through this strong, even if I have to drag you the whole way through."

"Patsy, thank you for being here for me. It really means a lot."

"Now don't get all soft on me."

They watch kids run and the duck's play, and Rosaleen imagines herself with two tiny kids and a yard filled with animals to chase around.

An ambulance and police car speed by with their sirens on, catching their attention.

"Hmm, I wonder what's going on." Patsy looks concerned.

"No telling. Let's get out of here and head home."

FORTY-TWO

Harrison is standing outside his house, pacing back and forth. "No, no, no. Not my Esther," he cries.

Patsy throws the car in park, and both women jump out and run over to him.

"Mr. Harrison. What happened? Where is Esther?" Patsy asks.

"She's gone . . ."

"You can't find her?" asks Rosaleen.

Harrison is sobbing too hard to answer.

Paramedics roll a stretcher out of their house. A white sheet covers up a body. The wheel hits a rock, and an arm falls loose, hanging from the bed.

"OH NO!" Rosaleen yells.

Patsy hugs Harrison, trying to console him.

"Please don't take my Esther. Please take me instead. Give her back," he pleads.

Patsy tries to hold Harrison back as he throws his arms around Esther's body. "Please wake up. Don't leave me. Wake up." He shakes her lifeless body.

"Mr. Harrison, they need to take her." Patsy pulls him off Esther.

Harrison puts his head on Patsy's shoulder, watching as the EMTs place her into the back of the ambulance.

"Come on, let's go . . ." Patsy takes his trembling hand and leads him to her car, motioning for Rosaleen to get in the backseat.

Harrison cries out for Esther as they drive to the hospital. "She has to come back. I can't make it without her. Please, God, give her back to me."

Patsy walks over to Rosaleen's house and sits with her in the kitchen.

"How is he?" Rosaleen asks, pouring some coffee for Patsy.

"I made sure he was in his recliner before leaving him," Patsy says and runs her finger across the top of the mug.

"Did you leave his lamp on by his chair?"

"Yeah, he said he doesn't want any other lights on. He said Esther always turned the lights out after him."

Rosaleen smiles. "She always fussed at him for leaving too many lights on in the house. That's why she got him that lamp—so he could see what he was doing without the big light bothering her." Rosaleen's smile fades. "I'm really going to miss her."

"Me too. Poor old fella talked like she was going to walk back in any second."

"He's not going to know what to do without her."

"One thing Esther taught us is to not give up. He'll be okay. It'll just take him a minute." Patsy stands from the table. "I'm going home now. Try to get some rest."

The next morning, Patsy walks up to Rosaleen in Esther's back yard. "What on earth are you doing?"

"I'm watering the rose bushes. What's it look like I'm doing?" She pours water over the lifeless plant.

"I've been searching all over for you."

"Well, here I am," Rosaleen snaps.

"Woman, you left your back door wide open. I thought something happened to you. Jeez." Patsy leans over and examines the plant Rosaleen is watering. "You know it's dead, right?"

"It's not dead!"

Patsy stands next to Rosaleen. "Okay now, just take it easy."

"Look at her roses." Rosaleen pulls a dead rose from its stem. "They look so battered and sad."

"They look exactly how they need to look when it starts to get cold out here."

"They're as battered as we are, Patsy."

"Okay. Why don't you come on in, and I'll make us some eggs and toast?"

"I can't. I promised Esther I would take care of her flowers for her. I can't just leave them abandoned. It isn't fair."

"Honey, nothing in life is fair. Come on in so I can tell you something. I think you should know." Patsy slowly grabs the watering can from Rosaleen.

"Okay . . ." Rosaleen gives in.

In the kitchen, Patsy sits across from Rosaleen, neither of them touching their breakfast.

"So, what did you have to tell me?" Rosaleen asks, breaking the silence.

"Just listen with an open mind, okay?"

"Sure."

"A few months ago, Esther sat me down and told me how she was recently diagnosed with stage IV pancreatic cancer. The cancer had already taken over multiple organs, so she chose to go home and live out her final days without treatment."

"So that's why Esther told me to take care of her flowers if something ever happened to her. I can't believe she didn't tell me."

"She didn't think you'd handle it well. And, well, she was right."

"She should have fought for her life."

"She would have been miserable. She was too far advanced. Harrison told me about their last conversation last night." Patsy picks up her toast, pulling off the crust. "Wanna know?"

"I guess."

"He told me that before bed, Esther started talking about the day they met." Patsy sets her toast down and pushes her plate away.

"Go on."

A smile travels across Patsy's face. "It's rather cute, actually. And you know how I hate all that mushy stuff." She takes a sip of her coffee. "Harrison was working in his old hardware store, and she walked in looking for plant fertilizer. He watched her go down a few wrong aisles before walking up to her to help. She laughed at his corny jokes as he led her to the right shelf. He said no one's ever laughed at his jokes like she did. As she was paying, their hands accidentally touched, and he instantly knew they were destined to be together. He said she was the prettiest woman he's ever laid eyes on. Even as they grew old and their bodies changed, he never lost that attraction to her."

"That's so sweet. I hope to be an Esther with a Harrison one day."

"That's real true love—what they had."

Rosaleen pops the yolk in the middle of her egg and dips her toast in it.

Patsy wipes a tear from her cheek. "He's taking it hard, but he's going to be okay. He has us."

"Our own little family." Rosaleen grabs Patsy's hand across the table and squeezes it. "I love you, you know."

FORTY-THREE

Rosaleen wakes up on Saturday morning ready to check out the town's nursery, in honor of Esther.

She walks through the main gates, ivy plants hanging above her head. There are a variety of fall mums in gold, rusts, and pinks. With so many other plants to choose from, Rosaleen finally decides on a color of mums and hostas to brighten up her flower bed. She grabs some extra fertilizer before she checks out.

Rosaleen walks up to a young girl sitting behind the counter, dressed in a long, baggy t-shirt and faded, torn jeans that are obviously too large. Her face is emotionless, like she doesn't have a care in the world, and her jet-black hair is a tangled mess. She can tell it hasn't been brushed in a long time, and Rosaleen's instincts kick in. She wants to grab a brush and brush the young girl's hair for her. *Maybe she doesn't have a mom.* She glances at her name tag. *Ruth. That's a pretty name.*

"Will this be all?" she asks Rosaleen, her tone jaded.

Jeez, this girl seems hopeless. Maybe she needs a hug.

Rosaleen points over to a small plant sitting off to the side by itself. "What's that?"

"Um, I'm not sure. No one really wants it because it's practically dead."

"Go ahead and add it to my stuff."

"You can just have it. It's a lost cause." She rolls her eyes, grabbing the plant and handing it to Rosaleen.

"You okay?" The words come out of her mouth before she can stop herself from asking.

"Ma'am?" The teen looks confused.

"Are you okay, sweetie?"

"Why would you ask that? You don't even know me."

She quickly thinks of something to say. "I'm Rosaleen. It's nice to meet you." She instantly regrets asking the girl anything. "You just look like something is bothering you. I'm sorry. You're probably thinking, 'why is this crazy lady you don't even know in your business.' Don't mind me."

The girl's facial expression quickly changes from disturbed to upset as she bursts into tears.

"Now, now. I'm sorry if I upset you. Please don't cry." Rosaleen sits her plant down and starts walking towards her, but before she makes it around to her, Ruth stops her waterworks as quickly as they started.

"Your total is $57.40."

Well, okay then. Rosaleen backs up and hands her a hundred-dollar bill. "Take it easy, okay?" She leaves before Ruth can hand her back her change. *She seems like she needs that more than me. Poor girl.*

Rosaleen gets home and plants her new purchases in her flower bed. She spends the rest of the evening in her garden chair, admiring the colorful beauty that surrounds her.

She's divorced and free.

So why do I still feel stuck?

FORTY-FOUR

Rosaleen walks to the mailbox to check the mail when she sees what appears to be red liquid dripping from it. She opens it, and a ton of flies swarm out. "What in the world?" She waves her hand in front of her face, shooing the insects away. She looks inside to discover a dead opossum, maggots filling its body. "Who would do such a thing?" She looks around, pulling the animal out by its tail and dropping it to the ground. Gagging, she pulls her shirt over her nose to shield herself from the smell.

Rosaleen pulls her water hose over, hoping she can get the smell out of the box. If not, she'll have to go to the local hardware store and order a new one.

Before spraying the inside, she notices a small, folded piece of paper near the back of the box. She picks up a stick, using it to pull the note towards her. Not caring about the blood, she unfolds it.

She grabs her chest when she realizes who it's from.

You'll end up like this animal as soon as I slit your neck and take your last breath. No one will be able to find you.

Rosaleen steps back and drops the note to the ground. Her heart races, everything around her spinning. Her hands are clammy, and she feels cold all over, despite the fact that it's still 80°F outside. *What should I do?* She runs inside, forgetting about the water hose running Her yard flooding is the least of her worries. She even forgets to shut the door behind her.

"Where do I hide? I need to hide." She panics as she runs from room to room. No where in the house feels safe. "The bed! I can hide under there." She crawls under her bed and tries to be as quiet as she possibly can, but her breathing is shallow and loud.

When Rosaleen's able to collect her thoughts, she realizes how ridiculous she is being. "This is not how I will live my life!"

Rosaleen goes and grabs the note, ripping it up and sending little shreds of papers soaring in the wind. "Come and get me! I want you to!"

She storms upstairs and flips her mattress over, throwing it completely onto the floor. Grabbing her gun, she walks over to her dresser, gets the magazine, and loads it. She sees the anger on her face as she passes the mirror.

Rosaleen hears her front door shut down-stairs. She racks and aims the gun toward the doorway, listening to the footsteps running up the stairs.

"You'll die before I do!" she yells out.

"Rosaleen! STOP! It's me, Patsy! Put that thing down before you kill me!"

Rosaleen's hands tremble as she lowers the gun. "Todd's coming for me, and I'm going to kill him." Her voice is so low, she almost sounds like a ghost.

"Just hand the gun over, okay?" Patsy reaches for the gun.

Rosaleen pulls back. "You just stay out of my way."

"You're okay. He's not here." She slowly places her hands on Rosaleen's. "You're safe. Let it go."

Rosaleen releases her grip, and Patsy takes the gun, ejecting the bullet from the chamber. "Here, let's clean this mess up." Patsy tucks the gun in her jeans and picks the mattress up, dragging it back onto the bed frame as Rosaleen staring blankly at the doorway.

"Come on, let's get some fresh air." Patsy loops her arm in Rosaleen's. They walk outside, and Patsy leads Rosaleen to the porch swing.

Rosaleen feels empty, and she just wants to be alone. She doesn't like the feeling of not being able to control her own emotions. For well over an hour, not a word is spoken. Eventually, Rosaleen breaks the silence. "Patsy, what's wrong with me? I'm so careless with myself, and it scares me." The words sound broken coming out.

"My husband used to make me feel that way. It scared me so badly because I realized I didn't know what I was capable of at that point."

Rosaleen sighs.

"Hey, why don't you come stay the night at my place? I don't think you should be alone tonight."

"I'm just going to lock up and go to bed. I'll be fine."

"Let me get your stuff." Patsy walks up to Rosaleen's room and starts grabbing clothes from her dresser, not giving Rosaleen much of an option.

"I'm telling you, I'll be fine." Rosaleen walks into the room behind her.

"Where do you keep your pajamas?" Patsy opens and closes all the drawers. "I don't see any."

Rosaleen points to the side. "In the bathroom hanging."

"I think there's a *Deadly Women* marathon tonight. We can binge watch it."

"Patsy, please. I just want to be alone. I can protect myself." Rosaleen can't think straight, and while she knows it's dangerous, she just wants to shut the world out.

Patsy laughs. "Come on."

Rosaleen gives in, knowing she doesn't have much of a choice. "Will there at least be coffee involved?" *There isn't any use trying to reason with her.*

"Well yeah, of course. You know me better than that."

Rosaleen slowly opens her eyes, continuing to lie in bed as she glances at the animal heads hanging in Patsy's guest room. She shivers, remembering the dead opossum Todd left in her mailbox last night.

She climbs out of bed and leaves the animals to themselves. She listens for the pitter-patter of the twins' feet, but the house is silent. *They must still be sleeping. We did stay up really late.*

Rosaleen throws on her robe and follows the smell of freshly brewed coffee to the kitchen. Patsy is nowhere in sight.

Rosaleen finds her place at the table. A stack of pancakes, with two eggs and a strip of bacon arranged in a smiley face sit waiting for her.

Rosaleen laughs as she pours syrup onto her pancakes. *It's never a dull moment with Patsy around.*

Rosaleen hears the kids playing outside, and Patsy yells, "Quit sticking them acorns in your nose, boys."

Rosaleen ignores all the excitement and enjoys her breakfast, not even attempting to see what's going on.

FORTY-FIVE

Belle greets Rosaleen as she walks into The Hideout. "Somebody left you a gift." She holds the box up to Rosaleen and teases her. "He was a looker too!"

Is it from Todd? Rosaleen pretends to be excited, unsure if she can trust what's inside. "Did you get his name?"

"No. He set it on the counter and asked that I make sure you got it. He said it was very important." Belle shakes the box. "Well, aren't you going to open it? I'm dying to know what's inside!" She hands it to Rosaleen, bouncing up and down.

What if there's something horrible in here? Whatever is in the box can't be good. "I'll open it later. We have a customer."

"Look, it's Mrs. Joy!" Belle stands in front of the register. "What can I get for you today?"

"The usual," Mrs. Joy says, handing her money to Belle. "Keep the change, sweetie."

"Thank you! It'll be right up."

"What are you two all cheery about this morning?" Mrs. Joy asks.

Belle grabs the box from Rosaleen and teases, "Somebody has a secret admirer. He left her this pretty box!"

"Well, isn't that lovely. Open it up, dear." Mrs. Joy watches as Rosaleen pulls the box back from Belle.

Here goes nothing. Rosaleen slowly pulls the bow loose and lifts the lid. A note sits on top of pecan clusters. She releases the breath she's been holding. *My favorite chocolates.*

Belle quickly grabs the note before Rosaleen can read it. "My heart longs to be with yours. Each morning—"

Rosaleen jerks the note back. "—and I'll take that back." She tucks the letter into her pocket.

Mrs. Joy grabs her cup from the counter. "I guess we don't get to hear the rest." She laughs. "You two have a fun day at work. I'll see y'all in the morning."

After she leaves, Belle turns to Rosaleen. "Sorry if I upset you. I'm just a sucker for romance."

Rosaleen isn't used to seeing Belle without a smile on her face. She wishes she could be like her. "It's okay. It's a long story. His name is Easton, and he works a couple of shops down."

"Oh?"

"Let's just say the man doesn't get the girl in this Hallmark story."

"Who does she get in the story?"

"Absolutely nobody. Just the way she wants it."

"That's a new twist. I like it!" Belle points at the box. "Do we at least get to indulge in the chocolate?"

Rosaleen hands her a cluster. "Of course! They are my favorites. How can we not." She bites into the caramel filled pecan cluster, bringing back memories of Christmas time.

One Christmas day, Rosaleen sat on her grandpa's lap, and ate them together while the rest of the kids ran around playing. Her favorite thing to do was crack pecans with him.

"Here, Rosaleen, hold these. Don't smash your little fingers when you break the pecan," her grandpa warned her.

"I can't break through it." Rosaleen knew her grandpa would give in and crack them for her.

She carefully watched him crack the shell as she impatiently reached for the nut, peeling it apart. She brought her grandma a piece, taking all the credit for cracking them. Her grandparents looked at each other and grinned.

FORTY-SIX

Rosaleen pulls up to her house after a quiet Saturday drive around town and sees Harrison outside. He is in his old straw hat, raking leaves near the side of his house. Rosaleen gets out of her car, and he tips his hat, waving at her.

She smiles and waves back.

Not wanting to interrupt him, she goes and sits on her front porch to watch. She tries to be subtle about it. She doesn't want the poor, old fellow feeling like she is babysitting him.

Patsy walks over with two mason jars of iced tea. She sits next to Rosaleen and hands her a tea. "Where have you been all morning?"

"Shh, don't spook him back into his house," Rosaleen whispers.

"Girl, he's been outside all day. I brought him some lemon water earlier. He drank it up and went right back to work. He just won't step foot in the backyard."

"Why not?" Rosaleen sips her tea.

"He says it's still too painful to remember all the years he gardened with Esther."

"Oh, wow! Maybe one of us can invite him over to visit sometime. It looks like a gust of wind could carry him away." Rosaleen is scared that he's going to grieve himself to death if they don't get him out more often.

"You know, that is actually a very good idea. We can make plans later this week."

Harrison works until the sun sets. He waves at Patsy and Rosaleen as he walks inside.

"Welp, that's my cue to head on in." Patsy walks down the steps. Halfway to her house she shouts, "Boys! Come on and get washed up! It's time to get ready for bed."

I guess I better do the same.

Rosaleen goes inside and flops down on the couch instead. *Who am I kidding?* She laughs to herself. Turning on the TV, she flips to the ID Channel for some background noise. She starts to doze off, but she hears a knock at the door. Alarmed, she stands, grabs her house-coat, and throws it over her pajamas. She ties the sash and walks to the door.

"Who is it?"

"Easton." His voice sounds a little muffled through the door.

"What are you doing here?" she snaps, swinging the door open.

"I needed to see you. Rosaleen, please. I want to hold you so badly," Easton pleads with her.

"No."

"I love you. Doesn't that mean anything?"

"It does, but I don't love you." Rosaleen clenches her fist in frustration.

"I can't stop thinking about you. You're my whole world. I don't know how to go on without you."

I can't handle this. "Now's not a good time, Easton."

Easton grabs her hand. "Please, Rosaleen. Please. Don't push me away."

She jerks her hand back. *He just won't stop. I'm sick of people overstepping my boundaries. I'll show him that I'm not who he thinks I am.*

Rosaleen steps back, leading him inside. She sits on the couch and undresses him with her eyes as he sits on the other end. *If he wants to keep stepping over me, I'm going to use him first.*

Rosaleen stands. "Want something to drink?" She knows where she's going with this and how wrong it is.

"Please."

"Let's go sit in the kitchen."

Easton follows her into the kitchen and sits at the table.

Rosaleen walks toward the icebox, pausing midway. *He had his chance to leave.* She turns back toward him and grabs him by the collar of his shirt. *It's his fault if this hurts him.*

"Rosaleen . . ." He stands up, meeting her face-to-face.

She puts her fingers over his lips and shoves his back against the wall.

I should stop. She kisses him firmly. *But why? He'd just use me like Todd did.*

She rips open his shirt. Buttons fly in every direction.

"Rosaleen, we should—"

I don't want to hear what he has to say. Cutting him off again, she pulls his body closer to hers.

"Rosaleen." He rubs his hands along her sides, looking her up and down before stepping back. "As badly as I want to, we should really talk first."

She continues to ignore Easton, shoving him onto the kitchen table. She yanks his belt and pants off, throwing them to the floor.

Dropping her house-coat to her feet, she pulls her pajamas off and straddles him. She stares into his eyes. *I don't need to be doing this.* Pushing the guilt back, she leans into his body and kisses him. He runs his fingers across her back, bringing their bodies closer together.

He should have respected my boundaries.

Easton flips them over, positioning himself on top and accidentally knocking over a chair.

The crashing of the chair startles Rosaleen. *I can't do this.* She shoves him off. "You shouldn't have come."

Easton stands, grabs his pants, and puts them on. As he walks out of her house, he pauses and turns to her. "What do I have to do to prove my loyalty to you?"

"Leave." Rosaleen doesn't mean to sound cold, but that night alone on the bridge changed her. She doesn't want to be like this.

I can't hurt people. I'm not Todd.

FORTY-SEVEN

What did Esther see in me that I can't?

Rosaleen misses their weekend morning chats. She misses seeing Esther's tiny, wrinkled hands that remind her so much of her grandmother's. Rosaleen feels like she's forgetting the sound of her sweet voice more and more each day and she cherishes the little pieces of Esther she has left.

Rosaleen decides to visit Harrison, and walks up to his front door, knocking.

He may not have heard me. She knocks a little louder.

Nothing.

Maybe he's in the backyard? She walks around and checks.

Still nothing.

She knocks on the back door this time.

Maybe he's taking a nap. Making her way back to the front of the house, she turns the door knob. *Hmm, it's unlocked.*

Rosaleen slowly opens the door.

"Mr. Harrison? I came for a visit. You awake?" she yells.

She can hear the TV blaring a commercial with an old Loretta Lynn song. *Does anyone order those CDs anymore?*

She enters the living room and sees Harrison reclined in his chair.

Rosaleen reaches out to tap his arm. Not wanting to startle the poor, old man as he peacefully sleeps, she gently places her hand on him instead. *Why is he so cold?*

"Mr. Harrison?" She shakes his arm.

Harrison doesn't budge.

"Harrison!" She shakes him harder. "Don't do this to me!" Her tears sting her eyes as she tries to hold them back.

She walks over to where Esther used to sit and grabs her quilt. She covers Harrison up to his chest. "You won't be so cold now. Esther will keep you warm."

Rosaleen walks into the hallway by the kitchen and stops all of the cuckoo clocks, stalling time. *It's the end for them.* Rosaleen's heart aches.

"I'll go get Patsy so she can say goodbye." Rosaleen wipes a tear away as she walks out.

"Don't tell me that, Rosaleen." Patsy races out of her house, and Rosaleen struggles to keep up. She bursts into the living room. Harrison looks so peaceful.

"Please wake up, Harrison! Don't leave us, too." Patsy pleads as she stands over him. She wraps her arms around him, hugging him tight. "He's just sleeping!" She frantically looks up at Rosaleen and then turns back to Harrison. "You have to wake up."

Rosaleen pulls Patsy off of him. "He's gone to be with Esther. Their souls belong together. He was lost without her." She pushes Patsy's hair out of her face.

"It's not true! Call an ambulance." She pulls on Harrison's arm. "Come on! You can't go like this. Get up!"

"Patsy, he's already gone, sweetie." Rosaleen rubs Pasty's back, trying to console her and not break down at the same time. *Someone needs to keep it together.*

"Why do the good ones go so soon?" Patsy's face is soaked with snot and tears.

"I don't know, Patsy. I don't know anymore."

She's right. The good ones always go so soon, while monsters like Todd are walking around destroying people like Esther and Harrison. It isn't fair.

FORTY-EIGHT

Rosaleen bursts through Patsy's front door and sees her lounging in a chair. "No! Come on! You promised you'd come to the tree farm with me!"

"I didn't think you were actually serious." Patsy changes the channel on TV. "Plus, all those trees mess with my allergies. I'll be sneezing for the next two weeks."

Rosaleen walks in front of the TV and turns it off. "Don't make me drag you there."

"Alright, alright. Let me go put some jeans on. But I'm not dressing up. You look like a Christmas wreath," Patsy jokes.

"Before you go change, hear me out." Rosaleen pulls out two Christmas necklaces from her dress pocket, pressing a button on both. They light up, flickering with different colors.

"No, no." Patsy laughs. "I didn't sign up for all this holly-jolly stuff."

"Awe, come on! You never do anything fun!"

"Can't you just get a fake Christmas tree?"

Rosaleen slumps her shoulders. "I can. It's just that Todd never allowed me to have a real tree. He said they were too messy."

Patsy rolls her eyes, grabs the necklace, and puts it around her neck. "I don't even decorate my own house with lights. Now I have to wear this stupid thing," she mumbles as she walks away.

Moments later, Patsy comes out in a long sleeved 'I heart Christmas' shirt and jeans. "I can't believe I let you talk me into this. Let's go before all the good trees are taken."

Rosaleen breathes in the strong smell of pine as she and Patsy walk through the tree farm.

She pulls some needles from the tree next to her and smells them. "I've always loved the scent of real pine. Here, smell this." She raises them up to Patsy's nose, and she sneezes.

A plump man in a flannel shirt and holey overalls walks up to them. "Is this you two love bird's first time picking out a tree together?"

Rosaleen laughs. "Oh, no. We're just friends." She waves her hands back and forth. "But its our first time picking out a real tree."

Patsy crosses her arms and looks the man over.

Rosaleen can tell she's ready to run her mouth, so she nudges Patsy in the side.

The man grunts out a laugh. "Sorry 'bout that. I was just checking because this lady here is lovely." He winks at Patsy.

Patsy balls her fist at her side, "Well, I tell you what, sir—"

Rosaleen jumps in before Patsy can go off on the poor man. "These trees sure are lovely. Don't you agree, Patsy." She nudges her again. "Right, Patsy?"

"Yeah, I'd like to swing that ax straight through something." She looks at the ax he's holding.

The man's eyes widen, and he lets out another grunting laugh. "Anyhow, I'll be near my booth if you two need anything." He walks off, whistling to the tune of "Jingle Bells."

"Look!" Rosaleen runs over to a scraggly tree. It leans to the right, and the top hangs down a little. "It's perfect!"

"You don't want one that stands a little . . . Well, taller?" Patsy looks displeased with Rosaleen's choice.

"Who wants a perfect one, when we can have one that is special in its own way?"

"Let's just look around a bit more," Patsy suggests.

"Fine! Only because I dragged you all this way."

They look at a few more rows of trees, but they all seem too perfect for Rosaleen.

When they get to the end of the lot, Rosaleen turns and looks at Patsy. "Look, just hear me out, okay?"

"Are you about to whine more about wanting that dysfunctional tree?"

"Well, yes. But—"

"Come on." Patsy walks in the opposite direction. "That tree it is, then."

"I knew you'd come around!" Rosaleen jumps up and down, clapping her hands.

"Ugh."

"One of us needs to wait by the tree so no one tries to claim it."

"Ain't nobody gonna want this scrawny thing." Patsy laughs. "I just need to find that weird worker to chop it down." She mumbles under her breath, "Or chop him down."

It doesn't take long for them to get the tree back to Rosaleen's house.

Rosaleen hands Patsy a pitcher of water as she walks out of the kitchen and into the living room. "Let me grab a few decorations from the attic while you water the tree."

Rosaleen goes upstairs and pulls down the attic stairs. She climbs up and shuffles around for her box of ornaments. Stepping back, she falls onto a taped-up box. As she pulls the tape off, the strong scent of cheap Aspen cologne hits her. *Daddy!* Unwanted memories flood over her, making her want her dad more than ever.

She opens the flap and pulls out a green and gray polo-striped shirt. She recognizes it as the one her father stored his reading glasses and cigarettes in, now covered in cologne. *I must have broken the bottle when I fell on the box.*

She picks up his shirt and hugs it tightly, soaking in the scent. "Oh, Daddy. I miss you."

Rosaleen sets the shirt aside and digs further into the box.

Her heart drops when she picks up his folded death certificate.

Am I ready for this now? Never having read it before, she unfolds the document.

Date of death: May 28, 2003.
Cause of death: Gunshot wound to chest.
Manner of death: Suicide
Time of death: Unsure.
Death time frame: Minutes.

She can't read anymore. The fact that the certificate states it took minutes for him to die hits Rosaleen hard. *What if someone could have saved him?* She folds the paper up, places everything back in the box, and reseals the tape on top. The wounds caused by her dad's death are still fresh. *How could he have been so selfish?*

Rosaleen locates the Christmas box and carries it back down the stairs.

"Ouch!" Patsy is trying to place the tree back in its stand when it comes crashing down onto her head.

Well, I made it just in time for the show. Rosaleen runs over and helps lift it off her. "What in the world?"

"Your perfect little tree was attacking me." Patsy backs up and rubs the top of her head. "Did you find the ornament box?"

"Oh, yes. Here we are." Rosaleen opens the box, then pulls out her phone. "Let's listen to Christmas music!"

Patsy sarcastically mocks Rosaleen. "Oh, joy." She presses the button on her necklace, and the lights start to blink.

"Don't be a Grinch. Todd hated Christmas music, but now I can enjoy it."

"You're just milkin' it, now. Here, hand me your phone." Patsy yanks it out of Rosaleen's hand and turns on "Rockin' Around the Christmas Tree."

"Now this is Christmas music." Patsy says, bobbing her head to the music.

Rosaleen tugs Patsy to the middle of the floor. "Let's dance it out!"

They playfully hop around to the music, hanging ornaments.

FORTY-NINE

With Christmas only a few days away, Rosaleen realizes she still hasn't completed her gift shopping. *I'll have to get Patsy and her boys something. Oh, and Mom.*

She picks up her phone, dialing her mother. "You know what?"

"I didn't miss your birthday, did I?" her mom jokes.

"Not this year. I just realized I still have some Santa shopping to do. How about we make a day out of it?"

"I thought you'd never ask. I'll get my things together and drive over there."

"I can come pick you up."

"Well, I'd actually love to see your house and how it's coming along. You can drive when it's time to go shopping."

"Okay. I'll get ready, too."

When her mom arrives, Rosaleen shows her around the house. Her mom admires the work Rosaleen and Patsy put into the remodeling. "It looks like a whole new house. It's beautiful!"

The affirmation makes her feel like she's accomplishing more than she realizes.

"Ready to go, sweetie?" Her mom grabs her purse from the bottom of the stairs.

"Let me grab my sweater."

On the way to town, they ride in silence until Bonnie breaks it. "Look, Rosaleen. I wanted to tell you I'm sorry."

"For what?" Rosaleen peels off some of the flaking rubber on her steering wheel. "I really need to get a cover for this old thing."

"You'll be able to get yourself a new car once you're completely on your feet. You'll be so proud of it." Bonnie fiddles with her shirt.

"This is going to be fun. We haven't done anything together like this since . . ." Rosaleen's words trail off.

"Yeah, about that. I wanted to apologize. I should have known. I should have picked up on the signs when you stopped coming around as much. I just thought you were busy building a new life."

"It's not your fault, Mom." Rosaleen places her hand on her mother's.

"I could have protected you. You're my baby. Mothers are supposed to protect their children."

"I lied to you; you couldn't have known." Rosaleen turns into the parking garage at the mall and parks. "Look, let's go have fun. We can't make up for the lost time, but we can pick back up where we left off."

After walking around the mall and picking out a few things for everyone, they fill Rosaleen's back seat up with shopping bags and grab lunch.

Bonnie plops down in the passenger seat. "I'm stuffed! It's time to head back now. I'm not young like you anymore. I need a nap."

"You're worse than a child." Rosaleen's joke turns into sadness when she sees a mom pushing her infant in a stroller.

"Your time will come, sweetie."

"I know. Sometimes I regret not having children with Todd."

"Stop that. You would have regretted bringing a baby into a toxic family. It wouldn't have been fair to that child."

"I guess so." Rosaleen drives home, enjoying her mom's company.

After arriving home, Bonnie leaves and Rosaleen decides to take a stroll down to the dead end of her street. She's never been down that far, and what else does she have to do on this beautiful, chilly afternoon?

The further she walks, the more she feels like she's in a fairytale, surrounded by cottages and gardens. *Why didn't I come down here sooner?*

She passes a tiny green cottage and notices Gareth reading under a magnolia tree. She hasn't talked to him since the awkward day she threatened to hit him with a hammer.

Gareth looks up from his book and waves at Rosaleen. "Hey there!"

She waves back. "Hello."

He stands and walks over to his little white picket fence, where Rosaleen meets him.

Gareth sticks out his hand, and she proceeds to shake it with hers. "How are the repairs coming along?" He meets her eyes as he's talking to her.

Did he forget about that incident? He's acting so normal. "It's slowly getting there. You should come check it out one day." *Did I seriously just invite him to my house?*

"I most certainly will, Ms. Rosaleen Hart."

Why does he call me that? "Well, it was nice seeing you, but I should head back before it gets dark."

"Goodbye. Enjoy this cool weather before it gets hot again." He makes his way back to his door and watches Rosaleen continue her walk.

Todd would flip if he saw me talking to another man. She knows she's single now, but she still feels like there are consequences for talking to another man.

Rosaleen goes back home and locks her door behind her.

Will I ever feel safe again?

FIFTY

Patsy walks up and sits beside Rosaleen on the swing. "Ain't it great?"

"What's not great is my ice melting in my tea because it's 80°F on Christmas morning!" Rosaleen takes a sip of her tea.

"Oh, no ma'am. We're not going to be Scrooges on Christmas, are we?"

"Ha! No. You were saying something was great?"

"Oh yeah. Our lives. Today. Right this minute. Being able to sit and smile without a care in the world. You know?"

For once she makes sense. "It really does feel good—peaceful. It's great not wondering when something is going to fly towards my head."

"I get it." Patsy laughs.

Rosaleen looks forward to the day she can put Todd completely in her past and laugh everything off.

"Welp, those pies won't bake themselves." Patsy stands, nudging Rosaleen. "You gonna sit there all day?"

"Alright. I'm coming." Rosaleen slouches down and pulls herself up. "Plus, my mom and sister are coming."

Rosaleen's mom and her sister, Adeline, arrive for their first holiday at her house.

Rosaleen and Todd used to go to her family's house for Christmas, but eventually they started staying home.

Holidays always made him twice as bad, and her family never understood why her mood tanked during the celebrations.

"What's gotten into you?" Her cousin asked.

Todd jumped in, "I don't know why she gets like this when we get around the family." He nudged her and pretended like he was having a good time. In reality, Todd whispered in her ear about how fat her aunt was getting or how awful her grandmother was.

Rosaleen shut down.

If they could have only seen the culprit behind the scenes.

This year is going to be different, though. She is going to start her own family tradition, Patsy and her kids included.

Patsy walks out of the kitchen. "Well, nice to meet you, Ms. Bonnie." Patsy extends her hand, and Bonnie reaches in and gives her a motherly hug.

Adeline walks in behind Bonnie. "Adeline." She shakes Patsy's hand. "You must be the famous Patsy who Rosaleen talks about all the time."

"That's me. Nice to finally put a face with the name. You don't seem like the annoying sister she makes you out to be," Patsy jokes.

"Never." Adeline laughs and points at Patsy. "I see Rosaleen's got you wearing those silly Christmas aprons."

Patsy shakes her apron, making the bells on Rudolph's antlers jingle. "Ha! Yeah. But we all know that wearing these things makes the pie taste better." She presses a button, and his nose lights up.

"Speaking of pie, it's about to burn, Patsy." Rosaleen walks out of the kitchen. "Mom, Adeline, y'all made it just in time. Patsy is about to show me how to make her homemade rolls."

Hunter runs in announcing, "Look, we made a chocolate pie!"

Beaux follows in close behind, holding a frisbee full of mud.

"Oh, that looks delicious. Come show me how you made that." Adeline looks at Rosaleen. "Guess I can't help in the kitchen. I'm about to make a chocolate pie outside." She leaves the room with the boys.

"You can't cook anyway." Rosaleen shouts behind her, joking. "Mom, why don't you have a seat, Patsy and I will take care of the rest. It's your turn to relax until it's time to eat."

"I can't argue with that." Bonnie sits on the couch.

"Rosaleen!" Patsy yells from the kitchen.

"She must be burning something. I'll be back in a little bit." Rosaleen rushes into the kitchen. "What's going on in here?"

"I forgot I left the sink on, and it ran over." Patsy says, grabbing every dish towel she can find and trying to contain the water on the floor.

"Here." Rosaleen takes over. "Go grab the mop, and I'll finish mopping this up. What am I going to do with you?"

Patsy goes to the pantry and grabs the mop. She goes to hand it to Rosaleen, but turns around too quickly. "Here ya go."

"Don't!" Rosaleen falls into the water.

"Easy there. It's just a little mess. We'll get it cleaned up." She soaks up some water with the mop. "See. No one's mad. Heck, you needed to mop anyway."

Rosaleen relaxes. "You just came toward me too fast. When Todd made messes, he'd make me clean it up and get mad if I didn't do it fast enough."

"Well, I'm not Todd. I'm your best friend." Patsy rings the mop out into a dirty mixing container by the sink.

"It's just that—"

"Nope, we aren't explaining ourselves today. Todd isn't going to ruin your first Christmas without him." Patsy grabs a handful of flour from the counter and throws it up in the air. It lands all over them.

"My hair!" Rosaleen looks at Patsy like she's crazy.

"See this?" She points to the floor.

"You mean the mess?"

"Yep. We are going to have a messy Christmas. With messes all over this kitchen." She hands Rosaleen the bag of flour. "Come on. Your turn."

"Ugh, okay." She grabs a handful and throws it at Patsy.

"Hey now!" Patsy empties the bag over Rosaleen's head as they both fall to the floor, laughing.

Bonnie walks into the kitchen and looks around. "What on earth?"

"We're cooking, Mom." Rosaleen puffs flour from her mouth. "See?"

"Y'all have gone bonkers." She scoots some flour over with her shoe. "Do I need to put you two in time out?"

"No, ma'am." Patsy dusts her hands off and stands up. "She started it." She points at Rosaleen.

"Hey!" Rosaleen pulls Patsy back to the floor. "Liar!"

"I'm going back to the living room where it's safe." Bonnie turns and walks back out, laughing. "You two are crazy."

The smoke alarm goes off. "Pie is done!" Patsy jumps back up. "Wait! No! The chicken is boiling over!" She lowers the temperature and lets the water sizzle down. "Time to make the roux. Hand me a wooden spatula, would ya?"

Rosaleen walks a spatula over to Patsy. "I thought we were using the jar roux today to save time?"

"Never! You didn't tell me your mom was going to be here. She deserves only the best of the best gumbo around." Patsy puts a heaping scoop of flour in the iron skillet of oil and starts stirring.

Rosaleen decorates the kitchen table with a red tablecloth covered in golden sparkles. She sets a bowl of rice, potato salad, and a pitcher of tea in the center of the table. Patsy pulls the pecan pie and apple crumble pie out of the oven and onto some pot-holders to cool.

Rosaleen sits across from her mom at the table.

Her mom leans over and grabs Rosaleen's hand. "You know. You looked so happy today. It's been a long time since I've seen you like this. I'm glad to have my daughter back."

I think I'm going to be okay.

The rest of the evening, they eat and open presents, enjoying their first Christmas together as a new family.

FIFTY-ONE

The next morning, Rosaleen walks around to the side of the house and hears scurrying in the bushes next to her. She gets ready to take off running as a brown dog darts out and jumps on her, knocking her to the ground. "Ouch!" She rubs her stinging arm.

He nudges her arm with his cold snout, as if apologizing.

"I'm okay. I should have raked these sticks up weeks ago." She wipes blood off her arm with her t-shirt.

The dog licks her scrapes.

"See, I'm okay. Where did you come from, little fella?" She pats the top of his head. "Are you lost?"

He sits and looks up at her, letting out a whimper.

"Look how boney you are. You must be hungry." Rosaleen stands. He stands tall, just above her knees. She taps her leg, calling the dog over. "Come in the house, and I'll feed and bathe you." He's matted with mud, but it is hard to tell what's mud and what's fur. The brown colors blend together. "You may be a mutt, but you're still cute."

With one ear bent over and the other one perked, he tilts his head. As though he understands what she is saying to him, he follows her inside, wagging his tail.

After bathing him, she feeds him some left-over chicken from the night before. "I'll get you some real dog food tomorrow." He nuzzles her leg.

Rosaleen sits on the floor and scratches him behind his ears.

He lifts his back leg, shaking it.

"Does that feel good, little fella?"

He barks in response.

"Do you have a name, boy?"

He lays his head on her lap and lets out a little whine.

"You're safe. This is your home now, too." She pats his head. "Hugh."

He looks up at Rosaleen as if acknowledging his name.

"Very well. That's your name, boy. Hugh."

Later that night, she climbs into her bed. *Ah. So warm and cozy.*

Moments later, Hugh comes prancing into her room and sits beside her bed.

"Oh, come on boy." She pats the empty space next to her, and he jumps up next to her.

Hugh sniffs, scratches, and circles the bed until he finds a comfortable spot. He lies curled at her feet, and they both doze off.

Rosaleen awakes to Hughs barking and growling.

"What is it boy?" She pulls the covers closer, and he jumps off the bed, staring into the hallway. "It took me a while to get used to the sounds of the house, too. Come on, boy." She pats the bed, trying to get him to settle. *Maybe he just barks a lot at night? He isn't used to this space.*

Hugh runs over to Rosaleen, nudges her, then runs back toward the hall and barks again.

"I guess I should follow you." She walks down the stairs behind him.

All of his fur stands on end by the time they reach the bottom.

"My door is open!" Rosaleen shuts the door quickly and locks it.

Hugh is still going crazy, whining and pawing at the door.

"What did you see, boy? What is it?" *I wish he could talk.* She turns her porch light on and watches the wind blow viciously through the trees. "Maybe we didn't shut the door all the way?" The only thing Rosaleen can figure is that the wind blew the door open. Everything else looks normal.

She does feel a lot safer with Hugh in the house. If someone did break in, they must have been spooked by the barking.

"Let's go back to bed." She walks back upstairs, but Hugh stays at the door, refusing to move. "It's nice and toasty upstairs under the blanket. Come on, boy. I'm tired."

As if sensing her determination to go back to bed, Hugh follows.

FIFTY-TWO

Something is off.

Rosaleen opens her eyes, feeling like someone is watching her. She looks at her phone. It's only been two hours since she'd fallen back asleep. She climbs out of bed, and Hugh jumps down behind her.

"It's freezing in here. I know I have the heater on." She grabs her housecoat and starts walking toward the thermostat. "Just my luck. The heater probably broke."

She walks out into the hallway when she thinks she hears a tapping from downstairs. Hugh goes ballistic. The fur stands back up on his back like it did earlier that night. Rosaleen stops to listen for more sounds, but she can't hear anything over the barking. "Hush, boy! There's nothing there!"

Just then, Rosaleen hears another tapping sound.

Hugh takes off downstairs.

The living room is too dark to see from upstairs, and she doesn't want to start turning on lights, just in case.

She runs back into her room and grabs her phone from the night-stand to use for the flashlight.

Hugh's bark becomes distant. "No, no, no!" She sees the front door is open again, swinging back and forth as she comes down the stairs.

What do I do?! She runs back up stairs and lifts her mattress up. *Where's my gun?* She remembers Patsy kept it the day Rosaleen had her meltdown. *Why did I act so careless?* Rosaleen looks around the room, trying to find something to use as a weapon. *This hammer will have to do.* She grabs the hammer she never put back after hanging pictures the other day.

She switches the light on and realizes that the front door has been kicked in. "HUGH!"

How did I not hear this happen? Rosaleen glances outside and sees a shadowed figure running into the woods across the street. "Hugh! Where are you?" Just then, Hugh comes running from the opposite direction of the shadow.

That was a person!

She runs back into the house, locking Hugh into the downstairs bathroom so he can't escape. He looks up at her with sad puppy eyes as she shuts the door. "Awe, don't do that to me. I'll be back soon." She bends down and pats his head. "You're a good boy." He puts his paw on her arm. "Stay here. Just for a little bit. I don't want you getting hurt."

Rosaleen grabs her flashlight and walks back outside. Thinking she hears something, she turns the light off, not wanting to be an open target. After a few moments of silence, Rosaleen walks inside and lets Hugh out of the bathroom.

She knows the figure was Todd. He already promised to punish her for the divorce. *Who else would do this?* She is about to call Patsy, but decides not to wake her. She can show her in the morning. Plus, if it is Todd, he's long gone now.

"Just another thing to fix around here. As if there isn't enough to do already," she tells Hugh.

She shoves a chair underneath the doorknob to hold it shut. "This will have to do for now."

Rosaleen lies on the couch with Hugh at her feet. While the sounds of nature usually soothe her, Hugh's ears perked up at every howl of wind or snapping branch. Nothing seems to alarm him.

"You're a good guard dog," she says as she doses off, unable to fight her exhaustion.

FIFTY-THREE

Rosaleen sits up, hearing the sound of drilling. "Patsy, it's too early for all that noise." She stretches her arms and lets out a big yawn.

"Well, good morning, sunshine."

Wait...

She instantly feels nauseous when she looks over and sees Todd standing in the doorway.

He sets the drill down. "That red-head next door won't be a problem, will she? I've seen her looking out her window a few times."

Patsy! I need her help. What do I do? Rosaleen looks around the room for a way out.

"The back is boarded shut from the outside, so don't try anything stupid." He picks the drill back up and tightens a few boards. "I really did a number on this door last night."

"Todd, you shouldn't be here."

"Oh, I should, though. I'm not going anywhere."

Rosaleen moves her legs and realizes Hugh is gone. "Where's my dog?"

"He probably won't be back for a little while. That stupid mutt got in my way last night when I came for a visit."

I knew it was him! "You better not have hurt him!" She sits forward.

"What does it matter? You have people thinking I'm some kind of monster anyway."

"You did that to yourself. I never had to say anything to anyone."

"Is this how you repay me for giving you such a luxurious life? You would have been nothing without me." He throws his drill at Rosaleen.

She ducks as it flies past her head and hits the wall, barely missing her. "I never needed you, Todd!" She looks for something to defend herself with and grabs the TV remote.

"I'm sitting here fixing your door right now. You don't see anyone else here, do you?"

"I don't need anyone! Especially you!" She chucks the remote at Todd, hitting him in the arm. "You're not gonna tear me down anymore!"

"Tear you down, huh?" He stands up, laughing as he stomps the remote to pieces. "Did you think that was going to hurt me?"

"That's all you ever did to me! You controlled me and stole my life! Well, guess what, Todd? This is my life now! You don't own me!"

Todd storms over to Rosaleen. "SHUT UP!" He raises his hand. "You're a woman, and it's time you learn your place!"

Instead of flinching, Rosaleen stands up and yells in his face. "DO SOMETHING, TODD! HIT ME!" Rosaleen can see Todd's face turning red, and the veins in his neck are pronounced. She's never seen him this angry.

"Sit down, you fool." Todd looks intimidated. She's never yelled at him like this before. "You're acting crazy," he says through his teeth.

She can tell he wants to yell at her. *Maybe I should back down.* Testing her limits, she pops off. "The only crazy one is you, Todd. You just don't know how to react to someone standing up to you." She shoves Todd in the chest, barely budging him. "How does it feel, asshole!"

The back of Todd's hand meets Rosaleen's cheek, sending her flying onto the couch. "Now, I told you to sit down, dammit! You will listen to me when I speak to you!"

Rosaleen grabs her throbbing face. *Why didn't I just keep my mouth shut.* The taste of metallic blood makes her feel queasy.

"Now, I'll go finish fixing the door to our new home." Todd starts walking back toward the entryway.

My home! She jumps back up. "You know what?"

He looks at her. "Ha! You just don't listen, do you?" He laughs, bending over to grab the tape measure. "Sit down and quit being stupid."

Not this time. No. He won't keep me down. Rosaleen clenches her fists. She runs at Todd and jumps on his back, wrapping her arms around his neck and squeezing as tight as she can.

Rosaleen's no match for Todd. He throws her off, flinging her against the wall.

"What the hell are you thinking?" Todd kicks her in the side with his steel-toe boot.

"You can't break me." Rosaleen forces the words out, ignoring the pain.

"Give it up already, Rosaleen. You know what's going to happen if you don't back down." He squats over her. "Look at how pathetic you look."

"You'll have to kill me before I give up."

"Be careful what you ask for." He grabs a fistful of her hair, yanking her up from the floor.

Rosaleen grits her teeth, trying hard not to groan from the stabbing pain. Todd doesn't deserve the satisfaction of seeing her hurt.

He shoves her onto the couch, just long enough to toss his pants off. He flings the top half of her body over his shoulder and storms upstairs.

"Put me down!" She kicks as hard as she can, but he is much stronger than her.

Todd kicks the door to her bedroom open and drops her on the floor.

Rosaleen feels intense pain as her head hits the metal bed frame. *Please, kill me now! Please!*

"You still tough now?"

The room spins, and she tries to sit up without falling.

"Get on the bed! Now!" He kicks her again.

The pain is unbearable, and she throws up.

"Look at you. You're disgusting." He drags her by her arm into the bathroom and throws her in the shower with her clothes still on. "Wash up." He turns the shower on.

The water is cold as it beats down on her, but she doesn't mind. It helps numb the pain.

Eventually, Todd shuts the water off and pulls her out.

All Rosaleen can think about is the mess he's making as he drags her from room to room.

"Get on the bed, now!" He drops her, and she falls back to the floor.

"No . . ." She can barely speak, her head and side hurt so bad.

Todd picks her up and shoves her on the bed.

"Please stop," she cries out. "I'm sorry. I want you back. I love you." Rosaleen tries reasoning with Todd, knowing if it doesn't work, then this will be the end for her.

Todd yanks her soggy dress off. The sound of wet clothes slosh against the wall.

Rosaleen lies on the bed exposed and naked. Never so vulnerable as she is in this instant.

Todd forces himself on her. She is too weak to try fighting back. *I hate him.* She squeezes her eyes shut, wanting him to be gone when she opens them again. It doesn't work, though. The monster is still here, taking what little bit of herself she has left.

Todd stands up and walks out of the room, leaving Rosaleen lying on the bed, feeling empty and hollow. She doesn't move or try to get up.

Todd wins, again.

"Get up and get dressed!" Todd yells.

Rosaleen drags herself up to get dressed and sees her hammer on the floor where she left it. *I can't go down like this.* She leans down and grabs the hammer.

As she reaches for it, Rosaleen freezes, feeling a cold, hard pressure against her temple.

"You're not getting dressed." Todd kicks the hammer across the room, sending nails flying everywhere. "You really think that hammer stands a chance against my gun? What were you going to do with that?" He presses the gun harder against the side of her head, and she falls to the floor.

Rosaleen screams. "Just get it over with, Todd. SHOOT ME!" She swallows hard and squeezes her eyes shut, ready for this to be over.

Todd leans in and whispers in her ear. "You see, if I shoot you now, then how do I get back all the months you took from me? You don't get to get away from me that easily." He removes the gun from her temple and shoves it into his waistband. "Now get up and get dressed."

Where's Patsy? Normally, she comes to visit me on Sundays. Please hurry, Patsy. Please.

"I said get up now!" He yanks Rosaleen up and throws some clothes from a pile in a nearby basket at her. "Put a sweater and pants on to hide those bruises. You look hideous." He roughly puts her shirt on for her.

She bends to pull up her pants. The feel of anything on her skin makes her want to scream.

"Let's go downstairs," Todd snarls, grabbing her arm.

Rosaleen limps down the stairs, using Todd as her crutch.

He shoves her onto the couch when they get back downstairs. "Where's the remote?" He looks around for a moment before looking at her. "That's right. You broke it."

No. He's not going to sit on my couch in my house. This is all mine! Maybe, I can make him think I want him back long enough to be able to get out of here. "I'm so sorry about what happened earlier, Todd. I don't know what came over me. I guess I just needed to be put back into my place. Would you like something to eat?"

"Egg sandwich. You know how I like it, so don't mess it up."

"Okay. Let me go make it for you." Rosaleen stands, and Todd grabs her, forcing a kiss. His stubble feels like razor blades on her busted lip.

She doesn't dare to resist him, allowing him to violate her. *I should have bit him.*

"I'll be sitting on our couch, waiting for my food."

My couch.

"Turn the TV on before you walk out." He leans back, placing his arms behind his head and showing off the armpit sweat soaking through the sleeves.

Trying not to glare a hole through him, she turns the TV on. *I want to bash his head in so badly.* Instead, she turns around and walks into the kitchen like a good little housewife.

FIFTY-FOUR

Todd walks into the kitchen behind Rosaleen. "How's the food coming along?" He wraps his arms around Rosaleen's waist.

Disgusting pig. "I'm warming the cast iron up so I can get an even temperature. Makes for better eggs."

"This is more like it. I knew it wouldn't take long to get you thinking straight." He releases her waist and leans in to smell her hair. "I've always liked the way you smell."

Rosaleen's so furious that she's shaking inside. She's mad because he left her battered and bruised. Mad because she promised herself she'd never let another man pick her apart. Mad because Todd forced himself on her, raped her, and left her vulnerable body lying there when he was done.

Rosaleen grips the skillet with a pot-holder. *Do it. Do it, Rosaleen. Just do it.* She clenches the handle. Turning, she swings the skillet at him, hitting him upside the head.

Todd falls to the ground, rolling around and grabbing his head. "You stupid bitch! I'm going to kill you!"

Rosaleen hits him in the head again. "I'm not stupid!"

Todd starts crying. "Please!" he shouts, pleading.

"You cry baby!" She keeps striking him steadily, anywhere she can land a hit. "If I don't get to cry, you sure don't get to cry. SHUT UP!"

Rosaleen comes to her senses when she hears a knock on the door, dropping the skillet to the floor. Staring at all the blood, she scrambles around the kitchen looking for a dish towel, finding a dirty one by the sink. She hurriedly splashes water on her face and wipes it. *So much blood.*

She stands over Todd and nudges him with her foot. "Todd," she whispers.

He doesn't move. *He's dead!*

Rosaleen jumps when someone knocks at the door again. *What do I do with him? I'm a murderer!*

Rosaleen slowly walks to the entryway. "Who is it?" She tries to speak as calmly as she can.

"It's Patsy. Open up."

Rosaleen opens the door partially just enough to hide the half of her face she doesn't want Patsy to see.

"Quit playing and let me in." Patsy tries pushing the door open.

"I had a long night. I'm just going to sleep in a little longer." Rosaleen tries not to sound winded.

"What on earth is wrong with your voice? And why are you so clammy?" Patsy's irritation turns to worry. "Rosaleen, why can't I come in?" She presses her body firmly against the door.

"I have to go tend to some things. I'll see you later, okay?" Rosaleen goes to shut the door and accidentally reveals the bruised side of her face.

"ROSALEEN!" Patsy shoves the door open, knocking Rosaleen into the wall. "I'm gonna kill that son of a—"

"PATSY! You don't have to. I already did!"

"Wait. Where's he at? Are you serious?" Her eyes widen as she searches the room.

"He's in the kitchen. I don't know what to do."

"Well, let's go see the situation first." Patsy walks into the kitchen and kneels next to Todd, feeling his neck for a pulse. "Welp, he's dead." She stands back up. "You still got them tarps we took off your roof?"

"Patsy! You're not suggesting we hide his body, are you?" Rosaleen panics, backing away from the scene.

"I have a few hiding places in mind."

"You're not serious, are you?"

Patsy looks Rosaleen straight in the eye, her face more serious that Rosaleen has ever seen her. "Dead serious. Let's walk over to my house. I have some latex gloves that will go up to our elbows."

"Maybe we should call the police? Let's think about this first."

"And tell them what? You murdered someone with a skillet? You're bound to go to prison."

"What about self-defense?"

"There's no self-defense here. Honey, you went overboard and acted like a mad woman. At least, that's what people will say." Patsy shrugs. "He had it coming." She lets out a dark laugh.

I don't think I have any other choice. "Let's go get them gloves and tarp. I won't survive prison."

They go next door to Patsy's house and grab the gloves.

"Hey, I just remembered that I have a brand-new tarp under my porch. I haven't even unwrapped it." Patsy walks outside. "Here, hold these." She hands Rosaleen the gloves and grabs the tarp. "Now, let's go clean this mess up."

They put their gloves on and walk into Rosaleen's house. "We can open the tarp in the living room and drag him over from the kitchen. We will have more space to wrap him up in there."

They walk into the kitchen, and Rosaleen's face drains of color. "Where is he!?" *He was dead!*

"Well, I be damned. He's still alive." Patsy points to the kitchen window, where a little bit of blood drips down the wall. "He cut himself up getting out."

Rosaleen sinks to her knees. *I can't do this anymore.*

Patsy opens a bunch of drawers, grabbin a rolling pin.

"What are you doing with that?" That's my good rolling pin." Rosaleen's attention shifts to Patsy.

"We gotta go finish him off." She slips her kitchen gloves on. "Don't wanna get blood all over my hands."

Has she lost her mind? Rosaleen stands. "Patsy, we can't do that."

"I can't let that coward get away with hitting you like that." She taps the pin in her hand. "This should be plenty heavy. Although he's so hard-headed, this may not crack that thick skull of his."

"Let's just stop and think about this first." Rosaleen tugs at Patsy's arm, trying to stop her.

Patsy laughs and jerks her arm away. "You obviously wanted to kill him. Why the sudden change of heart?"

"I didn't mean to go that far. Patsy, please," Rosaleen pleads.

"I'm going with or without you." She storms out of the kitchen. "We can follow his blood trail. He can't be far."

Rosaleen glances over at the skillet covered with blood on the floor and rolls her eyes. *Ugh, fine!* She grabs the meat cleaver hanging on the kitchen wall and follows Patsy.

"Hey," Patsy says looking back at Rosaleen. "Didn't I just sharpen that for you the other day?"

"Um, yeah." *Now that she mentions it, she did.*

"Nice selection."

They walk outside, around the house, and to the back door. They set the meat cleaver and rolling pin down. Patsy grabs one end of the board and starts pulling. "You just gonna stand there? Help me," she grunts. "Hurry, so he doesn't get too far."

Rosaleen tugs at the other end of the board, wiggling it loose. "Why are we doing this before we go and look for Todd?"

Patsy looks at Rosaleen like she's stupid. "Do you want to drag his dead body all the way around the house for people passing by to see?" Patsy puts her foot on the door and pulls harder. "I figure it will be easier for us to drag him straight on through to the tarp."

Why is she so good at this? "That's a good point." Rosaleen copies Patsy and puts her foot on the door, too. The board gives way, and the pair fling back.

Patsy jerks the door open. "Now, let's go find him." She sounds thrilled.

Rosaleen feels numb. *It's like she's done this before.*

Patsy points toward some underbrush near the woods. "There!"

Rosaleen looks over to see disturbed grass.

Walking over to the spot, Patsy squats down and touches something. She lifts her hand up to show Rosaleen the tips of her fingers, "His blood. There's a trail straight into the woods. Let's keep going." She wipes the blood off one the grass before she stands.

"What if it's animal blood?" *There's no way I did this to him.*

"Oh, Todd's an animal, alright." She pats the rolling pin in her hand.

What is Patsy about to do to Todd? Rosaleen remains quiet as they follow the droplets. *I can't believe I hurt him this bad. I just wanted him to leave me alone.*

Leaves rattle off to the side. Rosaleen stops in her tracks, glancing around, trying to listen for more sounds. *Any second, he's going to come out and grab me.*

Patsy turns around and grabs Rosaleen's shirt, yanking her forward. "You can't do that."

"What are you talking about?" Rosaleen asks, confused.

"I saw you hesitate when you heard that rabbit hop off. There wasn't any hesitation when you swung that frying pan." She starts walking faster. "See, there's some more blood. We are getting close to my deer stand. Maybe he's hiding out there."

"What if he's hiding and watching us from the trees?" Rosaleen steps on a twig and jumps. Anger floods over her. *Maybe Patsy's right. If I kill him, I'll never have to worry about watching over my shoulder again.* A frog jumps in front of Rosaleen, avoiding her step. "Ouch!"

"That frog didn't even touch you." Patsy continues to yank Rosaleen. "Would you just relax a little? You keep being paranoid like this, and he'll catch us off guard. We gotta be ready to take him down when we see him. We don't have a minute to lose. It'll start to get dark soon."

"Well, let go of me. I can't save myself if you're holding onto me like a dog." Rosaleen tugs her shirt free of Patsy's grip.

"Shh." Patsy stops just short of her deer stand. "What is that? A rag or something?"

Rosaleen walks up to it and picks up the blood-drenched fabric. "It's part of Todd's shirt."

A loud thud comes from Patsy's deer stand, making them both jump back. Rosaleen grabs Patsy's arm, causing her to swing the rolling pin at Rosaleen's head. Rosaleen ducks just in time. *Now who's jumpy?*

Patsy laughs. "Are you trying to get yourself killed?" She looks up, now mad. "That hollow-headed jughead better not be messin' up my box blind! He left my windows unlatched." She starts climbing the ladder. "I might just mistake him for a deer!" She jumps up onto the floor, skipping the last step.

Rosaleen isn't too far behind her when Patsy lets out a high-pitched scream.

HE'S TRYING TO KILL HER!

Rosaleen grabs the meat cleaver, ready to swing it as soon as she gets to the top. She stops and glances around. "Patsy, what? No one's in here."

"That idiot got blood all over my deer stand. Do you know how long it'll take to get the smell out of here? I'll never kill a deer this season unless I build a new box blind. They can smell everything!"

Rosaleen rolls her eyes.

"Dagnabbit, I'm serious." Patsy stomps her foot, her face as red as her hair. "First he messes you up, and now he messes with my blind? Nope. That's his last time messing anything up."

Rosaleen laughs. *Did she just compare me to a box blind?*

"Why are you laughing? You're going nuts."

"I tried to kill my ex-husband, and now we're standing in a box blind arguing about how his blood is going to mess up your hunting season. This is absurd."

Rosaleen catches sight of something out of the corner of her eye, and her heart skips a beat. *It has to be him.*

He's limp-running to the end of the woods. "Look! We have to get him!"

They take off down the stairs, running as fast as they can. As soon as they get to the paved road, they see Todd running to the black truck he has parked on the side. *That's the truck! I knew it was him all along.*

"SHOOT HIM!" Patsy yells at Rosaleen.

"I DON'T HAVE MY GUN! YOU NEVER GAVE IT BACK TO ME!" she yells back at Pasty.

"WELL, IF YOU HADN'T ACTED ALL CRAZY WITH IT THE OTHER DAY, I WOULDN'T HAVE HAD TO TAKE IT!" Patsy throws her hands in the air.

Todd jumps into the truck and peels out, leaving tire marks on the road as he speeds off.

"JUST LOVELY!" Rosaleen spins around and looks at Patsy, lowering her voice. "It's too late. He's gone." *I'm in for it now. I'm going to look like the abuser.* Rosaleen is angry he got away, because she lost her only chance to escape Todd. At the same time, she worries about who he is going to tell. *Should I get ready for prison?*

"Let's go get the Jeep! We'll catch up to him in no time if we run back."

"No, Patsy. The damage is done. He got away."

Suddenly, Hugh runs up to Rosaleen from the direction where Todd's truck had been.

Rosaleen wraps her arms tightly around him, Hugh licking her face in return of excitement. "I thought I'd lost you forever."

Patsy bends down, scratches Hugh behind his ears, then turns and gives Rosaleen a hug. "I'm sorry I yelled at you."

"Me too. We were just so close." Rosaleen clenches her fist, holding back tears, she shakes the emotions off. "I need to go clean up the kitchen. Wanna help?"

"Might as well. Too bad we aren't cleaning up a body amid the kitchen mess." Patsy laughs.

Rosaleen laughs, too. "I'll never understand your humor, but for some reason that was funny."

"Let me go grab your gun before I forget."

"Okay, I'll see you in a minute. I'll wait for you on the porch."

Patsy peels the soaked gloves from her sweaty hands. "I have to grab the boys from the sitter's house. You wanna ride?"

"That's okay. I really want to be home by myself. Plus, you need to spend time with the boys. I had you here all day cleaning up my mess."

"It's all good. Don't stay up too late. I wouldn't worry about Todd tonight. You really did a number on him today. I'm so proud of you."

I don't feel so proud, though. This isn't the end. He'll be back. I'm sure.

Rosaleen watches as Patsy walks home. As soon as she is in her own yard, Rosaleen shuts the door and runs into the kitchen. Slinging open her drawers, she finds the biggest butcher knife she can grab. She recklessly runs up the stairs and into her room. Stopping dead in her tracks in front of the bed, thoughts flowthrough her mind.

I'm used trash. She slides the tip of her finger down the blade as she stares at the sharp, reflective metal. *This is sharp enough to end it now.*

The cold metal gives her goosebumps as she traces the tip of the knife from her wrist up her arm. *It wouldn't take long—maybe only minutes. Then all my troubles would be gone.*

The tip knicks her, bringing her back to reality. "Ow!" *No! He's not gonna do that to me!*

The scent of Todd's cologne and sweat fills the air. She stabs the mattress.

Then again.

And again.

Every time the blade cuts through the bed, relief flows through her. *I will never let Todd or any man take my body away from me again!*

Rosaleen stands, staring at the cotton and fabric everywhere, out of breath. She turns around, drops the knife to the floor, and walks out, shutting the door behind her.

FIFTY-FIVE

Business is slow at The Hideout when Belle walks up to her. "Hey, do you think you can handle this place without me the rest of the afternoon? I have a date to get ready for." She flashes a contagious smile.

Rosaleen hasn't worked alone at the coffee shop yet, but given the lack of patrons, it should be a breeze. "Sure. You want me to lock up too?" She grabs a damp rag and wipes the counter.

"Yeah, would you? That way I wouldn't have to come back to town." She takes a key off her key-ring. "I'll just get it back from you tomorrow. You sure you've got this?"

"Don't worry, everything will be just as you left it when you get back tomorrow."

"You're the best." Belle starts to leave, but then turns back around. "If we stay this slow, you can go ahead and close early. The town festival is tonight, so everyone will be down the street."

Rosaleen remembers when she was as bubbly as Belle is. Todd took that innocence from her. She admires Belle's confidence. She never meets a stranger, prancing around and greeting people all the time. She's the kind of person who hums a happy tune regardless of what she's doing.

After Belle leaves, Rosaleen pours herself a cup of coffee and sits outside at one of the patio tables. No one has shown up for a while, so she takes the chance for a small break. She watches an occasional family walk by. One kid is throwing a fit because his balloon came loose from his wrist and floated away in the air. The smell of funnel cakes and popcorn interests her. She can't recall the last time she had a good funnel cake. *Maybe I can walk down there for a moment? But what would I even do there? There'd be all the town's people, but no one I know.* She grabs her empty cup and tosses it in the trash before taking the bag out. *Nah. I'll just clean up and go home.*

Rosaleen walks back in from taking out trash with every intention of locking up early. However, she finds Gareth sitting at one of the tables inside. She can tell something is off. His face is red and splotchy, and his mom's journal is sitting in front of him.

Has he been crying?

"Hey, you almost missed us. I was just about to close the store."

Gareth shifts in his seat and stands. "I'm sorry. I can leave."

"It's technically not closing time. Would you like something?"

"I guess a plain, black medium roast sounds good."

"That bad, huh?" Rosaleen goes to the counter and comes back with his coffee. Placing it in front of him, she slowly sits. "I see you've been reading your mom's journal. Did something happen?"

"She loved me so much before I was even here, and I'll never get to experience that."

"What happened to her?"

Gareth looks down and focuses on the mug in his hands. "She was murdered when I was a baby."

"I'm so sorry. Did they catch the person who did it?"

"Cancer murdered her. Took her away too soon. She was the most loving mother anyone could have had. She says in here that she would sit and sing me lullabies until I fell asleep. I bet she had the voice of an angel." Gareth is quiet for a moment before he continues. "She was six months pregnant with me when she found out about the cancer. When the doctors gave her the treatment options, she declined so I wouldn't be harmed. She still might be here if it wasn't for me."

"That's hard, but it's not your fault." Rosaleen puts her hand on top of Gareth's.

"It is. Unbelievably hard. She said I was her sunshine through dark, cloudy days."

"You are. I've seen you happy, and I can tell that's who you are. Your mom would be so proud of you."

"After I was born, it was too late for treatment. I was four months old when she died."

"But she got what she wanted the most before she passed. Just think about it. She really wanted you, and she got to hold you and have those few months with you. I bet when she went, her heart was fully satisfied. She gave you the gift of life."

Gareth takes the last few sips of coffee, handing Rosaleen the mug. "Sorry, I know you just cleaned up."

"That's okay. I'll stick it in the sink and wash it in the morning. One cup is not going to hurt anything." She walks to the kitchen and leaves it.

Gareth is holding his mom's journal close and tight when she walks back into the lobby. "I should get going now. Thank you for the coffee."

"Gareth, your mom sounds wonderful. I'd love to know more about her when you get done reading that."

He nods. "Rosaleen, have you lost a parent?"

"I have. My dad. But that's another story for another sad night."

Rosaleen locks up and goes home, bypassing the festival. As good as it smells, she doesn't want to have to deal with all the townspeople crammed in one small area. *I'd be the new girl in town or even worse. The poor girl who was beaten by her husband. These small towns can be pretty judgy.* Rosaleen isn't ready to have a new label slapped on her name.

She sees a large envelope taped to her door when she reaches the porch steps. *Must be some papers for the house title or something.* She gets inside, sits on the couch, and opens the envelope.

Pulling out the content, Rosaleen begins to tremble. *Why would he do this?* It's copies of their divorce papers with blood stains all over them. *Did he kill another animal?* She shoves the papers back into the envelope, barely managing to finish—her phone rings.

She picks it up and looks at the screen. *I've never seen this number before.* "Hello," she answers.

"I'm not done with you," Todd whispers out in a familiar, violent tone. Last time he sounded like this, their neighbor's dog got into their trash bin and threw trash all over the place. Todd's voice was calm, but chilling. When he told her to clean the mess up while he brought the dog back to its owner. He was gone for over an hour, when she washed his clothes that night, his pants were covered in mud. Rosaleen never saw the dog again.

Rosaleen drops the envelope and yells at him. "TRY ME!" Rosaleen hangs up and throws her phone onto the couch, picking up a pillow. Holding it tightly to her face, she lets out a scream so loud her throat stings.

Rosaleen comes back to when she hears her doorknob jiggling. The door swings open and she jumps off the couch.

"Rosaleen!" Patsy's eyes scan the room. "I heard all kinds of screaming from outside!"

"Todd just called my phone from an unknown number. He told me he isn't done with me. I'm afraid he's still watching me."

"I did see a vehicle screech off, but I thought it was some young teens since that festival is going on tonight."

"What did it look like?"

"I don't know. It was halfway down the road by the time I noticed it. But there's nothing we can do about it now, so just calm down. I have something for you, since it's your birthday and all." Patsy walks outside and comes back in with a funnel cake. "I figured you wouldn't go, so I brought you this." She sits next to Rosaleen. "You'll have to share it with me, though."

"You remembered my birthday!" Rosaleen pulls off a piece of the funnel cake and takes a bite. "Mmm."

"Of course I'd remember my best friend's birthday!" Patsy says, shoving some cake in her mouth. "So good."

With a full mouth, Rosaleen says, "You know, I wish I would have killed Todd the other day. I hate him so much."

"Funnel cakes sure do make you violent." Patsy laughs. "It's still not too late." Patsy shrugs and reaches for the envelope. "What's this?"

Rosaleen jerks it away from her. "Just some stuff Todd sent. I don't want to open it again."

"All I'm gonna say is that Todd's cornbread ain't done in the middle if he's brave enough to come 'round after what you did to him."

"Well, when you put it like that." Rosaleen can't help but be amused. She never knows what will come out of Patsy's mouth next. "Sometimes, I wonder what goes on in that brain of yours, Patsy."

Patsy shrugs. "Why don't you come over yonder to my house, where you'll be safer?"

"I'm going to stay here. I have a few things I need to get in order." Rosaleen knows she will have to go back to her room, eventually. It might as well be today.

"Very well, then. You know where to find me if you need me." Patsy says. "See you soon." Leaving, she shuts the door behind her.

Once she's alone, Rosaleen walks into the bedroom. It's the first time she's been inside since she demolished it.

Bending down, she grabs some fabric from the sheets. Dropping it, she turns toward the door and stops. *No, I'm doing this. I'm going to start this right.* She turns back around, staring at the mess. *I have to. I need to get these memories out of here so I can move on.*

After she takes what's left of her mattress to her burn pile, she grabs a can of gasoline from the shed and drenches everything. She throws a single match into the pile and watches the flames engulf everything, burning away the memories.

"Oh, my skillet." Rosaleen says aloud as she picks it up off the ground and walks over to the water hose. She attempts to spray off the old blood. *Great. It's going to take forever to get this blood out and season it back to perfection. Thanks a lot Todd, this was my favorite skillet.*

She is about to walk inside, but Patsy walks over. "I saw you outside, so I just wanted to see how it was going."

"I was just about to dry this off." Rosaleen holds up her skillet.

"You better season that before it rusts. Your grandma would be rolling over in her grave if she saw your skillet like that."

"That's what I'm going to do right now."

"Oh, hey, Rosaleen? Can you make yourself busy for a few hours this evening? I have a surprise for you, and you can't be home."

"Actually I—"

Patsy cuts her off. "I won't take no for an answer. Go visit your mom or something."

Rosaleen sighs. "Fine."

No telling what she has up her sleeve.

FIFTY-SIX

Rosaleen pulls up to her mom's house, noting immediately that her car is gone. *She must've had errands to run. Unless Todd got to her!* She rushes out of her car, grabbing the spare key from the shed.

Walking back to her mom's house, she unlocks the door and walks in. The curtains are closed, and it's pitch black in the house. She's never liked going into a dark house alone. Rosaleen feels around until her hand meets the smooth plastic of the switch, and she turns the lights on.

"SURPRISE!" A crowd full of her family pops out from behind furniture.

Rosaleen jumps back, startled. *I hate surprises.* She paints on a smile. "Awe, thank y'all!" she says, her body shaking.

Adeline walks up to her and drapes her arm around her shoulders. "I know you hate surprise parties, but your friend Patsy insisted that Mom throw one." The weight of her arm helps settle Rosaleen.

"A fair heads up would have been nice. Just wait 'til I see Patsy," Rosaleen says making light of the situation.

"Hey, now. Pasty's not someone I want to mess with, so I just went along with her plan," Adeline jokes.

"She's not so bad once you get used to her."

Adeline lets go of Rosaleen. "I have someone I want you to meet." A man walks up next to Adeline and grabs her hand. "This is Benjamin, my boyfriend."

He extends the hand that isn't holding Adeline's towards Rosaleen. "Nice to meet you."

Rosaleen shakes his hand. It's firm, and she stares at his clenched jaw making eye contact. *Todd's jaw does that when he's mad at me.* "Nice to meet you, Benjamin." She let go of his hand, realizing how tightly she was squeezing it.

"You can call me Ben." He pulls his hand back and rubs it. "Quite a firm grip you have there."

"So, Benjamin, how long have you known Adeline?" *I hate this dirtbag already.*

"About six months. We met at work." He balls his fist, tapping it against his leg.

Todd does that when he gets aggravated. "That's weird, she hasn't mentioned you." She crosses her arms, trying to intimidate him.

Adeline looks at Rosaleen, back at Benjamin, then back at Rosaleen. She leans over and whispers in her ear, "You're making him nervous. Back off some. Jeez."

"Were you surprised?" Bonnie asks, walking over and easing some of the tension.

"I was. Thanks, Mom." Rosaleen tries her best to smile, but she's still distracted by Benjamin.

"Let's go see your cake." Bonnie motions for Rosaleen to follow.

Rosaleen glances at her sister.

"Go. It's fine," Adeline mouths.

She combs the room, looking for anything off and making sure she keeps Benjamin in her sight at all times.

Admiring the double-layered strawberry cake filled with strawberry jelly, Rosaleen scoops a fingertip of pink, strawberry icing. "It's beautiful, Mom! Yum!"

"Hey! Save that for later." Bonnie playfully swats her hand. "I knew you'd like it."

Rosaleen notices Benjamin whisper something in Adeline's ear, nudging her in the side.

Furious, Rosaleen pushes past everyone in the room. "Stay away from my sister!" She shoves Benjamin back, knocking him to the ground.

"Hey!" He looks up at her, confused. "What was that for?"

Adeline gasps, "Rosaleen!" She helps Benjamin off the floor.

Bonnie walks up to them. "What's all the commotion for?"

The room falls silent as Rosaleen realizes everyone's attention is on her. She gazes around. *They don't know why I pushed him. I just look crazy in their eyes. That's what Todd wants.*

She shifts her attention back toward Adeline and Benjamin. "I'm not going to watch this happen." Without any explanation, she storms out the door, slamming it behind her.

Rosaleen speeds down the road. *What's it even matter.* She hits the steering wheel.

She comes to a dead stop. Rosaleen reaches up and grabs both sides of her hair and screams. *I just want to be free of him!*

After sitting for a moment, Rosaleen looks around and makes sure that no other cars are coming her way. *Thank goodness. I don't need anyone seeing me like this.*

The rest of the way home, Rosaleen can't help but wonder if she overreacted. *Who am I kidding? I really overdid it.* She sighs. *Not everyone is Todd.*

Rosaleen storms into her house as Patsy is walking down the stairs. "What are you doing here?" She asks rudely, not expecting to see Patsy in her house.

"What fiddled your faddle?"

"I may have blown up at my sister's new boyfriend by accident." Rosaleen sits and puts her head in her hands.

"Well, that's not good." Dismissing the whole situation, she waves her hand at Rosaleen, "Never mind that. Let me show you why I'm here."

Rosaleen doesn't budge.

"Look. Whatever you did, I'm sure it'll be fine."

"I made myself look like a lunatic in front of my entire family, but yeah, it's all fine and dandy."

Patsy laughs. "Okay, you've had your time to sulk, now come on before I burst from excitement. I've worked my tail off for the past few hours."

That catches Rosaleen's attention. She lifts her head up. "What did you do?" Sometimes, when Patsy tries doing something out of the kindness of her heart, Rosaleen has to go back and fix it.

"I got you a present. Now, can you just come upstairs with me?" Patsy looks like an eager child hyped up on twenty pounds of sugar.

Oh boy. Rosaleen follows her up the stairs to her room.

"Ready or not." Patsy pushes the door open.

Rosaleen stands, speechless. All her old furniture is replaced. The colors in the room are vibrant. Vintage, white furniture out against the subtle blue walls and navy curtains with yellow flowers.

"You like it?"

"I love it!" Rosaleen doesn't know what to say. "Wait, how did you move the old stuff out and get all of this in here so quickly?"

"Eh, I know some young teens down the road who didn't mind helping for a few bucks." She shrugs like it's no big deal. "Don't touch the walls. The paint's still wet."

"It looks like a whole new room. It's so bright and happy." Rosaleen sits on the edge of the brand-new bed. "And comfortable," she says, lightly bouncing. "Where did you put the old furniture?"

"Burned it. I burned everything that was in here. Well, besides your clothes. You'll have to fold them and put them back in the drawers." Patsy opens her closet, revealing a large basket filled with all of Rosaleen's clothes. "You know how much I hate folding."

Rosaleen runs over to Patsy, attacking her with a hug. "I love it, Patsy! I just don't know what to say. This is all so amazing!"

Patsy squirms. "Jeez, just say you'll actually sleep in your room from now on."

"I promise." Rosaleen holds up her pinky finger.

"Oh, and try to keep the knife away from these pillows."

FIFTY-SEVEN

"Just lovely."

Rosaleen puts her forehead against the cold window and stares out, watching the street flood. It hasn't stopped raining all day, and she forgot her umbrella. It is night time now, and the weather doesn't help with how dark it is outside. Normally, Belle shares her umbrella as they walk to their cars, but she has another date tonight. She left Rosaleen in charge of locking up again.

Rosaleen fogs up the glass with her breath and draws a heart. *Every week, Belle has a new date. How does she do that?* Rosaleen admires her courage. It's so simple for Belle. If there's something about a man she doesn't like, she moves on to the next one. One evening, a date didn't hold the door open for her, and she walked out before it even started. Rosaleen put up with the same nonsense from the same man for years. She only wishes she had whatever Belle has that gets her so much respect.

The work phone rings as she's cleaning up. "This is The Hideout. How can I help you?"

There's a click and then a busy tone. *Must be the weather.* Already a little spooked, the lights start to flicker, so she turns on the light from her phone and flips the main switches off. *I'm leaving anyway.* She steps outside and locks the door.

Hoping the rain might calm down soon, she stands under the patio umbrella for a moment before deciding to dart to her car. Water splashes up the backside of her dress as she runs. Completely drenched, she's more than ready to get home.

As she approaches her car, Rosaleen is jerked off her path. She squeezes her eyes shut, knowing Todd is about to kill her.

"Rosaleen."

It's not Todd. Her body relaxes, but she's angry when she looks up, seeing Easton standing right in front of her.

His cold hands reach her face.

The nerve! How dare he grab me like that! "No!" She backs up and slaps him. Her hand throbs. "Don't you ever handle me like that again!"

"You know, Rosaleen. You are so selfish, it's maddening." Easton clenches his jaw like Todd does when he's mad.

The thought is enough to make her want to bash his head in. "I'm not selfish. I'm tired of allowing men like you to walk all over me." Rosaleen balls up her fist and lifts her hand. As she's fixing to punch him, she stops.

I'm not Todd. This is something he would do.

"One day you'll beg for me to take you back, and it will be too late."

"Not a chance. You're too much like Todd for that to happen."

He walks away without looking back.

Normally, Rosaleen would regret saying something like that after seeing the hurt in his eyes. Tonight, after seeing Easton make a jerk of himself one too many times, she realizes it's all a game to certain types of people. They pretend to be the victims as the innocent ones suffer for it.

Not anymore. Not Rosaleen. *They will never change, no matter how much I alter my life for them.* She must be there for herself and not rely on the love of someone else.

FIFTY-EIGHT

The next morning, Rosaleen wakes up with a pounding headache and a stopped-up nose. *All because of that idiot holding me up in the rain.*

Rosaleen lies in bed for most of the morning with Hugh lying at her feet, resting his head on her legs. Around noon, Hugh jumps down and paws at the door.

"What's wrong, boy?"

He tilts his head, his eyes begging.

"Alright, I'll take you outside." Rosaleen throws her robe over her pajamas and slips into her slippers. "Let's go."

Hugh takes off running as soon as the door opens.

"Well, hey there!" Patsy calls over to Rosaleen. "Come see what I got."

One of the twins yanks the other down by their shirt, and they tackle each other.

"Y'all go on yonder and fight!" Patsy yells at them, and they take off to the back yard with Hugh.

So much for a quiet day. Rosaleen sits on the porch with Patsy. "What do you have there?"

Patsy lifts a crossbow in the air. "This here is my new baby. Just look how sharp these arrows are." She places one on the bow. "Wanna go see how far it can shoot?"

"Why not? I have nothing better to do."

"Here, hold it a minute." She hands the bow to Rosaleen.

"Oof." The weight is unexpected. "Why is this thing so heavy?"

"Because it's real." Patsy slips her mud boots on. "You aren't going out there in those pathetic slippers, are you?"

"Wait a minute, you never said we were going out where you hunt."

"Where else would we go?" Patsy laughs. "Come inside a minute, and you can use some of my hunting clothes."

"I can't hunt! I can't even kill a mosquito, much less a deer."

"Well, now's your chance to learn."

"Okay. I've always wondered how you do it anyway."

They walk inside, and Patsy hands Rosaleen some camouflage. "Here. Go put these on while I get the boys ready to go to their cousin's house. They'll be pulling up any minute."

"What cousins? I thought it was just you and them?"

"They're from their dad's side of the family."

"You're not worried about their dad trying to run off with them?"

"He's still missing, so I'm not too worried."

"What if he's hiding out, waiting for the right moment?"

"Not every abusive man is like Todd. I just have this funny feeling that bastard ain't coming back." Patsy looks around. "Don't let my boys hear you talking about their daddy, though. They ain't old enough for that conversation yet."

Rosaleen lowers her voice. "So, you trust his family with your kids?"

"His cousin, yes. As for the rest of his family, no. They don't even know where I live. His cousin walked in on me getting hit upside my head with a belt."

A car honks outside, interrupting Patsy. "Perfect timing. This discussion was going too far."

"I didn't mean to—"

Patsy cuts her off. "Come on, boys! Jasper is here!" Patsy yells to the twins. They both dart out the door like firecrackers. "Doesn't Momma get a kiss?"

"Come on, Momma!" the twins yell at her.

"You go on and get them clothes on. I'll be right back in."

What else do I not know about her.

After changing, Rosaleen walks out, tugging at her pants. "This is ridiculous. Why do I let you talk me into this crazy stuff?"

"Awe, you'll feel better once I spray my lucky perfume on you." Patsy laughs, pulling a bottle from her vest and spraying Rosaleen's shirt.

Rosaleen waves her hand in front of her face. "What is that? It's awful!" She covers her mouth, trying not to gag.

"It's deer urine."

"What!"

"Yeah, buddy. It's supposed to help us attract a buck." She sprays herself a few times.

"Why would you spray that in your house?" She grabs the bottle from Patsy and examines it. "This is disgusting."

"Ah, stop your whining. You'll get used to it. The smell goes away fast."

Out in the woods, Rosaleen doses off on the box blind while Patsy stares into her scope. Patsy nudges Rosaleen and whispers, "Look at that!" She points ahead of them.

Rosaleen leans forward. "You aren't going to shoot that one, are you?" she whispers back.

"No, that's just a baby. There's a big buck back here somewhere. I saw him last night when I was leaving."

Rosaleen sits back, bored. *What is so fun about watching something for so long just to kill it?* Thinking about it makes her think of Todd. He is pretty good at following her like a hunter. That's all he ever does—'hunt' her. *He'd kill me like this if he could.*

Rosaleen pictures herself in the deer's position. *Where is Todd right now? He could be watching me this very moment for all I know.* "I can't do this!" Rosaleen jumps up. "I'm not going to sit here and watch you stalk these poor, innocent animals like some kind of serial killer." Rosaleen slings the door open and goes down the ladder.

Patsy watches, looking completely lost. "Hold on a minute." She follows Rosaleen. "This is different than that."

"No, it's not! They don't even know that you're watching them."

Patsy sets her bow and arrows against a tree and catches up to her. "Hey, now. People who stalk someone for no reason or hurt somebody ain't right in the head. You know that."

"Where's your husband, Patsy?" *I shouldn't have asked that. For all I know, she could be on Todd's side. Why would she bring me out to the place where Todd ran off on the day he got away. I should have hit him a few extra times. He wouldn't be somewhere out there ready to find me.* "And why are you so sure he isn't coming back?"

"Hey! Now you wait a damn minute. I'm not the bad guy, Rosaleen." Patsy points her finger at her.

"How do I know? You always change the subject when your husband is brought up." Rosaleen puts her hands on her hips. "You're always trying to tell me what to do, like I can't make my own decisions. How do I know you and Todd aren't working together?"

Patsy steps back and puts her arms over her chest. "Rosaleen! Just listen to what you're saying." She swallows hard. "I hate Todd. Probably as much as you do." She looks like she's about to cry. "I was just trying to protect you. You're my best friend." Her voice crackles.

"Well, I don't want your help any more. I'm sick of it. I'm sick of you! I'm sick of Todd! I'm sick of Easton! All of you!"

"I never meant to make you feel this way. If you would have just said something . . ." Patsy shuffles her feet in the leaves. "You're all I have besides my kids. I just wanted to make sure I never lost you. I'd never hurt you like that."

"You hear that? You, you, you. It's all about what's convenient for you. Well, what about me!?"

"Just—"

"No! It's still my turn to talk! You all try to decide what's best for me. I can make my own choices. I know what's best for me!" Rosaleen throws her hands in the air, continuing to yell at Patsy. "I didn't even want to go hunting in this stupid box blind."

"I'm sorry, I shouldn't have forced you to come." Patsy slumps against a tree. "I'm sorry. I thought you would enjoy it, and we could have something in common." She puts her head in her lap and starts to cry. "I'm sorry, Rosaleen. I'm sorry."

I made Patsy cry. She'd never take Todd's side. The poor thing has had a life just as bad as mine, and here I am tearing her down. Patsy never cries. Rosaleen sits next to her and puts her arm around Patsy. "It's okay. I shouldn't have yelled."

"I would have backed off. I swear."

"I know." She pats her back in a reassuring way. "I thought it was going to be fun, too. That's why I came. I could have said no."

"I didn't give you the chance." Patsy wipes a tear from her cheek.

"I don't know why it reminded me of Todd."

"Because that man has you so messed up. Rosaleen, I'd never help Todd. I'd probably kill him if I saw him."

"I know. I'm sorry I accused you of that. My mind was just flooded with thoughts, and I felt trapped. I know you'd never do that. You're my best friend, too."

Patsy wipes her face with her sleeve, blowing snot out her nose and onto the ground. "Well, that's enough of this whining stuff. Let me grab my bow, and we'll go back home and make some tea." She turns to Rosaleen. "That is, if you want to."

Rosaleen smiles. "I'd love to. Or we can go back up there. I want to see you get your buck."

Patsy laughs. "Even if we wanted to start hunting again, it's too late. We've already scared every living creature out here with all this sappy stuff."

"Let's go get that tea."

FIFTY-NINE

Hugh ran in circles, barking at the birds flying around. It is a beautiful day for a walk down the street, and Rosaleen wants to take advantage of her day off.

Rosaleen and Hugh walk back home, taking their time. Approaching home, she sees Patsy in her front yard with a leaf blower. *Patsy never does yard work.* "Come on, boy, let's go see what she's up to."

Hugh wags his tail.

"You want to play with the boys, huh?"

He jumps up on her, and she scratches his ears. "Go get 'em!"

Hugh takes off running toward the twins as she walks over to Patsy. "What are you doing? You have a visitor coming?" Rosaleen jokes. Patsy never has anyone over to her house.

"Ha! Who's gonna come to our neck of the woods to visit?" She sets the leaf blower down. "I'm making a mountain of leaves for the kids to jump in. Grab that other rake and give me a hand, will ya?"

Rosaleen finds the rake. "You can blow the leaves toward me. And I'll collect."

Patsy points the machine at Rosaleen, blowing her hair every which way.

"That's it!" Rosaleen laughs. "Payback!" She throws the rake down and shoves Patsy into the pile of leaves.

Patsy pulls Rosaleen into the pile with her, and they throw leaves at each other.

The twins run up from the back, laughing, and jump into the leaves with them. It's not much longer when Hugh lunges into the pile, trying to catch the leaves with his mouth as they come falling back down.

Patsy stops, looking over at Rosaleen's house. "Who's that at your gate?" Patsy asks.

"I have no clue." Rosaleen climbs out of the pile, trying to make out who it is. "Oh, that's Gareth," she whispers. "I'm not sure why he's here."

"Want me to walk over with you?"

"Yeah."

Patsy and Rosaleen walk over to the fence where he's standing.

"Hi, Gareth. Is there something you need?" Rosaleen asks him.

"I was just strolling by and stopped to admire your house and how nice it's looking."

Patsy chuckles "I'm sure," she mutters under her breath.

Rosaleen nudges her in the side.

Gareth looks at them both. "I see you're busy right now. I also wanted to see if you'd like to have coffee with me later today, Rosaleen."

"Well, sure. Patsy can even join us."

"Actually, I think I have something to do in a little bit."

Rosaleen turns and glares at Patsy. "You're not busy at 7:00 tomorrow, remember?" She smiles at Gareth. "How's 7:00 in the morning?"

"Um, sure." He looks at Patsy and hesitates, instantly looking like he regrets coming over.

"See you then, Gareth. Have a good evening."

Once he's gone, Rosaleen looks at Patsy and laughs. "He's probably just lonely and needs a couple of friends."

"But he's so weird." Patsy rolls her eyes. "Why did you have to go and pull me into this?" Patsy whines.

"You wouldn't want your best friend to be alone with a complete stranger, would you?" Rosaleen nudges Patsy's arm. "Plus, you owe me."

"For what!?"

"For dragging me to places I don't wanna go." Rosaleen walks back toward the pile of leaves.

"Oh, alright." Patsy follows.

"Plus, I feel bad for the poor guy. I couldn't tell him no."

"He is kind of handsome." Patsy teasingly winks at Rosaleen.

They both know he doesn't have a lot going for him when it comes to looks.

"Oh, hush." She shoves Patsy back into the pile of leaves.

That evening, Gareth walks into the yard to meet them.

"Well, come on in." Rosaleen says.

They inside go and sit in the kitchen. Patsy grabs three mismatching mugs and pours them all some coffee.

She's doing that on purpose. Rosaleen glares at Patsy. She can't stand when things don't match, especially in situations like this. It's another thing she learned from Todd.

Patsy leans over. "Time to change things up, you think?" she whispers.

Rosaleen sighs and takes a sip from her mug. Nothing in her life matches anyway, which helps her feel more at ease.

Rosaleen can tell that Gareth is here for a reason. He probably wants to talk more about his mom, but Rosaleen doesn't want the emotional burden right now. She has plenty on her mind already. *Where is Todd? I haven't seen him lately.*

"So, Gareth. Do you work or anything like that?" Rosaleen asks, attempting to figure him out.

"I work from home. I'm a writer."

She stands and walks to the counter. *Just like his mom. He likes books too.* "Oh? What do you write?" She pours some creamer.

"I write fantasy, romance, and mystery. I have several books published." His face instantly lights up.

"I've never heard of you before. Maybe you can show us some of your books." Rosaleen sits back down next to Patsy.

Patsy pinches Rosaleen's leg under the table and whispers, "You must want to see this hottie again after all."

Rosaleen pinches Patsy back.

"OUCH!" Patsy jumps, and they both start laughing.

Gareth looks at them, confused.

After talking over coffee for a good and awkward thirty minutes, Rosaleen cuts into the visit. "Well, I must go to work now. It was a nice morning visit with you two. Hope to see you again soon." She turns to Gareth. "You know where to find me."

Patsy gets into her vehicle, and Gareth starts to walk home. He turns back toward Rosaleen as she climbs into her car. "I'd like to discuss some stuff with just the two of us again sometime."

She hesitates. "About your mom's journal, right?" If it's only about that, she doesn't mind. Every time she's ever gotten close to a guy, he's turned into a jerk.

"Of course." He turns back around and leaves.

SIXTY

Rosaleen walks up to her front door after work and notices the door cracked open and the living room light on.

"Hugh, come here, boy."

Nothing.

"Hugh!" She whistles.

Still nothing.

Maybe Patsy came by to get something, and she let him out? Rosaleen calls Patsy and asks if Hugh is over there.

"No, I haven't seen him today."

Rosaleen walks into the house, sensing that something is off. Hugh is gone, and the house is too quiet.

She walks into the kitchen. "Hugh?"

The wind catches the kitchen door, and swings it open. *Oh no. Why is it open?*

Rosaleen turns, running to her room to grab her gun and checking every room in the house on her way back down.

Maybe Todd came by and saw that no one was here? This time, she has her gun on her, and she isn't going to let him get away.

Rosaleen makes sure all the doors and windows are locked and then walks out her back kitchen door. She calls for Hugh for about thirty minutes.

Finally, she sees Hugh running out from the trees. He limps over to her.

"Let's get you inside, boy."

He lets out a whimper.

"You're going to be alright. I got you now." Rosaleen picks him up and carries him inside, laying him on her bed. "There isn't any bleeding anywhere. That's a good sign." She rubs his head. "What happened here, boy?"

He nuzzles her hand, almost as if trying to tell her something.

Rosaleen cuddles him closer. "I wish you could tell me."

SIXTY-ONE

The next morning, Rosaleen wakes up to Hugh jumping and licking her face. She sits up in bed, and he grabs the blanket with his teeth, dragging the blanket off her.

"You're not limping anymore. Are you feeling better now, boy?"

Hugh barks at her and jumps back on the bed, his tail wagging.

"I'm so excited to see you playing around."

Rosaleen hears a knock on the door. "Hang on! I'm coming!" she yells down the stairs.

She cracks the door open, and Gareth is standing there, smoking a cigarette. "Oh, Gareth. Hey. I wasn't expecting you." She waves the smoke away.

"Sorry." He turns and puts the cigarette out on the porch post. "I saw you weren't working today, so I wanted to see if you needed help around the yard again?"

So much for a lazy day. "Might as well, since I have some help." She opens the door all the way. "Want some coffee first?"

"Sure." He awkwardly walks in behind her.

As soon as they finish their coffees, they go outside and get to work. Gareth throws debris down from her roof, and Rosaleen picks up,

The day passes quickly, and just as the sun is about to set, Gareth calls to her. "Rosaleen, come see."

"Whatever it is, I can wait 'til next time. You should come down before it gets too dark."

"Just come here." Gareth waves her up. "Come on."

She climbs up the ladder to Gareth. *Why is he sitting?* "What is it?"

"Sit right here and watch." He pats the spot next to him.

"Okay?" Rosaleen sits.

"Watch the sunset. It's beautiful from up here."

This is a first. She's never met a man who just sits and admires something like the sun going down. "It's going to be dark while you're walking home."

"Shh, that's okay." He scoots closer to her. "Just watch."

It's a chilly evening, and the heat from his body helps keep her warm. For the next thirty minutes, they sit in silence as the sun slips below the earth.

"Wasn't that beautiful, Rosaleen?"

"It was. I haven't taken the time to watch the sun set in years."

"Now look at that gorgeous moon. It's almost full. Just a few more days."

"It's so lovely." Rosaleen stands, not really wanting to move away from his warmth as the wind blows around them.

"It never gets old. It's as if seeing it for the first time each time." Almost as if Gareth can read her mind, he loops his arm around hers. "It's cold out here."

"Yes," Rosaleen says, easing away from Gareth. "We should get down."

After Gareth leaves, Rosaleen goes inside and checks her phone. She has a text from Patsy.

Come check this out. HURRY!

Rosaleen runs to Patsy's house. She is sitting on her front porch, holding a bundled-up towel. "Come look."

She steps closer and pulls back the fabric. Two little beady-eyed racoons stare up at her. "Aw, look how cute. Where'd you get them?"

"They were under a bush near the side of the house." She strokes one of the baby raccoons' heads. "Hugh might have gotten ahold of the mom. Now, they are orphans."

"That Hugh! Where's he at now?"

"I put him in the house. He needed a timeout."

"Those poor babies."

"They'll be fine. I'll bring them down to the feed store in the morning, and they'll take care of 'em." Patsy stands from her rocker. "I think you ought to let me make a hunting dog out of him."

"I think so too. Maybe it'll calm him down some."

"Yeah. You should have seen it. I had racoons running everywhere, stuff flying left to right, while the twins chased after the dog, and the dog chased after the momma racoon." Patsy laughs. "Hugh grabbed the mom and took off to the woods, and the twins got in the way of me running after him. I flew forward to the ground and landed on my face." She points to her lip. "Hence the busted lip."

Rosaleen covers her mouth and laughs. "How did I miss all of this?"

"You were out there letting man bun distract you."

"Be nice." Rosaleen focuses her attention back to the racoons. "They are so cute. Let me hold one." She grabs the baby racoons from Patsy. "Let's bring them in. They're probably cold." She walks into Patsy's house, baby-talking the raccoons. "I would have paid good money to see all the commotion y'all's momma caused with Hugh. It's okay, you'll get taken care of."

Hunter and Beaux come running into the house, leaving the door wide open.

"Shut that door. Y'all are wasting electricity."

Rosaleen laughs. "You sound like my pawpaw."

"Help, Momma!" Beaux yells.

"What in tarnation is going on?" Patsy laughs with Rosaleen.

"He ate something!" Hunter screeches out.

Rosaleen jumps up. "Well, what was it? Someone better tell us right now."

"He ate a grasshopper!" Hunter tries not to gag.

"Well, it'll build his immune system. Good for his growth," Patsy jokes with the twins. "It's always something. Y'all run along and go play, you hear. He is just fine." Patsy shooed the kids off. "Go catch some fireflies for my mason jar."

SIXTY-TWO

Rosaleen wakes to the sound of her phone ringing. Rubbing her eyes, she glances at the screen to see who called. *Three missed calls?* This time the number isn't blocked.

"What? Todd. NO!"

Maybe, I can call the police, and they will catch him. On second thought, he'd probably talk his way out. Plus, I did hit him with a skillet. That wouldn't look good, and he always finds a way to get himself out of trouble. He has that charismatic personality that can charm anyone over.

Should I call him back?

Before she can decide, her phone rings again. Her heart races with fear. She lets it ring for a moment and hits the green button.

Rosaleen remains silent.

"Rosaleen?" He says in a low, calm tone. "You there?"

"What do you want, Todd?" she says, irate.

"Can we talk? I swear it will be civil. I need to talk to you. I've changed, Rosaleen. I went to my first counseling session. I just need to talk to you in person so you can see my face when I tell you what I want to tell you."

"No." Rosaleen hangs up. *I've heard enough of his lies over the years. It's the same old story.* Rosaleen turns her phone off. *He says he's changed, then it's back to the same old thing a week later.*

Rosaleen has an unsettling feeling. *There is no way he will ever let me get away with what I did to him in the kitchen.*

She walks over to the window and looks outside, but it's too dark to see anything. The street light has been out for the past week. She can't shake the feeling that she's being watched, and she goes downstairs to make sure all of her doors are locked. *I know he is coming for revenge. I can just feel it.*

The door knob rattles as she walks away from the door. She hesitates. "Who is it?"

"OPEN UP. NOW!"

Todd is back, and he sounds more aggravated than ever.

"Go away! I'm calling the police!" Rosaleen inches back from the door, ready for whatever he's about to do.

"They'd never get here in time, you idiot."

A loud BANG echoes through the house.

Todd grows quiet.

Rosaleen freezes, then frantically searches the door. *Did he break it again?*

Another BANG sends Rosaleen into a panic. *A gun!*

She searches the door again for bullet holes.

Still nothing.

Patsy's voice thunders through the chaos. "Back up, Todd. Nobody needs to get hurt tonight."

Todd slams his fist on the door. "Rosaleen, you better tell her to shut up."

Rosaleen smiles to herself. "I wouldn't upset her, Todd."

Patsy clicks loudly as she cocks her shotgun. "Back on up and leave, Todd. GET!"

"Mind your own business, lady!" Todd kicks something across the porch, but Rosaleen is unsure of what it is.

Rosaleen hears Patsy laugh. "You ain't stupid enough to do something now, are you?"

Rosaleen looks out the window just as Todd balls his fist up and raises it into the air.

"You better put that fist down, boy. This ain't my first rodeo with a coward like you." Patsy's voice sounds closer now. "You really don't want to mess with me. It's past my bedtime, and you already woke me up. So now I'm cranky."

"You don't want to get in the way, lady. Go back to your house."

"You're wrong, there. What I want to do is shoot something right now. You don't want it to be you, do you? Get on out of here and leave that girl alone."

"Rosaleen, you are only digging yourself into a deeper hole. You don't know what you're doing. Tell your lady friend she better leave us alone!"

Rosaleen jumps at the sound of another gun-shot. *Oh no, he really ticked her off now.*

"Get on out of here before this 'lady friend' shows you how a real lady shoots. Next shot is going to be through that thick skull of yours. What's your choice? Leave or get some lead."

Todd gets into his truck, flinging rocks and dirt behind him as he speeds off.

Rosaleen opens the door, and Patsy runs up to her.

"Thank you, Patsy. I don't think he would have left if you hadn't been out there. Why haven't the cops arrived yet?"

"I didn't have time to call them. He would have killed you before they got here. Plus, from where I was standing, it was hard for him to see me. He looked more scared than anything. I had no choice but to handle up on him."

Just the thought of Todd fearing someone satisfied Rosaleen more that she thought possible.

SIXTY-THREE

Rosaleen tries brushing a section of her hair, but the brush keeps catching on what she thinks is a knot. After several attempts, she pulls the strands of hair to the side to see what she is dealing with.

"GUM!?" Rosaleen shouts.

One of Patsy's twins must have had gum the day before, and somehow got it in her hair.

She tries putting peanut butter in her hair to work it out, but it doesn't work. It's smeared near the top of her head, and there is no way the gum can be cut out without it looking like she chopped her hair up.

Rosaleen starts to cry. She let her hair grow long as a symbol of her freedom. Todd used to yank her by her hair if he couldn't grab her fast enough. He would pull her hair so hard that handfuls would fall out and her scalp would bruise and bleed.

Since she left Todd, the feeling of her hair, waves flowing in the wind, have made her feel free. Something she's more than likely about to lose.

Rosaleen goes to Patsy's house with a pair of scissors, feeling defeated. She will have to keep her hair short, above the shoulders. She walks into Patsy's house crying.

"Oh no, girl. What happened now?"

"I need you to help me cut my hair." Rosaleen hands the scissors to Patsy.

"Why?"

"One of the kids must have left gum somewhere, and it's stuck in my hair."

"Them dang boys. Hang on. Hang on." Patsy sets the scissors down. "What have you tried?"

"Peanut butter."

"That's it?" She puts her hand on her hip.

"Well, yeah. It obviously didn't work, or I wouldn't be here needing you to chop all my hair off!"

"Hang on." Patsy walks out of the room. Moments later, she comes back carrying a small glass jar.

"What's that?"

"Coconut oil. It'll help soften the gum, and we can work it out." Patsy grabs a kitchen chair. "Come on. Let's go on outside and sit on the front porch."

"OUCH!" Rosaleen jerks her head forward as Patsy yanks the brush through her hair.

"Well, if you'd sit still, I wouldn't have to pull so hard. You're worse than a child."

"You try having gum stuck in your hair!"

"Oh, I have. Now, sit still or I'm gonna pop you with this brush."

The two laugh as Patsy works the gum out of Rosaleen's hair. After some time, Patsy has the gum completely out of her hair.

"Once again, Patsy, you saved me."

"That's what I'm here for. I have nothing better to do."

"I really am grateful. My hair is just one less thing Todd can take away from me."

"I really do understand." Patsy's face shows remorse. "Say, you wanna stay for dinner?"

"I see what you're doing."

"What? We can't let him control your emotions anymore."

"Ugh." Rosaleen rolls her eyes at Patsy. "Whatcha cooking?"

"I was thinking about Jambalaya. I haven't made that since . . ." Patsy shakes her head, as if trying to erase a memory. "How's that sound?"

"That sounds really good." Rosaleen grabs her chair to take it back in. "I wanna watch you make it. I've never made Jambalaya from scratch."

"Even better." Patsy's still looks a little distraught.

Patsy's mixing ingredients in when she accidentally touches the side of the pot. "Ouch!" Patsy grabs the hot pot with her bare hands and chunks it to the back of the stove.

"Hey!" Rosaleen says, watching as Patsy jumps back. "What is wrong with you?" She grabs Patsy's hand and examines it. "You blistered your hand pretty badly. Are you okay?"

"Yeah, I've got an aloe plant on the window-sill. Will you grab it for me?"

Rosaleen snaps a piece of the plant off and squeezes some aloe out. "Here." She applies some to Patsy's hand.

"Thanks, let's just not talk about this." She grabs a pot-holder and puts the pot back on the burner.

Maybe cooking this is a major step for her. Rosaleen knows that simple tasks can become traumatic after a toxic relationship. *They really ruin small joys for people like us.*

Rosaleen and Patsy are eating supper, pushing through the awkwardness, when they hear a knock at the door.

"Who on earth could that be?" Patsy gets up and answers the door. Moments later, she walks back into the room with a police officer following behind her.

"Mrs. Ashter."

My married name? "Yes. Sir?" *That's odd.*

"I was told I'd find you here if you weren't home. Can I ask you a few questions?"

"It's Ms. Hart. I no longer go by my married name. Questions about what? Did something happen, officer?"

"Mrs. Hart, Todd Ashter has been reported as a missing person. His family feels something might have happened to him. They said that you're likely the last person to see him."

The last time I talked to his family was on our wedding day. "He came by a few nights ago, and I made him leave. I haven't seen him since. I'm sorry, am I being accused of something?"

The officer opened his notebook, took a pen out of his pocket, and jotted something down. "Do you mind if we look around your house?"

"That won't be necessary, officer. He never came in. Last time I checked, I was the one in danger."

"Very well. That's all the information I need for now."

"Thanks, officer." Rosaleen is more irritated than anything.

"I'll see myself out, ladies. Enjoy the rest of your dinner."

They wait until they hear the door shut to start talking again.

"This tea sure is good." Patsy gulps some down.

"Not talking about this either, right?" Rosaleen says, referring to Patsy refusing to talk about her accident earlier.

"Nope." Patsy spits her drink out as she bursts out laughing.

"At least we know Todd didn't go to the police after what happened."

"How could he? He broke into your house first. Don't forget that."

"Yeah . . ."

"Let's eat before our food gets cold. Or something else happens."

"I'm stuffed!" Rosaleen plops down on Patsy's couch, kicking her feet back.

"You took my spot! Scootch over." Patsy wedges herself in.

"Hey! I was comfortable!"

"Too bad."

Patsy holds up the remote to turn the TV on.

Rosaleen grabs it from her. "I'm company, so I get to choose the channel."

"It's my house." Patsy steals it back.

Rosaleen fakes a sad face. "But my remote is broken."

"I don't feel bad, not one bit. Although, you did throw it at that ass-hat, so I'll give you that one." She hands the remote back to Rosaleen. "You better not pick any of that sappy Hallmark stuff."

Rosaleen flips it to the ID Channel. "No way. Not today."

"Hey, whatever you're planning, I'd hate to be in your way. Especially with you watching all these killer women." Patsy mimics cutting her throat with her hand.

"Nah, he isn't worth my time anymore." Rosaleen turns the volume up. "Shh, I can't hear it."

"What attracted you to him the first place?" Patsy asks her a hard question, and it really makes Rosaleen think.

"Well, I felt like he was Mr. Right. He had the looks and the charisma. I thought it was a fairytale come true, you know? Someone like me gets Mr. Perfect."

"Yeah. Mr. Not-So-Perfect."

"I mean, I thought he was at one time. I thought I was lucky. You know. . . Handsome guy. Good money. He loved me. I had it made." Rosaleen mutes the TV. "The first time he hit me, it caught me off guard. Surely, he didn't mean to. Not Todd. But then it became an everyday habit for him." She puts her hand on her arm and lifts her sleeve to reveal a scar. "I look at this every day and regret not leaving sooner."

"That's a big scar." Patsy looks sympathetic.

"Yeah, I know. I always make sure my sleeves are long enough to cover it. It's so embarrassing."

Patsy puts her hand on the scar. "Don't let it be. It's not your fault. It shows how brave you are."

"I don't want people to see what I let him do to me." Rosaleen pulls her sleeve down, and Patsy moves her hand.

"Girl, don't be ashamed, I have my own scars too." Patsy pulls her pant leg up. "He cut my leg with a machete. Swung it at me and cut me clear to the bone." She pulls the pants leg back down. "It wasn't our fault."

"But this is my fault. I could have left before we got married. It would have saved me so many complications."

"It seems like that would have been the perfect time to leave, but he might have killed you, Rosaleen."

Rosaleen pauses a moment. "He always loved me extra hard after he hurt me. Eventually, I lived for those moments. That's when I felt like he cared for me the most."

"I understand. I'm sorry you had to live like that."

"Patsy, can I ask you one more question?"

"Might as well."

"What really happened to your husband?"

"Listen here . . ." Patsy falls silent.

"You don't have to."

"I had no intention to kill my husband, you know? I was just sitting in my room one evening, sewing my son's jeans. He'd ripped them on our old. Anyway, I was minding my own business. The kids were asleep upstairs. Ace, that was his name, stumbled into our bedroom. He had been drinking, and I could smell the rum on him from across the room." Patsy pauses and wipes away a tear.

Rosaleen grabs her hand. "It's time to get this off your chest. You've been holding onto this for far too long. You're my best friend, and I will never judge you."

"Well, he took a few steps toward me, and one of his arms was behind his back. He pulled a wooden board out from behind him, and I knew at that moment if I didn't kill him, he would have killed me." Patsy is sobbing now, tears pouring down her face.

"It's okay, Patsy. It's okay. Let it out." Rosaleen rubs her back.

"I had started carrying a gun in my bra. You know, ole Sally? I pulled it out and begged him to step back so I didn't have to shoot him. He started yelling at me, saying he was gonna kill me. I didn't shoot until he came running at me, swinging the board."

Rosaleen realizes Patsy has been reliving these moments all day. *No wonder she's been so upset. I can't imagine having to kill someone I loved for so long.*

"I still have nightmares. It was horrible. I called my dad, and he helped me get rid of his body and clean up the mess. We fed him to some gators down the old Sabine River. My dad was the only one who knew. He took it to his grave and didn't even tell my mother." Patsy blows her nose into her shirt. "We can't go around feeling sorry for ourselves, though. It's all about rebuilding and starting over." She grabs the remote from Rosaleen and turns the TV sound back on.

"But we have a right to think about it and grow from there. It happened, and we can't change that. It's okay to talk about it."

"I guess you're right. That's one thing Esther taught me while she was still alive."

SIXTY-FOUR

Rosaleen hears a sound coming from the front yard—a horn. "Who could that be?" Her heart races. *Please don't be Todd.*

"HEY!" She hears a loud, obnoxious voice. Her sister, Adeline is walking onto the porch.

Rosaleen gets up and runs over to her. "Whatcha doing here, stranger?"

"I had to come see my favorite sister! I haven't seen you in forever!"

Rosaleen laughs. *I guess she's not mad at me for pushing her boyfriend over.*

"Plus, I need to see what's in your icebox to snack on. It's my right, since you ran my boyfriend off and all. Now my cabinets are empty." Adeline laughs. This is nothing new; she always digs into her sister's snacks.

They walk inside, and Rosaleen sits at her kitchen table while Adeline scrambles around her kitchen. Rosaleen is relieved her sister isn't holding what she did at her surprise birthday party against her.

"About that night I shoved your boyfriend down. Look, I'm sorry. I was going through a lot."

"Girl, that's okay. He was such a whiny baby. It just gave me an excuse to break it off with him. He complained about his elbow hurting him for days." Adeline finds some chocolate syrup and grabs the milk out of Rosaleen's icebox. She snatches up a bag of Doritos from the cabinet. "It's all good."

"What? I didn't push him that hard," Rosaleen teases. "Why don't you sit and visit for a while?"

"I just needed something to snack on before my long drive." With her hands full of junk food and chocolate milk, she starts to walk out. "My new boyfriend and I are going to Tennessee."

"Already?"

"He's different, you know?" Adeline shrugs. "So don't go pushing this one. If I get tired of him, I'll just throw you another surprise birthday party." Adeline winks. "Bye, girl."

Rosaleen follows behind her. "I'll add all of that to your tab," Rosaleen jokes. "You're welcome!"

"Oh! Thanks, girl!" Adeline climbs into her car, and a man in the passenger seat waves.

"You were too scared to bring him in?" Rosaleen calls out to her.

Adeline pops her head out the window. "I told you I wanted to keep this one."

"Y'all be careful!" Rosaleen laughs and waves until they are no longer in sight. *She's so crazy.* Rosaleen wouldn't expect anything less of her, though. *Maybe she stopped by to let me know she wasn't mad at me after all.*

Adeline is the only one in the family who saw straight through Todd's phony act. Todd would get so mad because Adeline never put up with him. She would always call him out on his bluffs. Todd hated the confrontation. Rosaleen could tell he wanted to hit Adeline. He'd ball up his fist and hold them straight by his side. Rosaleen wished he had tried. Adeline would have eaten him alive.

Adeline hated Todd, and she made sure Rosaleen knew how much she disliked him too.

Rosaleen shrugged Adeline off. At that time, Rosaleen felt like it was too late, and she was stuck where she was forever. She didn't realize that, one day, she would be brave enough to leave.

Looking back now, Rosaleen sees how much she's grown. She can see how her hard work is paying off. Finally, for once, she sees that everything she's been fighting for is well worth the effort. She never quit, and she's thankful she kept pushing. If she hadn't, she probably wouldn't be here now. She would be long gone, washed away by the Mississippi River by now.

SIXTY-FIVE

It's late Friday evening, and Rosaleen has to close up The Hideout again. Belle has another date, but this time with the same man as before. "He must be a good one for you to keep him around this long," Rosaleen teases Belle.

"I've never met one like him. He even ran around the car to open the door for me." Belle blushes.

Rosaleen's never seen her blush. "Go ahead. I've got it here." *It really isn't safe for me to be alone, but why ruin her night?*

"I owe you big, Rosaleen!" Belle hugs her tightly, prancing out the door.

Rosaleen calls out to her, "Y'all don't have too much fun!"

Rosaleen notices the sun slipping away and looks up at the clock. 6:00. She decides to start cleaning the place up and close the shop. It's been an hour since the last customer left, and she doesn't want to get stuck alone in the dark again. Ever since Easton caught her that night, she's been making it a point to leave before it is completely dark outside. *I can't believe that jerk did that to me.* Rosaleen stops wiping the counter down after she realizes how hard she was scrubbing. *He isn't worth the anger.*

She's about to leave when the phone rings. She walks over to it and answers. "This is The Hideout. How can I help you?"

The person on the other side of the phone is silent.

Hmm, this has happened before, just as I was closing up. "Hideout," she repeats.

Still no reply.

"Look kids, if you're going to play phone games, call the tax firm down the street. They're more fun to mess with."

Someone breathes heavily into the phone, sending shivers down Rosaleen's spine.

"STOP CALLING!" She slams the phone down. *I can't stand prank callers. Jeez. These kids get weirder every year.*

Something about that phone call leaves Rosaleen creeped out. *I'll take the trash out in the morning. It's only half full anyway.*

She looks at the clock on the coffee maker. 6:15. *I promised Patsy I'd watch a movie with her this evening.* She hurries to finish locking up.

Walking to her car, Rosaleen pauses when she thinks she hears someone walking behind her. *Is Todd following me?*

She puts her car key between her fingers, ready to punch him with it if it comes down to saving herself.

As she's about to unlock her door, a loud crash comes from someone to her left.

She jumps around, ready to defend herself.

A lid from one of the metal trash cans topples to the ground. "Show your face!" Rosaleen grasps her car door, now ready to make a run for it. *I have no chance against him, alone out here.*

A kitten jumps out of the trash cans and runs up to Rosaleen, meowing. It rubs its head on her leg.

"Hey cutie, you scared me." She stokes its head down its back. "I have to go. My crazy friend is waiting on me."

Rosaleen gets into her car and watches the kitten run behind the trash cans.

She checks the radio clock. *6:44. I was supposed to be there by 6:30.* Rosaleen takes her phone out of her pocket and calls Patsy. *I'll call and butter her up until I get there.*

Patsy doesn't answer.

Rosaleen sets her phone down on the passenger's seat. *She's probably putting the boys to bed.* She looks down at her apron and coffee-stained blouse. "I'll get out of these dirty work clothes before I head over."

It's so creepy out here tonight. Rosaleen hates the nights when the drive home feels eerie and unsettling. Nothing ever happens; it's just the way she feels sometimes, now that she's left Todd.

She pulls up to her house and goes inside to change.

Hugh greets her at the door.

"Hey, boy!" She pats him on the head. "How was your day?"

He runs around in circles, then rolling onto his back.

"Hang on, boy." She rubs his belly and starts to walk off. "I have to hurry. Patsy is waiting on me."

Hugh barks, jumping up and scratching at the door.

"Sorry, boy. You can't play with them tonight."

Hugh runs over to his tennis ball and whines.

"The boys are already in bed. You'll stir them up, and Patsy will be mad at you. You stay here, and I'll be back in a couple of hours."

Rosaleen goes upstairs and changes, then tries calling Patsy one more time before the screen goes black. "Dead, of course." She tosses her phone on the dresser and starts walking downstairs. *She's probably mad at me for being so late.*

Hugh stands by the door, blocking Rosaleen from the exit. He lets out a little whimper.

"I know, Hugh. You just can't go play tonight. You can play with Beaux and Hunter in the morning." She scratches behind his ears. "Now, go be a good boy and lie down."

Hugh tucks his tail and walks away from the door.

"Aw, don't do that. I'll be right back. What's wrong with you tonight?"

Hugh lies on the floor and doesn't look back at Rosaleen as she walks out.

Rosaleen notices Patsy has her burn pile lit up as she walks between their houses. The fire lights up half the back-yard. *Patsy always overdoes it with her burn pile. Looks more like a bonfire.* She takes a deep breath in. *Smells like smores!* She remembers the fun camping nights she had with her father during the summer. *Maybe I can talk Patsy into making smores before the movie.*

Rosaleen approaches Patsy's front door. *The boys must've left the door cracked open. I'm surprised Patsy hasn't realized it yet and started yelling about the mosquitos.* She laughs to herself and walks into the living room, shutting the door behind her.

"Patsy?" The lights are out, and a football game is muted on the TV. *Patsy doesn't watch football.* "Where are you? You forget about our movie?" Rosaleen takes a few more steps into the living room.

Patsy doesn't answer back.

She sees a light shining under the kitchen door and can hear the sink running. "Whatcha cookin'? I sure could use some iced tea," Rosaleen calls out as she walks closer to the kitchen. She stops *Why is she not answering me?*

"Patsy . . .?" She hesitates, placing her hand on the door. She's ready to open it and then backs up, turning around.

Her heart starts to race. *Wait, what's missing?*

Rosaleen looks at the wall. That's strange. *Her deer mount is gone.* After further inspection, she notices the deer head is on the floor, one of its antlers broken.

"Patsy . . . what happened to your deer? It looks like a war zone in here," she calls out. *That's not like her to leave something so precious to her on the floor in this manner.*

Rosaleen hears the sink turn off in the kitchen. "Patsy?"

She can make out the sound of heavy, slow footsteps getting closer to the door, and the light under the door disappears.

"Quit messing with me, boys. Hunter? Beaux?" Rosaleen slowly pushes the kitchen door open, her eyes having a hard time adjusting to the dark.

Her hands begin to tremble when she feels something wet and slippery on the wall as she moves her hand around, searching for the light switch.

She switches on the light and notices her hand is red. She smells it. The metallic scent makes her stomach turn over.

BLOOD!

What is happening? Her whole body grows weak.

"PATSY!? THIS ISN'T FUNNY!" Her heart stops, and she goes cold all over. She pushes the door open the rest of the way, meeting an unbearable sight. "NOOOOO!" Rosaleen lets out a horrific, piercing scream.

Patsy is tied to a chair with duct tape wrapped around her mouth. One eye is swollen shut with a big black and purple bruise around it. She can see the dried-up blood through her fiery red hair. Patsy looks up and pleadingly shakes her head no, trying to mumble something.

"PATSY!" Rosaleen rushes over to Patsy as she still frantically shakes her head.

"Who did this to you?" Rosaleen can sense someone behind her. *Todd's here!* She turns around and sees Todd kicked back in a chair, his feet on the table. The hair on her arms stands straight up as she looks Todd in the eyes.

Scratches stretch across his cheeks and down his arms.

Rosaleen can tell Patsy put up a strong fight. *But where are the twins? Did he kill them?*

"Hey, Rose. You're just in time," Todd's voice echoes. A stomach-turning smile spreads from one cheek to the other. "Your little girlfriend can't save you this time." He laughs, the sound vile.

Rosaleen clenches her fists. "What did you do to her?" she growls.

"What needed to be done." Todd leans forward and pulls his feet down from the table. "You see, women like you and this bitch here deserve to be kept in place." He pats the chair next to him. "Come sit with me and have a drink. Patsy made us tea." He grabs a glass pitcher from the center of the table to in front of him.

Rosaleen looks at Patsy, who moans in pain. Blood is running from Patsy's nose down to her shirt. "You didn't have to hurt her like this, you monster." She starts to walk to the kitchen sink to grab a rag, not caring if Todd gets irritated with her.

"I wouldn't help her if I were you." Todd stands.

Rosaleen freezes in her tracks, knowing that Todd isn't messing around this time. He promised Patsy that he'd be back. Now here he is, back with his kept promises.

"Can we just talk about this, Todd?"

"You've had your chance. It's too late for talking now."

Rosaleen looks desperately around the kitchen for something she can use to fend him off. Patsy's knife block is gone. *He must've cleared out anything that could be used against him.*

"Momma," a little voice from the living room calls. "I'm thirsty."

Rosaleen sighs in relief to hear Hunter. *He's still alive! Where is Beaux?*

"Who the hell is that?" Todd turns towards the voice.

He doesn't know there are children in the house? I have to make sure they stay safe.

Patsy looks at Rosaleen hysterically, tears streaming down her face.

Rosaleen whispers to Todd. "Please, Todd. He's just a child. Can I at least tuck him back into bed so he doesn't see his mother like this?"

"Why should I care?" Todd laughs.

"Momma," Hunter calls out for Patsy again.

"Please, Todd. Please." She folds her hands together and pleads. "What if this was your kid? You wouldn't want your own child to see something like this, would you?"

"You took the chance to have kids away from me. You think I'd forget about finding your birth control?"

"Please, I'm begging you. He's just a child."

"Hurry up! If you take too long, I'll tie that kid up next to her." He spits on the ground toward Patsy. "Trash."

Patsy hangs her head, sighing in relief.

Rosaleen rushes into the living room and swoops Hunter up.

"Where's my momma?" he says, sleepily.

"She had to run to the store to get you a surprise. You can only have it if you stay in bed all night." She carries him back to his room.

"Okay." He rubs his eyes. "My cup is empty, and I'm thirsty."

"Let me get you some water." She lays Hunter down and tucks the blanket in around him. "Snug as a bug. I'll be right back." She looks over and sees Beaux sleeping. She walks over and runs her thumb over his cheeks. Rosaleen's heart aches. *These sweet babies might never get to see their mom again.*

Rosaleen walks across the hall to the bathroom and fills the cup with water from the sink. She walks back into the twin's room, and Hunter is sound asleep again. She sets the cup in between the beds on the nightstand. She can't help but worry about them. Their mom could be dead by the time they wake up, and here they are both peacefully sleeping. *We will all be dead if I don't find a way out for us quickly.*

"Take your time," Todd calls out from the kitchen.

Rosaleen can hear what sounds like a slap and Patsy groaning.

She hurries back, pausing in front of Patsy's room. *She normally keeps her pocket knife next to her bed.*

She rushes into the room and shuffles through a few things on the bedside table. *Why can't she be more organized?* Rosaleen locates the knife and slips it into her dress pocket, hoping Todd won't see the bulge.

Rosaleen hears another slap. *I have to hurry!*

Rosaleen walks back into the kitchen. Patsy's head hangs down, and she looks defeated.

"Todd, please let her go. I'll do whatever you want," Rosaleen pleads.

"It's too damn late!" Todd stomps his foot on the ground. His hair is a mess, no longer perfectly combed back with hairspray. Sweat falls from his reddened forehead, veins showing through his temples and neck.

Rosaleen hardly recognizes the man unraveling before her. *He's completely lost it.* She knows their time is running out. "Please. She didn't do anything to you. It's me you want. Not her."

Todd starts pacing back and forth. "If it wasn't for her, you'd be back at the house with me, in bed where you belong. But no, you had to let her brainwash you and make you think it was okay to treat me the way you do." He walks up to Patsy. "You ruined my marriage, you freak!" He slaps her in the face, and she lets out a grunt. "I told you to stay out the way! Did I not?" He yanks her by the hair, almost flipping her over in the chair. "You wanted her for yourself!"

"TODD, PLEASE!" Rosaleen whisper-shouts, so she doesn't wake the twins. "It's not her fault. It's mine! Tie me up. Let her go. I'm begging you." She grabs his arm to stop him from hitting Patsy again.

"Let go of me!" He turns, grabs Rosaleen, and throws her to the floor.

She stands almost instantly and backs up in front of Patsy. She taps her pocket. *Please notice. Please!*

Patsy slowly raises her hand and grabs the knife.

Hurry, before he notices! Rosaleen knows Patsy is in an extreme amount of pain, but if she doesn't use this second of opportunity, this could be the end for them both. *What will he do to the twins?* She can't imagine Todd hurting them too, but he is completely besides himself. *There's no telling what he'd do.*

Todd flips a table chair over, breaking off one of the legs.

Rosaleen is too scared to move, unsure if he saw the exchange or not.

"Get away from each other! Rosaleen's mine!" He clenches his fists and puffs up.

Rosaleen moves across the room, out of Todd's reach. She can feel her blood rushing throughout her body. Her heart quickens. *I have to distract him so she can free herself.*

A look of surprise fills Todd's face. "Where do you think you're going? You'll never learn, will you?"

He didn't see Patsy get the knife. I have to get him out of this house and get my gun.

Rosaleen's eyes meet the front door. *There's little to no chance He's so much faster than me.*

Todd notices her glance. "Don't you dare."

SIXTY-SIX

Before Todd can reach for her, Rosaleen takes off running out the front door. She can hear Todd yelling, but she's unsure of what he's saying. *Run! Run! I have to get my gun! Run faster!* Her legs feel like they are about to give out as she reaches her front door. She scrambles in her pockets for the key, knowing Todd is getting closer with each step. She flips through her keys, trying to find the right one.

Why do I have so many stupid keys?

She finally gets the door unlocked and runs in, shutting it behind her. She's unable to latch it, but it'll buy her a couple of extra seconds to get to her room, where the gun is.

She darts up the stairs two at a time, almost stumbling. Midway up, she hears Todd burst through the door. "I'm going to kill you. Just give it up." His boots sound like steel weights behind her.

She barely has time to make it to her room, but she shuts the door and locks it.

Hugh jumps off the bed and runs to her side. He starts barking aggressively at the door as Todd steadily kicks it in.

"Hugh! Go hide!" *Where's my gun! Hurry!* She looks up as the door starts splitting down the middle.

She lifts her mattress up higher and is finally able to reach the gun.

Todd punts the door in, and Hugh latches onto him, shredding his pant leg.

"Move, you stupid mutt!" Todd kicks Hugh in the side.

Hugh lets out a yelp, runs, and hides under the bed.

"Hugh!" Rosaleen has no time to get to him before Todd runs over and shoves her to the floor.

Todd jumps on top of her, reaching for her gun.

She holds onto it for dear life, trying to wrestle away. "LET GO!" She hits him over the head, and he stumbles back.

Hugh runs back out from under the bed and bites Todd's hand as he tries to strike Rosaleen again.

Rosaleen scrambles up and out of bedroom, trying to get to the stairs.

Todd follows closely behind, pulling Hugh by his tail and throwing him over the railing.

Hugh hits the floor and lands on his side. His body jolts, and blood instantly pours from his nose and mouth.

"Hugh!" Rosaleen grabs onto Todd's shirt and rips it. "You killed him!"

He swings back at her, barely missing her head.

Rosaleen claws at Todd's face, scratching him in the eye as he screams out.

Patsy stands at the bottom of the staircase and cocks her gun, getting Todd's attention. "It's time you go, you uncultured swine!" The words crack out through deep breaths. Patsy fires a shot, but misses and hits the railing.

Rosaleen, seeing that Todd is distracted, uses the opportunity to kick him in the back.

He rolls down the stairs, hitting his head several times.

Rosaleen follows him to the first floor and sees blood running out of his ear.

"DO IT NOW! SHOOT HIM!" Patsy yells at Rosaleen as she attempts to reload her gun.

Rosaleen points the gun at Todd, who lies there staring up at her. She kicks him in the ribs, and he wails. "Ahh!"

She squeezes the trigger tightly, and nothing happens.

Todd's wail instantly turns into an evil laugh. "Kind of hard to shoot someone with the safety on." He swings his leg around and trips Patsy before she can finish loading her gun.

Already fragile, she falls over, dropping her shotgun.

Todd stands, looking disoriented, and braces himself on the wall to keep his balance. He kicks the shotgun across the room and puts his hand out to Rosaleen. "Give me your gun, idiot."

Rosaleen steps back toward the doorway and shakes her head. "No." Tears start streaming down her face as she looks at Hugh and Patsy. *Todd is taking everything I love away from me.*

"Why are you crying? Not so tough after all, are you?" He steps unsteadily toward Rosaleen.

"You're wrong." Rosaleen wipes her face with her arm.

"Run," Patsy tries to say through her heavy breathing.

"Hand it over." Todd looks down and steps on Patsy's hand as he continues to creep closer toward Rosaleen.

Rosaleen cringes at the sound of her bones popping.

Patsy lets out a low moan and hardly moves as Todd laughs.

She barely reacted to that! "You monster!" Rosaleen a run out the door, desperately looking for a way out. There's no one around to help, unless she runs over half a mile down the street. *I would never make it in time, and no one would hear me screaming. Patsy is wounded, and my only other neighbors are dead.*

She looks around and sees the fire still burning in Patsy's backyard. *Thank you, Patsy! Maybe I can get him close enough to push him in.* She runs in that direction.

Where is he? She looks back and doesn't see him behind her until she sees Todd's truck speeding closer to her.

He turns on the headlight's brights, making it harder to see. *HE'S ABOUT TO END ME!* She switches off the safety on the gun.

She stops dead in her tracks. *If he is going to run me over, I won't go down without a fight.*

She lifts the gun and fires a shot, sending a bullet through the windshield and shattering the glass.

That doesn't stop Todd; he is still coming at her, not giving up.

She fires another shot, hitting the front tire. She aims and shoots the other front tire. The truck loses control, veering side-to-side before coming to an abrupt stop.

That's three bullets. I better make the last three count. She fires two more shots at the windshield.

Todd screams. "You fucking shot me!"

Rosaleen's hands tremble as she lowers her guns numbly. *I actually shot him!*

The night stands still with no movement coming from her house or the truck. *Did I kill him?* It's hard to see anything with the headlights blinding her.

Rosaleen takes a mental note of how close she is to the fire now and slowly walks towards the truck.

She gets close, and Todd is nowhere to be found. *No! I want him gone!* "WHERE'D YOU GO, TODD! I WANT YOU MORE THAN DEAD!" Rosaleen screams.

"ROSALEEN! RUN!" Patsy's voice crackles through the night as she limps toward Rosaleen.

Rosaleen turns, but it's too late.

Todd grabs her, pinning her against the truck. He yanks the gun out of her hand and tosses it.

Rosaleen watches the gun land near the fire. *I can't reach that.*

He holds her by her wrists with her arms up in the air.

"No, Todd. Please stop!" She tries to push him off, but she can't escape his tight grip.

He forcefully kisses her, putting his tongue into her mouth and gagging her.

Rosaleen wants to vomit. Disgusted, she bites his tongue, breaking free from his kiss. "You're sick!" She spits the blood she drew from him in his face.

Todd lets go of her wrists and puts his hands around her neck, choking her.

Rosaleen stares into his dark, blood-shot eyes. He looks evil and ready to kill. *I can't fight. He's going to win.*

Patsy runs up behind Todd, yanking on his shirt and trying to pull him off Rosaleen.

He turns and punches Patsy in the head with one hand while his other is still around Rosaleen's neck.

Patsy falls to the ground, not moving.

Rosaleen tries to scream, but only a high pitch squeal escapes her throat as Todd puts his other hand back around her neck.

She claws at his face, causing her nails to break. *I have to fight or die. I can't . . .*

She feels her feet lift from the ground as he lifts her up and presses her neck even harder.

I quit . . . The world starts to spin around her.

Todd grunts, but he doesn't ease up. "I told you no one else would have you."

A calm, serene expression passes over his face as she stares into his eyes. She remembers how every waking minute was miserable with him. Every hit, every name he called her. *That's no way to live.* Her breath slows, and everything starts getting dark. Her agony is turning into dull pain. *It's going to be over soon.* Her thoughts start to get cloudy. *It's so quiet.* Her tense body starts feeling loose.

She can faintly hear him laughing as her head gives in and falls forward. *I made it this far. It can't end with him being this satisfied!*

She gives her legs one final swing with the little bit of fight she has left in her.

Todd drops her to the ground, and he falls over.

Her chest stings as she gasps for air. Her head is throbbing, the world spinning, as she tries to stand straight.

Her vision pulsates as she focuses on Todd. He's rolling around on the ground, holding his crotch as Rosaleen stands over him. *How did I do that?*

She looks over at Patsy. *She still isn't moving.*

I'll come back for her. Rosaleen takes off running in the opposite direction. *My gun is near the fire! There's one shot left. I have to make it count. For Patsy!*

Todd's knees wobble as he stands. Blood pours out of his shoulder from where Rosaleen had shot him.

She grabs the gun off the ground as Todd staggers closer. "Stop right there, or I'll put a bullet through your brainless waste of space." Rosaleen prepares herself, taking a deep breath.

"My, oh, my. You sound just like your dead little girlfriend over there."

Rosaleen wants to look over, but she's afraid to take her eyes off Todd. One wrong move, and he'll be in control again.

"She's dead, Rosaleen. Who do you have now?"

Tears stream down her face. *Don't let him get in your head.* "I'm not going to listen to you any more!"

"Don't believe me? Look for yourself." Todd walks away from Rosaleen, a few feet over to Patsy.

The whole time, Rosaleen stays standing near the fire, aiming directly at him. *If I stay here, he'll have no choice but to get near the fire, just in case I miss.*

Patsy's body moves lifelessly as he pushes her with his boot. "Dead." He laughs, turning back toward Rosaleen and slowly stumbling towards her.

Rosaleen stays in place, still pointing the gun. *This is my chance.*

He walks right in front of her, now holding his shoulder where he was shot. Blood seeps through the cracks of his hand. Cuts covers his face, and his eyes are blackened. His lip busted, his teeth red from the blood inside his mouth. He doesn't look like Todd anymore. Instead, he looks like a real monster. The ones you only see in horror shows.

He sticks out his bloody hand. "Hand it over, Rosaleen. Give it up." He reaches for the gun, but she pulls it back.

"NO, TODD!"

He steps closer to her, and she freezes.

"You don't have the courage. Coward." He places his hand over the top of the gun. "You missed your chance." He jerks the gun from her, shoving her to the ground.

She barely misses the fire and can feel the warmth burning her arm.

He aims the gun at her, and she tightly squeezes her eyes shut at the sound of a loud bang.

He shot right next to her, into the ground.

"Oops, the last bullet is gone." He tosses the gun into the fire. "Say, what if you accidentally fell into the burn pile? Hmm." He rubs his chin, taunting her. "Like I told your little friend earlier, fire can be dangerous if you aren't careful."

Rosaleen looks over toward Patsy's body, but she's not there. *What? Is she alive?* A sense of relief gives her the extra push she needs. *I can't let him win. I just can't.*

Rosaleen looks around, searching for any way out. Anything that can buy her time.

A stick sits next to her, partially inside the fire. She grabs it and swings it at Todd. "You're right, Todd. Fire is very dangerous." She jumps up, and hitting him in the face.

"You psycho bitch!" he yells, grabbing his face.

She hit him again in his back and arm. His shirt catches fire as she beats him with the stick until he falls to the ground.

"AHH!" He screams, rolling. "HELP ME!"

He stops moving after the fire is put out and slowly turns over onto his back, revealing his face. His right eyelid is burned off and both of his eyebrows are completely charred. There's no more skin left on his nose, and she can see his bone.

Rosaleen throws up, holding the stick away from her. She can't handle the smell of burning flesh or the crackling sound of his skin.

"Rosaleen," Todd barely gets the words out through his moaning. "I loved you."

She bends over Todd and presses the stick firmly into his gunshot wound. Blood bubbles out, and this time Rosaleen doesn't cringe to the sight. "I hated you."

Todd screams in agonizing pain. "NO!" His body trembles and his legs recoil. "Stop . . . please."

She can barely make out what he's saying. *Music to my ears.* "What's that? Oh, wait. No one lives close enough to hear you, Todd."

She digs the stick deeper into his wound, and he doesn't react this time.

"I'll be sure you never hurt me or anyone else ever again."

Patsy limps, covered in blood, from the other side of the fire and stands next to Rosaleen. She rocks back and forth, barely able to stand. "When running isn't a choice, you have to stand and fight." She pushes the words out between deep breaths. "Here. It's time." She hands Rosaleen her shotgun.

BANG.

The shot echoes through the night.

Todd instantly stops moving.

Rosaleen looks at Patsy and drops the gun. She falls to her knees, taking a deep breath. Years of fear and resentment escape Rosaleen's body as her hands tremble, but not from being scared this time. She won't have to look over her shoulder every time she walks outside. *I'm free!* After years and years of abuse, she will finally have the life she's always dreamed of. Todd won't be around to prevent her from living her life to the fullest. There will always be his voice in the back of her head, but now she won't have to be afraid to stand up to it. He no longer holds control over her. She isn't his property anymore, and most importantly, she can start fully loving herself.

Knowing her past life will be buried, she feels the freedom of her new life beginning. She relaxes her shoulders, letting out a breath that she feels like she's held in forever. *I'm truly free.*

Patsy turns and limps away. "I'll go get the shovel."

Battered Roses

About the Author

Growing up in a small town in Louisiana, writing has always been a passion for Christina. Since elementary age she has been writing poetry. However, she realized she had something valuable to share with the world and decided to write her first novel "Battered Roses."

She's inspired by her favorite Author Lurlene Mcdaniel and hopes her stories will make a difference in someone else's life like the stories she has read.

When not writing words at her favorite coffee shop, she's chasing children, parrots, ducks, turkeys, geese, and an occasional dog or two.

Maybe it's because she's always chasing after something, her characters are always feeling like they must run for their lives.

Follow Me!

facebook.com/ChristinaRozeline

instagram.com/christina_rozeline/

tiktok.com/christinarozeline

Website and Newsletter Sign up:
www.christinarozeline.com

Acknowledgements

I'd like to thank the following people for making this book possible:

My Momma, who kept pushing me and believing in me.

Beth Savoie, my writing bestie, who stayed by my side through the whole process from my "VERY rough draft" til publishing.

Lauren Loftis, Tally Ink, who not only copy edited my story, but gave me the needed encouragement and support.

Colleen Mitchell, Tally Ink, my Author Coach, whose instructions was invaluable, especially with character charts.

The following businesses who helped support the publishing stages:

Michelle LeJeune, Scentsy consultant.
Beth Savoie, Author of the Compton and Murray Mysteries.
Christy McCann, Mary Kay consultant.

Cotina Holland & Janet Caswell, Lucky Tees Creations.
Penny Borel, Paparazzi consultant.
Brittany Brossette, B's Crafts & more.
Lindsey Doucet, Pink Zebra consultant.

Go Sparkle and Shine!

Made in the USA
Columbia, SC
13 February 2024